Bringing down the thunder . . .

Jim looked at Tom and said, "You better get your horse and just ride on out of here. You don't want to buy in on this."

Tom smiled. "Reckon I wouldn't get far. Maybe as far as the horse before you'd put a bullet in me."

Roy smiled lazily. "Now, why would we want to do that?"

"Witnesses," Tom said. "You wouldn't want to leave one behind now, would you?"

"What makes you think we would be afraid of witnesses?"

"Like I said, you don't have badges," Tom answered.

"Damnit! This here's my badge!" Jim shouted, and reached for his pistol.

Tom tilted the Spencer forward, the barrel slapping into the palm of his hand as he pressed the trigger. The heavy bullet slammed into Jim, knocking him off his horse. Tom slipped to the side, levering another cartridge into the Spencer. For a second, he thought he was too late . . .

THE
OUTCAST.

Luke Cypher

BERKLEY BOOKS, NEW YORK

THE BERKLEY PUBLISHING GROUP
Published by the Penguin Group
Penguin Group (USA) Inc.
375 Hudson Street, New York, New York 10014, USA
Penguin Group (Canada), 90 Eglinton Avenue East, Suite 700, Toronto, Ontario M4P 2Y3, Canada
(a division of Pearson Penguin Canada Inc.)
Penguin Books Ltd., 80 Strand, London WC2R 0RL, England
Penguin Group Ireland, 25 St. Stephen's Green, Dublin 2, Ireland (a division of Penguin Books Ltd.)
Penguin Group (Australia), 250 Camberwell Road, Camberwell, Victoria 3124, Australia
(a division of Pearson Australia Group Pty. Ltd.)
Penguin Books India Pvt. Ltd., 11 Community Centre, Panchsheel Park, New Delhi—110 017, India
Penguin Group (NZ), 67 Apollo Drive, Rosedale, North Shore 0745, Auckland, New Zealand
(a division of Pearson New Zealand Ltd.)
Penguin Books (South Africa) (Pty.) Ltd., 24 Sturdee Avenue, Rosebank, Johannesburg 2196,
South Africa

Penguin Books Ltd., Registered Offices: 80 Strand, London WC2R 0RL, England

THE OUTCAST

A Berkley Book / published by arrangement with the author

PRINTING HISTORY
Berkley edition / June 2007

ISBN: 978-0-425-21596-8

BERKLEY®
Berkley Books are published by The Berkley Publishing Group,
a division of Penguin Group (USA) Inc.,
375 Hudson Street, New York, New York 10014.
BERKLEY is a registered trademark of Penguin Group (USA) Inc.
The "B" design is a trademark belonging to Penguin Group (USA) Inc.

PRINTED IN THE UNITED STATES OF AMERICA

10 9 8 7 6 5 4 3 2 1

*For I will pass through the land of Egypt this night,
and will smite all the firstborn in the land of Egypt,
both man and beast; and against all the gods of Egypt
I will execute judgment . . .*
—Exodus 12:12

*And I beheld when he had opened the sixth seal,
and lo, there was a great earthquake;
and the sun became black as sackcloth of hair . . .*
—Revelation 6:12

/C

*We must remember that even God has need of
an avenging angel who wields a mighty sword
and has his seat at God's left hand.*

1.

THOMAS Cade lolled lazily on the cool grass bank of Plum Creek, watching the bobber on his fishing line move gently in a tiny circle in the slow current. The sun was warm on his shoulders and chest, and the Indian summer scent from the changing leaves of the oak and ash trees in the Tennessee hills left him feeling sleepy. Dimly, he could hear the contented grunts of pigs as they rooted through the mud in their pens on the other side of the Osage orange grove that his father, the Reverend Micah Cade, had planted to act as a windbreak when the blizzards came into the hills. The pens and corral where the milch cow and Hampshire pigs were kept were the same soft silver-gray color of weathered wood as the cabin—like all the other cabins in the hills where they lived a short distance from his father's Church of the Navarene. The planks of the cabin were twelve inches wide, grooved and pinned, and overlapped each so chinking had not been necessary.

The roof had cedar shingles and was set at a single pitch
for the rain to sluice down. From a distance, when the sun
was full upon it, it shimmered like a translucent gray pearl.

"Thomas!"

He grimaced as he recognized his father's voice, then
sighed, and pulled in his fishing line, wrapping it carefully
around the cane pole. He stripped the worm he was using
as bait from the hook and tucked the hook under two turn-
ings of the line.

"Thomas!"

There was an edge to his father's voice now, but still
Tom didn't hurry as he made his way back to the grove and
slipped through the Osage orange trees.

His father stood on the porch of the cabin, his hands on
his hips, white patriarchal beard bristling in the noon sun.
He had dressed all in black, with the exception of the white
Wesley collar he affected although he did not believe in
the teachings of John Wesley. His blue eyes narrowed as
he watched his son amble slowly across the clearing to the
bottom of the steps.

Tom planted the cane pole by his bare feet and looked
up at his father. "Yes, Pa?" he asked.

His father shook his head. "Thomas, didn't I tell you to
keep an eye on the cow?"

Tom glanced at the empty corral next to the springhouse
filled with black widows and hornets. The gate stood wide
open, the shuttle bar nudged back far enough to slip from
its lodging. He sighed and nodded. "Yes, Pa, you did. But
I told Matthew to watch her for an hour or two."

Micah studied his son, tall and gangly, with large bones
that promised the man to come. His blue eyes seemed to
bore into the back of people's minds and read their
thoughts there. His hair, the color of a raven's wing, was

long and shaggy, and a shock of it continually fell down over his forehead.

Sixteen years old, Micah thought. The bloom of my seed. The one upon whom I hung such high hopes. Micah took a deep breath and let it out slowly, resisting the impulse to lash out at his son. Those days were numbered now, and he could tell from the resentment that built up within his son's eyes that many more tongue-lashings would not be tolerated.

"Thomas," he said quietly. "The job of watching the cow was one given to you to do, not for you to give to Matthew. That was your responsibility and you shoveled it off on another. Remember the parable of the faithful and unfaithful servant."

"Yes, Pa," Tom said dutifully, but his father was lost in his own thoughts.

"That parable illustrates that the servant teaches not only that you must be faithful to your master, but with that faithfulness comes additional and greater responsibility. You must accept responsibility and not pass it off on your brother or anyone else."

Tom's blue eyes looked like agates set in a wooden face as he listened. Inside, he burned with a resentment born from past lectures when his father would rebuke him for being different from his brothers, Matthew, Mark, and Luke.

"You are the oldest son," Micah continued. "And the others look to you to see what you will do."

"Yes, Pa. I'll just go get that cow now," Tom said. He turned to go.

"I'm not finished," Micah said quietly.

Tom turned back, the muscles at the corners of his jaws

working angrily. Micah started to speak, then changed his mind.

"You'd better check out Mr. Johnson's cornfield first," he said resignedly. He felt defeated at such moments. "Remember what Mr. Johnson said he'd do the next time he found our cow in the cornfield."

"She does have a liking for sweet corn," Tom said.

"Her liking is not a concern of mine," Micah said. "That cow has a mind of her own and it's going to get her in trouble someday. Some people are like that too."

"Meaning me?" Tom said. His eyes had turned darker as he felt anger bubbling close to the surface.

"A wise man learns from everything around him," Micah said. "You go find that cow now and bring her home. We'll talk more about this later. After you have read Matthew 24:45–51 and Luke 12:41–46."

"Yes, Pa," Tom said resentfully. Always, these talks ended with assignments to read the Scriptures or the works of dead poets his father was fond of quoting as if they too were gospel, as if he wanted to make the son the image of the father and his father before him, Grandpa Jonas Cade, who wore the same type of black suit with Wesley collar as his offspring and preached the same narrow tracks of fire and brimstone and the saving of only a handful of God's creatures who were deserving of His grace.

Tom leaned the cane pole against the side of the house and walked down the narrow lane to the dirt road leading past the church. He trudged along it, feet kicking up tiny puffs of dust that hung in the air and made him cough until he felt trapped deep in dust. He pulled the frayed and broken straw hat off his head and squinted up at the sun high in the sky, a bright orange ball. He glanced down at his patched overalls and the thin linen shirt that was missing a button at the collar, which he closed with a pin whenever a lady came calling on his father. Since the death of his mother two years this coming Christmas, there'd been no one to sew buttons on shirts except himself and his father.

A rattlesnake announced a warning as Tom passed, and for a moment, Tom was tempted to go back and hunt him down in the tall bluegrass beside the road. The last one he'd found had gone a good five feet, and he'd sold the skin to Al Perkins, who owned the general store in Bundren Gap, for a dollar. Perkins added the amount to the account that Tom kept at the store, where he sold the muskrat and raccoon skins from his traps in the woods. By his reckoning, he had nearly enough to buy the used Spencer .54 that Perkins had taken in trade for performing his undertaker's duties on a traveler who had been killed in a knife fight in the shanty behind the sawmill on Plum Creek, where the Steppins brothers sold their moonshine that had such a bite to it that it could knock the eyes out of a rooster.

Bundren Gap was a four-building town that consisted of Perkins's Store, Watson's Saddlery, Tull's Tavern, and Doc Henry's place that doubled as a surgery, but pickings were slim for Doc Henry as old Widow Wilson, who lived up on Raventop, had been midwifing for more years than anyone around knew. Her potions, backed by a healthy jolt of the Steppinses' first-run-through corn mash, had more respect than the medicine provided by Doc Henry's apothecary skills.

"Good for stomachee and rheum-tis-me and general choler," Widow Wilson would announce, and if a soothing seeker needed a potion for something else, she cheerfully added to the list of ailments that could be cured by one of her tiny black bottles.

The rattler buzzed again, but Tom moved regretfully on down the road, watching his shadow grow long on the road as he followed it west toward the Johnson place. Maybe on the way back from rescuing the milch cow the rattler would still be there, lazing around in the cool grass from the heat.

Tom reached the edge of the Johnson field, and could see where the cow had managed to knock a railing off and step over it into the corn. For a moment, he thought about trying to take the cow out of the corn without Johnson knowing about it, but if his pa found out he'd collected the cow without admitting to the damage in the field, another parable would be forthcoming. He wasn't really certain how many parables there were, but by his reckoning, he'd had at least a hundred over the years, and that wasn't counting the books on philosophy that his pa insisted he read as well.

Tom walked on down to the lane leading up to the Johnson cabin. Johnson's oldest girl, Eula, was sitting on an old wicker rocker on the front porch, running a brush through her long yellow hair. When she saw Tom approaching, she raised her hand and drew it down her hair, arranging it to fall in large curls over her melon breasts. Tom always felt nervous around her as when he looked at her, her eyes seemed to become secretively all-knowing, and he was pretty certain that eternal grace and salvation were not upon her—at least at that moment.

He stopped at the foot of the steps leading to the porch and touched the brim of his hat.

"Afternoon, Miss Eula," he said. "Your pa around?"

Eula stretched one long shapely leg out in front of her, pointing her toes so her homespun dress draped and Tom could look up into the shadows.

"Now, what you be wantin' him for?" she asked huskily, as if she had too much smoke in her voice.

"Reckon I've gotta beg his pardon again," Tom said. He looked away from the shadows beneath her dress. "Our milch cow's managed to get into his cornfield."

"Pa ain't gonna like that," Eula said. She leaned forward, and Tom could see the damp circles her breasts made against the front of her dress.

"Yes, ma'am, I know," Tom said. "But that cow sure has a liking for sweet corn and your pa's got the nearest field around."

"She sounds like a smart cow," Eula said. She bit her lower lip, making it appear more bee-stung than normal.

"If'n she's so damn smart, she'd realize that your pa's ready to pepper her hide with buckshot," Tom answered. "He around? I reckon I'd better apologize and figure out some sort of restitution with him."

"Well, he ain't here," she said sullenly. "He went possum hunting last night with Old Hank and hasn't come home yet. Chances are he's holed up back in the swales with a jug or two. He dearly loves to top off a night's hunting with mash whiskey. Says it makes him feel foggy and cool inside. He'll be sleeping up right now, I reckon. Probably won't be home until eventide. You want to wait? I've got a goat fried up inside."

"I'd better get that cow out from the corn," Tom mumbled. "Pa'd have my hide stretched on the springhouse if I let anything happen to that cow."

She pouted. "Well, you can tie her up and then come on back up to the house."

"Yes, ma'am, I could do that. But if your pa came home and found that cow tied off, he'd figure out what had happened pretty quick. I think it better if I just take her on back home. Not that I don't appreciate the offer," he added quickly so as not to offend.

Eula ignored him. She tugged at her dress until she pulled it down well over her breasts.

"It shore is hot, ain't it?" she said. "Be nice to cool off down under the willows by the creek."

Her eyes changed expression and looked like two candles guttering down into the sockets of iron candlesticks.

"Want a drink of water?" she asked, rising lazily.

"If it's not too much trouble," Tom answered.

"Water's right here," she said, using her shapely toes to nudge a bucket by the porch post. She crossed to it and filled a gourd, handing it to him. "Water always tastes better when it's set a while in a cedar bucket, don't you think?"

He had to admit that the water had a warmish-cool taste to it like the smell of cedar trees in a hot July breeze. He handed the gourd back and she dropped it into the bucket.

"Tell you what," she said, stretching her arms and arching her back. "How about I help you with that old cow and we go on down to the creek for a swim to cool off? It'll be hot work getting that cow out of the cornfield when she won't want to go."

"That cow does have a mind of her own," Tom said, feeling foolish at having nothing more clever to say. But when Eula got to acting like this, it made him feel all hot and flustered inside, like he was coming down with the fall fever and had to be dosed with castor oil.

Eula smiled lazily and stepped down off the porch. She stood so close to Tom that he could smell the soap on her skin and the faint sweat smell of the woman beneath. He became suddenly conscious of the stories he'd heard about her from his friends while sharing corn-silk cigarettes behind the church after Sunday services.

"Eula likes a sampling in her men," Billy Eston had said, coughing up the words from lungs filled with smoke. "And there's a lot of men who've enjoyed the sampling."

Knowing nods came from the others, but Tom kept quiet to not draw attention to himself.

"Maybe we'd better go get her out of that corn," Eula drawled. She turned and walked away, her backside switching under her thin dress like two raccoons wrestling in a gunnysack.

Swallowing hard, Tom followed her down the slight slope to where the cornfield began. They could hear the cow rustling among the tall stalks.

"You go down the left, and I'll come in from the right," Eula said. "We'll push her back to the end of the field. I reckon she came in where that corner railing don't fit so well?"

Tom nodded. "Yeah. But she's a stubborn cuss. We'll have to keep her from doubling back and around on us. She knock down any more of your pa's corn and he'll know for certain that she's been in it. Fact, he'll probably know anyhow," he added gloomily.

"Cows don't move until they're pushed," Eula said, moving off to the right.

Tom slipped down the rows, jumping back and forth between them as he narrowed down on the milch cow. He could hear Eula slipping through the stalks on his right, the wrinkled leaves of the corn brushing against her dress like a gentle wind across sunburnt skin.

The cow saw them coming and tried to move around them, but they stepped in the cow's path, turning her with waving hands and shouts of "Whoo bossy." The cow flung

a slather over her shoulders and turned and moved back the
way she'd come, walking fast and stiff-legged along the
path of downed stalks, her milk bag swinging from side to
side.

When they came to the fence, she came to a scuttering
halt and made one last try to get past them, but then lowered her head and stepped resignedly over the bottom railing and turned down the road, ambling slowly into the sun
back toward the Cade place.

Eula swung into step beside Tom, breathing hard, her
breasts heaving so hard her nipples showed like ripe
huckleberries. "That pussel-gutted bitch gave us a time,"
she said.

Tom watched her breasts strain against the thin fabric
and swallowed. His face reddened, and he lowered his
head to stare at the road and the dust sifting like flour over
her highly arched bare feet. She caught his stare and a
strange smile curved her lips.

"What you thinkin'?" she asked. But before he could
answer, she waved her hand in front of her like a fan and
said, "Whew, but it's a hot one."

He looked at the fine sheen of perspiration formed on
her high forehead and cheeks and how it seemed to flow
like a thin sheet of water down to the top of her breasts before soaking into her dress. He felt the trickle of sweat
moving down his spine, between his shoulder blades, and
soaking into his coveralls.

"Too hot to be out in the sun like this," she said, fanning
herself with her hand. Her eyes flickered to his, hot and
warm.

"Want my hat?" he asked.

She pushed damp tendrils of hair off her forehead and

smiled at him, her lips curving deep into her cheeks. "Then, what'll you wear?" she asked playfully.

He shrugged. "Sun don't bother me that much. And we're coming down to our place now. Be under the shade in no time."

"I can wait," she said. She reached over and took his hand, and he nearly jerked away, feeling like he'd been scalded by her touch. But she tightened her grip, and his heart began to hammer in his chest like it was trying to break through the breastbone.

"Little jumpy, ain't you?" she asked. Her eyebrows arched suggestively.

"A bit," he admitted. He looked over at her. It wasn't that he hadn't seen her before and felt all flustered for some reason around her. It was just that he was looking at her differently and she was looking at him differently with those tiny fires like guttering candles in her eyes.

She laughed and squeezed his hand as they came up to the lane leading to Tom's home. The cow turned obediently into the lane and ambled up as if she'd been planning on doing that once she'd eaten her fill at the cornfield. Tom waited until she'd stepped into the corral, and then drew the latch bar across the stilt poles and wedged it in place with a wood chip.

"Now, let's see you get outta that one," he muttered at her.

The cow ignored him and walked over to the water trough and lowered her head, drinking.

"Come on," Eula whispered. "I'm hot. Let's go cool off down at the creek."

Tom cast a quick eye at the cabin, hesitated, then nodded. Boldly, he took her hand, feeling the calluses on her palms, and they ran lightly together down the slope strewn

with bluebells and white clover. They slipped past the
black raspberry bushes, and came to a halt under an old
willow tree whose branches draped over the water like a
lacy green curtain. Eula halted under the branches and
backed against the trunk. Her eyes were shining now like
sun-struck glass. He stood a few feet away, watching her
breathe deeply like she couldn't suck enough air into
her lungs. Then she laughed, and in one motion pulled her
dress over her head and stood naked before him. He gasped
as she laughed again and ran lightly past him, cleaving the
creek water in a smooth dive that took her down deep into
the water. She came up and used her palms to push her hair
smoothly back from her forehead.

"The water's nice," she said. "Come on in."

Then he was naked, and the water was cold upon him
before he realized he'd stripped down and Eula was up
around him, her legs locked around his waist, her lips kiss-
ing him with a hunger that was both frightening and filling.
Above them, a jay shrieked and squirrels chattered warnings at the jay to stay away from their nests in the boles of
the oak trees.

Later, when they were dozing, wrapped in each other's
naked arms under the canopy of willow, a deer came down
to drink at the creek. Tom moved slightly and the deer
paused, one foot lifted for quick flight. But the deer heard
no further noise that was strange to him, and he bent his
slender neck for a drink as Tom slipped his lips close to
Eula's neck and drank the salty softness in the hollow
there.

2

MICAH sat on his rocker on the porch, rubbing his knees as the bullbats came swooping through the near dark. He was getting old, he reflected, as his arthritis had begun bothering him on a nightly basis despite the slippage in weather. For a moment, he remembered with a pang of regret the death of Lisa, his wife, five years ago. Had she still been alive, she would have rubbed liniment on his knees and warmed his bed on the cool nights that settled in like damp blankets before the first snowfall. But most of all, she would have made all the difference in the raising of the children, especially Tom. She had a way of tempering his lectures to the boy and softening his anger, which, he had to admit, often came away with punishments too harsh for the offense. Yes, it took two to raise a family to its finest moment, and the absence of one often created a deep gap in the family that could never be filled.

It's not as if you haven't tried, he told himself as the

twilight deepened. But Tom's different from the others. There's a strength in him that just naturally causes him to seek his own way despite what you tell him. It seems at times that he wants to make his own mistakes and not learn from the wisdom of his elders.

Movement came to him out of the darkness lit by a quarter moon. He squinted, feeling his muscles tighten with warning, then relaxed as he recognized the gait of his oldest son. He fumbled his watch out of his pocket and held it against the moonlight to check the time. When he opened the case, the familiar tinkle of "Eroica" sprinkled through the night.

"A bit late getting home, Thomas," he said as the boy came up to the steps.

Tom paused, one foot on the bottom step. Moonlight gleamed off his hair, still wet from the creek and pushed back flat off his forehead.

"Just swimming," Tom said.

"You missed supper."

"That's all right. I'm not hungry."

"A growing boy needs his food," Micah said, mildly reproving. "You need to fill out some before you start going without."

Tom shrugged. "Man doesn't live by bread alone," he said.

Micah felt his lips tug, then said, "Perhaps not a man, but you are still a youth studying to be a man."

"I'm old enough to do a man's work," Tom said. He couldn't keep the defensive note out of his voice.

"And you squander your time in play," Micah said. "The Lord gives only so much time to a man and it is up to him to spend it wisely."

The screech of a hunting owl made both look toward the dark woods. Suddenly, Micah shivered.

"Someone's walking on my grave," he said.

"The nights are getting cooler," Tom answered.

"It isn't that. There's just something about this night that seems all wrong. I can't put my finger on it. Sort of like a sense that there's evil coming and I won't be able to do anything about it."

"You getting superstitious, Pa?" Tom asked.

"No, I'm not," Micah said. "But sometimes I get these feelings and I can't get shut of them." He sighed. "Guess I'm just getting old. And you'd better be getting to bed. Matthew milked the cow tonight, so you need to get up early and take the morning milking for him. Fair is fair. Make certain that you do that reading I gave you. Hear now?"

For a moment, Tom was tempted to tell his father to let Matthew do the milking steadylike, but the memory of Eula under the willow and in the water tempered his tongue. He nodded, and the boards creaked on the porch as he walked past his father into the house.

Micah sat a long while, studying the moon and the Big Dipper. A shooting star made a long white arch like a spider's filament over the night.

"Thou shalt not be afraid of the arrow that flieth by day, nor the terror that cometh by night," he said softly. "Remember the days of thy youth."

The fireflies had come out now, from the thick grass leading down to the Osage orange grove. For a second, he thought he saw a will-o'-the-wisp, but decided that it was only fireflies glowing through a slow fog rising from the creek.

"Enough, old man. You're letting your imagination run

away from your common sense," he said. He rose, stretched, then moved into the house, carefully locking the door behind him.

• • •

Three weeks passed, and it was the day that Tom turned in to Perkins the skin of a doe he had caught in a deadfall a month earlier, and collected the used Spencer .54 that he had been coveting for over a year and one box of ammunition, when Eula and her angry father came to call on Reverend Micah Cade. Matthew, Mark, and Luke were chasing fireflies down at the creek, while Tom and Micah were in the house finishing supper in the late afternoon when they heard Johnson clumping on the porch like he was wearing iron shoes.

"Cade!" Johnson hollered. "Where's that no-account son of your'n?"

Micah raised his grizzled eyebrows at Tom, then quietly placed his coffee cup on the table, rose, and stepped out to greet the red-faced Johnson. Johnson backed down the steps, his jackboots planted in the dust of the front yard.

Micah stood on the porch, gazing down at the red-faced Johnson, who was holding a shotgun in the crook of his arm. Beside him stood his daughter, sullen-faced, a huge bruise covering her left eye and spreading down like an obscene spider across her cheek.

Micah's face tightened, but he forced his voice to remain quiet and calm as he addressed the angry man.

"Yes, Mr. Johnson, what can I do for you?" he asked.

Johnson gestured violently with the shotgun.

"It ain't you I want! It's that son of your'n. Where he at?"

"What is it you wish with my son?" Micah asked quietly.

But the quiet observer would have observed how the muscles along his back tightened and how the anger he felt at seeing a young girl so abused made his frame become rigid and taut.

Johnson reached over and grabbed the girl by her elbow. His grip made her wince with pain, but before she could try and jerk free, he threw her contemptuously at the foot of the steps leading up to the porch. Her head struck the bottom step and bounced, and she cried from the pain.

"There's no call for you abusing your child, Mr. Johnson," Micah said. His voice had dropped tellingly, but Johnson was beyond listening to the quiet sounds of warning around him.

"Yer son has been having his way with my daughter! And now she's with his child! And I want to see that sumbitch out here right now!"

Johnson's hand tightened threateningly on the shotgun, the barrels coming up to waver and hold on Micah's chest. But Micah refused to budge as his eyes burned from the soft blue in the iris that moved others to feel comfort to the steel-gray that made the guilty of his congregation shiver in fear of their souls.

Micah looked down at the girl cowering on the ground, and stepped down from the porch to raise her gently by the hand. He looked into her eyes, but she ducked her head away, refusing to meet his gaze. He reached with thumb and forefinger and forced her face back to his. She closed her eyes.

"What is it, Eula? What has happened?" he asked.

"Tom and me, well, you know what," she said. She stepped back from him and stared at him defiantly. "We been together for a spell."

Micah stared at her for a long moment. Her cheeks

burned red under his gaze, and she shifted her weight from one bare foot to the other and pulled at a tendril of yellow hair that curled down by her cheek.

"You gonna call that boy out here or am I gonna have to go in and git 'im?" Johnson asked angrily. "This thing don't set well in the hills, y'know. Our kin ain't gonna like it one bit."

Micah sighed and called, "Thomas! Come out here."

He heard the creak of the porch boards as Tom stepped out of the door and came up beside him. He turned his head and looked at the boy, seeing for the first time that the boy was near to being a man. Briefly, he wondered about the passing of time, seeing in the boy the history of himself and knowing the wildness that had run through him in his youth until his own father had caned it out of him.

"Thomas, you heard what Mr. Johnson said." Tom nodded. "Is there something you want to tell me?" he asked quietly. He nodded toward Johnson and his daughter.

Tom shook his head.

"No, sir," he said.

"Mr. Johnson says that Eula is going to have your child. Is that true?"

Tom took a deep breath, then met Micah's gaze. "No, sir. I don't think so."

"You damn whelp!" Johnson said threateningly. He raised the shotgun. "Y'all saying my girl's lying about you having your way with her?"

"No, sir" Tom said. "But we only been together like that a couple weeks now."

Micah heard the strength in his son's words and knew Tom was telling the truth. He shook his head and sighed deeply.

"What are you saying, Tom?" he asked quietly. "Best to

get it out in the open in plain language so we all know where you're standing."

Tom turned his attention back to Eula. She stared back, and he could see in the depths of her eyes a glimmer of triumph. For a brief moment, he had a glimpse of his future in the cutting of firewood and wash pots and the small cabin they would be sharing and the fields he'd be plowing and planting and the sprawl of children clambering over each other and the loathing that he would feel for her in the years to come.

"We've been together," he said quietly. "But I wasn't the first, and I reckon we can all count, can't we, Eula? You just pick my name out of a hat?"

Her face flushed hotter and she shook her head, not trusting the words she wanted to speak. But her father spared her that.

"You accusing my daughter of sleeping around with others before she walks to the altar?"

"Reckon that's up to Eula to claim," Tom said. "But the truth is that we haven't been together long enough for that child to be mine." He turned back to his father. "You remember the last time when the milch cow got out and you sent me to Mr. Johnson's place to get her out of his sweet corn?"

Micah nodded slowly.

"That was the first time I ever spent time with Eula." Tom looked back at Johnson. "I ain't ducking responsibility, Mr. Johnson, but this ain't right."

"Right is what y'make it," Johnson said. He gestured toward Eula. "Truth is, she's having a child and y'just admitted that y'been with her. Now, I reckon y'just have to marry her 'fore talk runs through the hills and spoils her r'ppetashun."

Eula's eyes glinted with satisfaction as she looked up at
Tom. The shotgun in her father's hands held the resolution
to her problem. That, and the Johnson kin that numbered
greatly in the hills, would insure that Tom would have to
marry her to keep a feud from breaking out between the
Cades and the Johnsons. Feuds were long and costly and
the Cades were short-numbered. Besides, the reverend
wouldn't allow such bloodshed to happen, given his preach-
ing against the feud between the Wallaces and Stevenses
that had taken its toll on both families before Long Stevens
settled it by putting a ball through the head of the last Wal-
lace, leaving him facedown in the dusty street before
Perkins's store. She saw the resignation in the reverend's
face, and knew he was thinking the same.

The truth was that Eula had no idea who was the father
of the child she carried, but she knew that taking the son of
the reverend as her husband would lend her respectability
and make her a woman to be counted among the families
eking out a hardscrabbled living in the hills. Tongues
would be wagging behind closed doors and in quiet corners, but no one would say anything where offense might
be taken.

Micah shoved his hands in the pockets of his trousers
and spread his legs. The dying sun touched his white hair,
making him look like a prophet who had just stepped from
the pages of the Bible. Muscles worked at the corners of
his jaw as he stared down at Johnson and the shotgun.

"There'll have to be a wedding," he said quietly. "But
I think we'd better know the names of the other men before we come to a decision about who will be marrying
whom. Tom was wrong in what he did, but that doesn't
mean he should pay for the dalliance of another. You
know that's right, Mr. Johnson. Things just don't add up

that way, and you waving that shotgun around doesn't make any difference."

"That y'final word?" Johnson asked.

Micah nodded.

"Then, I reckon that y'all have brought what's gonna happen down upon your own heads," Johnson said.

He raised the shotgun and centered it on Tom's chest, but before he could trigger a barrel, Micah stepped in front of his son.

"You don't want the law coming down upon you, Mr. Johnson," Micah said quietly. "And it will if you fire that shotgun. Now, turn around and go back to your home. I'll come over tomorrow and we'll sit down and talk after you've cooled off and see if we can't figure out the proper way to solve this problem."

"There ain't gonna be no sittin' and talkin' when doin' has to be done," Johnson said. But he lowered the shotgun, knowing that a load of buckshot in the reverend's chest would bring all the people in the hills down upon him and his kin despite anything he could claim to the contrary. "Your boy's gonna marry Eula here. Now, or later, and that's a fact. Even if my kin has to haul him over to the next county. Or"—he paused deliberately—"these hills are gonna run red with Cade blood."

He spat, and the spittle curled into dirt balls as he turned and took Eula by the arm, spinning her around and sending her stumbling forward a few steps before she caught herself.

"Y'git home now," Johnson said. He looked up at the reverend, still standing in front of Tom. "This ain't over with. Not by a long shot. Reverend or no reverend."

Father and daughter walked away. Micah watched until they turned the corner in the road leading back to the

Johnson place before he turned to study his son. Tom met his eyes, head held high, and Micah sighed and placed his hand on Tom's shoulder.

"I'm sorry, Pa," Tom said.

"I confess that sometimes I don't understand the Lord's doings," Micah said softly. "But I think I have a pretty good idea about man's doings after spending some time in this world."

He glanced off into the darkness in the direction the Johnsons had disappeared.

"Mr. Johnson isn't going to let this alone," he said sadly.

"I swear that I'm not the father, Pa," Tom said.

Micah squeezed his son's shoulder and said. "I know that, Thomas. You were wrong, but two wrongs don't make a right. Mr. Johnson is looking for respectability by having his daughter marry the son of the preacher man. I have a hunch the two of them know the father and decided you were the best choice. Or," he added after a moment's deliberation, "the only choice given another."

Tom remained silent as Micah stood in the dark, considering.

"We cannot have another feud in these hills," Micah said at last.

"I'm not afraid of the Johnsons," Tom said defiantly.

Micah squeezed Thomas's shoulder hard.

"That's not the point!" he said sharply. "You have a lot to learn yet. A lot. There's a big difference between being afraid and being cautious, and one don't necessarily mean the other. But"—his voice softened—"I reckon I'm plumb out of time to teach you. You'll have to go away, Thomas. That's the only way I can see a chance to avoid bloodshed and wrong. I'm sorry, Thomas, but that's the only way."

Tom nodded, a lump forming in his throat. But at the same time, excitement began to race through his veins.

"You've had a good education, Thomas. The best that I could give under our situation. But don't forget that you still aren't finished learning. Read, Thomas, read. And keep your knowledge to yourself. Don't offer information to others and let them realize how much you know. Some men will use what you know against you if they can. It's a different world outside these hills, and I'm not certain that it's a better world as there is an evil at work in the land where men make their own law away from God's commandments." He reached and placed his hand on Tom's shoulder. "Remember, son, to trust God above what others tell you and you won't go wrong. You won't be the most popular among men, but you will be right and that's enough for any man."

His hand fell away. His eyes suddenly misted and Tom looked away, embarrassed by his father's sense of loss. A sadness seemed to fall upon the night that edged away the excitement that he felt, and he too began to feel the same sense of loss that his father was feeling.

"I wish," Micah said softly, "that I would have made more time for you. But we are all subject to the Lord's doings and to question His plan for us is to question ourselves. Maybe that's the way it's supposed to be. The older I get, the more I realize I don't know and the more that I'll never know. Be careful, Thomas. You're the oldest, but you're still young and time will run away from you before you know it, and you'll have to live the rest of your life with regret for what you could have done and what you should have done. Act wisely. But remember that even Solomon, with all the wisdom that the Lord gave him, made mistakes. Don't dwell on your mistakes, but learn to live better because of them. I reckon that's all I can give you anymore."

He turned and walked slowly into the cabin, his shoulders slumped like an old man feeling the burden of his years upon him as an unbearable load that would have made even Job wince.

Tom stood for a long moment, watching the fireflies play along the edge of the creek and listening to the sounds of the night as crickets spoke to each other. A lump came into his throat, and a premonition that he would never again see his home came upon him like a dreadnaugbt inching its way up the creek.

That night, the Leonids showered through the heavens as Tom shouldered his pack, took his rifle, and slipped away through the night, working through the hills on a long detour that would take him around the Johnson place, yet holding steady on a westerly direction. The moon came up blood-red, a hunter's moon that gave the dark woods a strange luminescence. Dark limbs lifted like withered arms to the sky. Somewhere an owl hooted and there was the sudden screech of a nighthawk hunting, but they were all familiar and sad sounds to young Tom Cade.

• • •

Tom made his way through the hills, avoiding the roads as much as possible, until three weeks later, he stood on a hill overlooking St. Louis. His belly was empty, although he had made a breakfast out of acorns and blueberries that he'd picked as he came down through the mountains. Twice, he'd seen deer and twice he'd raised the Spencer to his shoulder, only to lower it as he realized how far a shot could be heard in the mountains if someone was following him. No one was, but he did not know that the angry John-

son had been forced to abandon his matrimonial plans for
his daughter when he learned that the planned husband-to-
be had left during the night for parts unknown. He did not
know that Ed Wilson's boy had been tapped as his replace-
ment, and that Wilson's clan was large enough to not fear
the Johnson clan, and the beginnings of a feud that would
spread like wildfire over the hills for the next five years
had begun when Young Wilson told his father that as near
as he could figure, there were at least ten other young men
in the hills that could be the father as well. Since Ed Wilson was a practical man and not used to bartering for goods
that had seen more than fair usage, he refused to be swayed
by Johnson's threatening shotgun.

During the weeks Tom worked his way west, he had
passed blacks working in the fields, their hands moving
crablike as they picked cotton and corn, but the newly
freed paid him no attention, for their freedom was only
marginal despite the government's assurances and to stare
too long at a white man could still bring hate and explosive
anger to some sullen whites who remembered the ways of
their world that had been shattered by war.

He stared out over the land to where the skyline appeared as brown paper edged by deep blue, then sighed and
moved down out of the hills into the town.

He found work on a steamboat moving upriver, but that
lasted only two months. A hard-shouldered man who had
a reputation for brawling up and down the river thought the
quiet boy to be fair pickings for his brutish and bullying
ways, until one day the boy beat him down and threw him
into the river. The captain was angry that he'd had to stop
the boat and fish the man from the water, and at the next
stop for firewood, the boy took half wages and began
working his way west through Kansas to where he'd heard

the Union Pacific railroad was hiring men to lay track. At first, the foreman was reluctant to hire the boy, but the breadth of the boy's shoulders made him think again. Still, he hesitated until the boy took a sledgehammer and moved into line, swinging effortlessly with the easy movement of one who has spent many years chopping firewood. The foreman reconsidered and put the boy at the end of the finishing line where he would seat spikes that had not been driven fully into the ties.

Slowly, the track crawled across Kansas. Railheads sprang up and became towns, and the foreman discovered that the boy was an excellent shot with the Spencer and moved the boy from swinging hammers to hunting wild game to feed the men.

Tom was happy with the change for he was given the use of a mule to ride out on the prairie away from the camp in search of deer or antelope or buffalo to keep the cook pots full. Hunting was a full-time chore as the hardworking men built up huge appetites that had to be eased to keep the men from fighting amongst themselves.

At first, finding game was easy, but as Tom killed more and more, the animals drifted away from their old grounds, forcing Tom to go farther and farther afield in search of them.

One day, as he was riding south, he came upon a wounded man lying near death in a buffalo wallow. He approached the man slowly, and turned him over. The man wore a white shirt with a black string tie and black trousers. A black frock coat lay where he had shrugged out of it. Around his waist was a heavy black gunbelt. A Navy Colt was in the holster. The man moaned and his eyes fluttered open. The light seemed to darken, and Tom looked up at the sun and saw the beginning of a solar eclipse, a black ball moving across the sun's path.

"Who . . . are . . . you?" the man gasped.

"Tom Cade," he answered.

But the man did not hear Tom's words as darkness came over his vision when the sun turned black and covered the earth in early twilight. The grama grass turned silver in the light and a lone wolf howled in the distance.

Tom loaded the man on his horse and, mounting his mule, rode down to Cottonwood Creek. Instinct told him that the man needed sanctuary, and Tom found a place where the creek had carved a deep hole in the side of its bank where the horse and mule could be kept and Tom could care for the man. He unsaddled the man's horse and his mule and made two pairs of makeshift hobbles from his rope to keep the animals from wandering off. He made a pallet for the man with dead leaves and the man's saddle blanket and soogan, which he'd tied behind his saddle.

He made a small fire and stripped bark from a willow tree to form a crude pot, wrapping the sides with green willow shoots in the way he'd been shown by an old Cherokee Indian. The water would keep the bark from burning. He heated water and then turned to care for the man. He found that the man had torn his shirt and used pieces of it to plug four gunshot wounds. He bathed the wounds and gently worked the plugs out. The man moaned and tossed his head from side to side. Perspiration made his face and chest slick as firelight flickered off him. Tom bathed the wounds and bound them with cotton strips he tore from the man's shirt. After he finished, he took his Spencer and slipped out into the dark, hunting.

He found an antelope drinking about a mile downstream and killed it with a single shot to the neck. He quickly skinned the animal and took the choice cuts and made his way back to the camp, pausing to pick some wild rose hips and some prairie smoke whose roots he would pound to make a poultice to treat the man's wounds along with wood sorrel and globe mallow. Later, he found some hoary puccoon whose powdered root was good for gunshot wounds, and gathered that too along with some wild onion.

The man held the Navy Colt in his hand when Tom slipped under the overhang. The man's eyes were bright with fever, but he held the pistol steady on Tom.

"Who are you?" he asked hoarsely.

"Tom Cade. I found you on the prairie a few miles back and brought you here."

"I heard a gunshot."

Tom swung the antelope skin off his shoulder and dropped it on the ground.

"I shot an antelope about a mile downstream." He casually lifted the Spencer and crooked his thumb around the hammer. The man's eyes narrowed as he followed Tom's movement.

"Best take it easy," Tom said. "You're hurt bad. You don't want to make any mistakes right now."

The man studied Tom closely for a long moment, then said, "This your camp? Any others?"

Tom shook his head. "No. I hunt for the railroad."

"They'll be expecting you back soon," the man said.

Tom shrugged. "Maybe. Game's getting scarce around here. Sometimes, I'm gone for a day or two."

The man nodded. A small smile flickered across his thin lips. His eyes looked hollowed in his gaunt face above his salt-and-pepper beard. Tiny crow's-feet spread out from the corners of his eyes. He gestured with the pistol.

"You bothered with this?"

"Somewhat."

"But not afraid."

Tom shrugged. "A man's a fool if he's not afraid when someone points a gun at him."

The man lowered the gun and placed it on the blanket beside him. His lips tightened with pain as he slumped back on the ground. He gasped and bit his lips.

"I'll make some broth," Tom said, moving to the campfire. "I don't have much to work with, but we got to get something inside you."

"You haven't asked how I got shot," the man said.

"None of my business," Tom said. "You want to tell me, you'll tell me. I don't go hunting trouble."

The man tried to laugh and gasped from pain. "You may have bought yourself into my trouble by helping me. Smart thing for you to do is to climb on your horse and ride away."

"Only have a mule," Tom said. "And you're in no shape to ride anywhere for a while."

He cut pieces of meat and dropped them into the crude bark pot. Using a stone, he crushed the rose hips and sprinkled them in the pot, then added some of the globe mallow and wood sorrel.

"You know what you're doing?" the man asked.

"Back in Tennessee, my father befriended an old Cherokee Indian once. He showed me. The Indian, I mean," Tom said.

"You know how to make a poultice? For my wounds?"

"If I can find the right roots," Tom said. "I'll look in the morning."

"Look in my saddlebags. You might find something useful there. There's some coffee and beans. You find my packhorse?" he asked suddenly.

"Nope. He must've wandered off. I'll look for him to-morrow too."

"Why are you doing this? You don't know me."

Tom smiled. "My father is a preacher. I must've heard the story of the Good Samaritan thirty times while I was growing up. I guess it just stuck with me."

"You don't care who I am?"

"Doesn't matter. You need help. I'm here. That's enough."

The man remained silent for a moment, then said, "I'm Sam Kilian. That mean anything to you?"

Coyotes began yapping in the distance downstream. Tom looked out into the darkness. "Guess they found the kill. Yeah, I've heard about a gunman named Kilian from down Texas way. Heard he killed eight men in a shoot-out near Pecos."

The man tried to laugh and gave it up. "I heard that too. Folks do like to add to stories. There were only two of them. Nobody kills eight men in a shoot-out. Not even Wild Bill was that good."

"I figured that," Tom answered. "Still, I heard there were others."

"Yes," Kilian said. "There were others. Too many. But I never killed nobody that didn't need killing and came hunting for it."

Tom nodded and rose, walking to Kilian's saddlebags. He rummaged in them and removed a blackened tin cup and a spoon.

"These'll come in handy," he said, returning to the fire. He stirred the stew carefully, then ladled some in the tin cup and carried it to the man. He spooned the broth be-tween Kilian's lips, waiting patiently while he swallowed painfully. He made a face.

"Doesn't taste very good."

"Didn't have much to work with," Tom said.

"Needs salt."

"Later. Right now, this is what we got to get into you. Then, you better sleep. I'll stand watch." He nodded at the bandaged wounds. "And we'd better hope that those don't begin to fester or I'll have to open them up."

"You still haven't asked how it happened."

"Later. You rest now," Tom said.

The man nodded and lay back wearily once he finished the broth. He sighed. His eyes flickered and his hand dropped down to rest upon the Navy Colt beside him. Then he sighed again and Tom watched as his chest begin to rise and fall gently. Then Tom rose and returned to the fire, and cut a slice of meat and stuck it on a sharpened willow branch and held it over the fire, turning it around patiently while it seared.

After eating, Tom checked the hobbles on the horse and mule, then took the Spencer and moved just beyond the edge of firelight and rested his back against his saddle, slipping the saddle blanket around his legs. He craned his head, studying the night heavens. He picked out the Big Dipper lying on its side, and followed the line of stars up to the Little Dipper and North Star. He studied Orion's Belt for a bit, then lowered his eyes and watched the fireflies play along the edges of the creek. Crickets sounded, and he could still hear the coyotes fighting over his kill. But he heard nothing that didn't belong to the night and the prairie, and after a while, he slipped into a light sleep.

3.

DAYS passed as Tom stayed with Kilian, caring for him. Twice, he had to open the wounds to drain them while Kilian tossed and moaned on his bedroll in fever. Tom found sassafras roots and willow and sorrel leaves, and made poultices that he laid upon the wounds to help them heal. He shot a sage hen one day and made a soup that he managed to spoon into Kilian during his lucid moments. He knew that the Union Pacific had probably written him off their records and his job was gone, but the wounded man needed attention and he couldn't bring himself to leave Kilian alone.

On the seventh day, the gunfighter opened his eyes and looked around him. His eyes were bright and clear and Tom knew the fever had passed, although Kilian was still weak and vulnerable, too weak to protect himself against the man or men who had put the bullets in him. Tom's eyes felt gritty from lack of sleep as he spent most of the nights watching the older man and listening for those who might still be hunting him.

The sun shone brightly and wildflowers were showing their colors along the creek bank and out on the prairie. Wrens sang in the branches of the cottonwood above their camp, and squirrels scampered through the chokecherry bushes that lined the creek on either side. He had staked the mule and horse in a nearby clearing so they could graze. Tom had found Kilian's packhorse and had picketed him as well with the others. He'd been relieved to discover a coffeepot and skillet in Kilian's pack along with some beans and coffee, and had supplemented their meager fare with Kilian's supplies.

"Morning," he said when Kilian's eyes lit upon him.

The gunfighter gave a faint smile. "You been here all the time?"

"You needed help," Tom said.

He poured a cup of coffee and carried it to Kilian, who levered himself up and held his head for a moment until his senses stopped swimming. Kilian took the cup and took a deep swallow, swearing softly as the hot coffee burned his tongue.

"How you feeling?" Tom asked.

"Like hammered buffalo shit," Kilian said. But he drank the coffee. He looked at the fire and studied the camp. "And hungry."

"I fried up a rabbit this morning. Think you could handle some?" Tom asked.

"Lead it on," Kilian said.

Tom nodded and rose to ready a tin plate for him. He heard a click and glanced over his shoulder, and saw the gunfighter checking the Navy Colt that Tom had left beside him.

"It's loaded," Tom said. "I charged it again this morning

in case the dew got to the powder. The caps seemed all right."

Kilian studied him curiously. "You did that? Why?"

Tom shrugged. "Whoever shot you must have had their reasons, and if the reasons were strong enough to shoot you to begin with, they probably want to make certain you're dead. I didn't want any surprises."

He nodded at the Spencer leaning against the cottonwood. Kilian smiled and leaned back against his saddle, holding the pistol in his hand.

"How old are you?" he asked.

"What's that got to do with it?"

"You seem pretty young to be thinking that way."

"Common reasoning," Tom said. "If I'd been the one who shot you, I'd want to make certain that you were dead. A wounded man's like a wounded bear. Both dangerous, but the man has a long memory and he doesn't forgive those who hurt him."

He rose to take the plate to Kilian and glanced at the animals. They had stopped grazing and stood with their ears pricked, staring down the creek. Tom gently placed the plate on the ground and stepped over to the Spencer. He picked the rifle up, cocking it.

"What's wrong?" Kilian asked.

"I don't know," Tom said. He nodded at the horses. "They know something, though."

The sound of horses splashing through the creek reached them, and two riders hove into view. Their unshaven faces were hard beneath their battered hats. They wore pistols on their left hips, butts canted forward. They pulled up when they saw Tom; then the one on the left nudged his horse away from his partner to put distance between them.

"Hello the camp!" the taller one said. He sat his horse

easily, hands resting on the pommel of his saddle. The other one held his reins in his left hand, his right resting lightly on his thigh.

"Hello yourself," Tom said easily.

The rider's eyes moved around the camp and stopped on Kilian, half-sitting, half-reclining against his saddle. A cold smile touched his lips.

"Seems like you've had a bit of trouble," the man said conversationally.

"No trouble," Tom said easily. "But you never can know."

"Uh-huh," the man said. He glanced over at his partner and then at the Spencer Tom held easily by his side.

"What can I do for you?" Tom asked.

"Could use a cup of coffee," the man answered.

"Sorry," Tom said. "We just ran out."

The man's eyes narrowed. "You're not very hospitable, boy."

"Well, the Good Book tells us to keep an eye out for the enemies of the Lord," Tom answered.

The man frowned. "What's that supposed to mean?"

"I reckon the Lord isn't the only one who has enemies. You two strike me as trouble. This is a peaceful camp and I intend on keeping it that way. So, why don't you and your partner just ride on."

The man smiled. "We look like trouble to you?"

"If you weren't, why'd you come riding down the creek. Strange way of getting from one place to the other unless someone was looking for you or you were looking for someone," Tom said.

"The kid's got a smart mouth," the other rider said.

The man looked at Kilian and his face tightened. "Well, I think we can just take care of any trouble by taking that man off your hands. He's a wanted man."

"Wanted by who?" Tom asked.

"The law."

"I don't see any badges on the two of you."

"They don't have any," Kilian said. "That's Jim and Roy Hardesty. They bushwhacked me down the trail some. Roy's the one on the left," he added.

Roy nodded at Kilian. "Seems like we didn't do a good enough job."

"Some men just don't accommodate others," Kilian said. "Then, there are those just not worth accommodating. Reckon you fall into both categories."

Jim looked at Tom and said, "You better get your horse and just ride on out of here. You don't want to buy in on this."

Tom smiled. "Reckon I wouldn't get far. Maybe as far as the horse before you'd put a bullet in me."

Roy smiled lazily. "Now, why would we want to do that?"

"Witness," Tom said. "You wouldn't want to leave one behind now, would you?"

"What makes you think we would be afraid of witnesses?"

"Like I said, you don't have badges," Tom answered.

"Damnit! This here's my badge!" Jim shouted, and reached for his pistol.

Tom tilted the Spencer forward, the barrel slapping into the palm of his hand as he pressed the trigger. The heavy bullet slammed into Jim, knocking him off his horse. Tom slipped to the side, levering another cartridge into the Spencer. For a second, he thought he was too late, but Kilian's bullet struck Roy in the shoulder, half-turning him, and his shot went wild. Tom fired again and the bullet struck Roy just above the belt buckle. He grabbed for the pommel as his horse began to buck, but he couldn't hold on and fell off his horse into the creek.

Tom levered another bullet into the Spencer and ran forward, splashing into the creek. He approached the fallen men carefully and rolled them over. Jim was dead, but Roy moaned, then cried out, clutching his belly where the heavy Spencer had blown a hole through him.

"Damn you! You've . . . killed . . . me!" he gasped.

Tom grabbed his collar and pulled him out of the creek. Roy cried with the movement, holding himself tightly against the pain. Tom laid the Spencer near him and ripped open the man's shirt, pulling his hands away from the wound. Blood gurgled out and Roy grabbed himself again.

"Let me see what I can do," Tom said, but Roy shook his head.

"Belly wound. Ain't nothing nobody can do. I'm . . . finished!" he said.

"He's right," Kilian said from his pallet. He tried to rise, but fell back, too weak to move. "A belly wound from that Spencer pretty much finishes one."

"You sonufabitch!" Roy said, gritting his teeth. "The others are coming. They'll . . ."

His eyes slipped out of focus. He drew a deep, rattling breath, and died.

Tom shook his head and folded Roy's hands upon his chest. He sighed, then rose and went back out into the creek and fished Jim out of the creek. His bullet had smashed a hole through Jim's chest, killing him instantly. Tom stretched him out beside his brother and stood, silently looking down at the two of them.

"They the first?" Kilian asked.

Tom glanced at him and nodded.

"I've never killed anyone before," he said.

"Strange," Kilian said. He took a deep breath and let it out slowly. "It seemed to come natural to you. I'd a-figured you for at least one or two before, the way you handled yourself and all. Most men freeze for a second. But you didn't."

Tom shrugged, and remained silent, staring down at the bodies of the brothers.

"You all right?" Kilian asked.

"Guess so," Tom said.

"You didn't have any choice," Kilian said. "They would have killed you for certain. That's what the Hardestys do."

Tom lifted his head and said, "Why were they after you?"

Kilian said, "I was marshaling down by Pecos and tried to arrest their cousin. He didn't cotton to that and tried to pull a gun."

"You killed him."

"Yes." Kilian remained silent, watching Tom as he stood by the brothers. "There's something you need to know." Tom looked up. "There's no going back from a killing and the Hardestys are a killing family. They'll come after you. And me. It won't be finished until they're gone or we are."

Tom nodded. "A feud. We had those back in the hills."

"Then, you know. You'd better catch up their horses."

Tom turned and waded back into the creek. Roy's horse shied away from his approach, but Tom talked softly to him until the bay stopped quivering and let him approach. Tom gathered the reins and stood beside the horse, speaking softly and rubbing his hand down the bay's neck until the bay relaxed and nudged him with its nose.

He led the bay out of the water and tied him off to a willow branch, and then went after Jim's horse, a white-faced sorrel that stood quietly where its rider had fallen. The reins trailed in the water, and Tom gathered them and led him out and tied him next to the bay. He pulled the saddles from both and stacked them under the cottonwood.

He went back to the bodies and said, "Well, I guess there's nothing for it but to bury them." He shook his head regretfully. "Sure wish they would have ridden away."

"Their kind never does," Kilian said softly. "I'm sorry, boy, but some people just don't have it in them to back away. They figured you for easy pickings. After you, they would have killed me."

"You still hit one," Tom pointed out.

"A lucky shot," Kilian said.

Tom studied him for a moment, then said, "Somehow, I don't think luck played much in it."

He kneeled beside the pair and unbuckled their gun-belts, then went through their pockets.

"What are you doing?" Kilian asked.

"Looking for someone to notify," Tom said. "People should know what happened to their kin. It's the decent thing to do."

"Decent has nothing to do with it," Kilian said. "Survival has everything. You notify them of your name and you brand yourself for them. Best to just bury them and leave it at that. Besides, the Hardestys will figure I did it. Nobody knows about you."

"God does," Tom said automatically.

"God?" Kilian shook his head. "Son, I don't know anything about you but I can tell you that out here, God has a tendency to look the other way. It's best if you get used to that."

Tom didn't answer, but stood and grabbed Roy by his ankles and began to drag him from the clearing.

"There's a little gully down the creek a ways. I'll put

them there and collapse the bank over them. That's the best I can do with no shovel."

Kilian shrugged. "Suit yourself. They're beyond knowing."

"But I'm not," Tom said quietly, and went to work.

•   •   •

That night, Tom sat cross-legged in front of the fire, looking at the pistols he'd fished from the creek. Roy had had a Navy Colt similar to Kilian's, but Jim had used a Smith & Wesson Schofield .45.

"You know anything about pistols?" Kilian asked.

Tom shook his head. "Nope. Never fired one. Couldn't afford anything but the rifle and a rifle's better use in the hills. Some men had pistols they carried in their waistbands, but most everyone depended upon rifles."

"Bring them here," Kilian said, elbowing himself up against his saddle.

Obediently, Tom gathered the pistols and rose, carrying them over to Kilian. He squatted beside the gunfighter and laid the pistols in his lap. Kilian picked up the Navy Colt and disassembled it, laying the pieces out carefully on the blanket. He picked up the barrel and squinted through it, rolling it between the palms of his hands. Then, he selected the cylinder and examined it closely before checking the trigger assembly.

"The Navy's in pretty good shape," he said finally. "But"—he lifted the Schofield—"I think the Schofield is in better shape."

He broke it apart and checked it carefully, then reassembled it and handed it to Tom. "About new, I'd guess. I doubt if more than twenty or thirty rounds been fired through it. Try it."

Tom gripped the pistol and raised it, sighting down the barrel at a willow branch.

"No," Kilian said. "You grip it like you would the handles of a plow. Like this."

He took the Schofield from Tom and swung it smoothly, sighting, his hand curving naturally and effortlessly around the grip.

"A pistol's not a rifle. You don't force your hand around the grip, but let it follow the curve of the grip naturally. If you grip it too tightly, you throw your sight off. You must let the pistol come into your hand; not your hand taking the pistol."

"That doesn't make any sense," Tom said.

"Perhaps," Kilian said. "But the pistol is a different weapon from a rifle. You must think of it differently and treat it differently. Don't grab for it. Drop your hand to it and let it come into your hand. Try that. Put it in your lap and drop your hand and let the butt curve inside your hand."

Tom tried again, but when his hand touched the butt, he tightened his grip and raised it quickly.

"Look at your knuckles," Kilian said. "See how white they are? You can't aim a pistol when you have a death grip on it. Try it again."

Tom tried it again, but still his hand squeezed itself around the grip.

"Think of the pistol as a living thing," Kilian said. "Would you squeeze a kitten that way when you pick it up?"

"This is just a hunk of steel," Tom said. "There's no life to it."

Kilian shook his head. "No. The pistol chooses the man as much as the man chooses the pistol. Some men like Colt Navy pistols, some Smith & Wessons, others Remingtons, and some Manhattans and Deringers. It doesn't matter. Some men are good with a Navy, while some can't handle a Navy but can a Remington or even a Smith & Wesson Russian. Some folks," he added, "think that's the best pistol made."

He reached over and lifted the Schofield from Tom's lap.

"I would not be as good with this pistol as I am with a Colt Navy. And I have to work with my Navy all the time."

"Maybe the Schofield isn't the right one for me," Tom said, half-joking, still not believing what the gunfighter said.

Kilian nodded soberly. "Maybe. But I have a feeling that it is the right pistol for you. You just haven't learned how to handle it yet."

He reached over and laid the pistol back in Tom's lap.

"Now, just let your hand rest on the butt. Don't try to pick it up. Just let your hand lay on the butt like you were going to scratch a kitten behind its ears."

Tom dropped his hand lightly on the pistol, his fingers folding automatically around the butt. He held it loosely in his hand, still resting on his lap.

"Tell me," Kilian said, "why did you come out here? A mountain boy like you belongs in the mountains."

"It's a long story," Tom said.

"Uh-huh. Well, I got the time."

"I came out here to avoid a feud," Tom said. "Leave it at that. My father is a preacher and didn't want our family to become involved in a feud. There's been enough killing in the hills over the past years. There's no sense adding to the tally."

"What brought you out here?"

Tom made a face. "Well, I had a job—probably long gone by now—hunting for the railroad. But I've been gone long enough that I reckon they've written me off the rolls.

So, I suppose I'm footloose again." He glanced over at the animals. "Of course, I reckon I should take that mule back. It's railroad property."

Kilian made a gesture of dismissal. "Had you collected your wages before your left?"

Tom shook his head.

"Then, I reckon what they did is just write off that mule against your wages. If someone wants to make a case against you stealing that mule, you can always make a case against wages you're owed. And the Union Pacific is a big enough company that they aren't going to worry about one lost mule, given the daily expenses they have to account for. You and the mule are just a mark in a ledger, and the smart bookkeeper will let one cancel the other out to keep the company from falling into the red."

"You sound like you've been in business sometime back," Tom said.

Kilian nodded. "I was. Briefly. I owned a store down in Arkansas, but one day, a couple of saddle tramps came through and tried to rob us. They killed my wife."

He fell silent, staring into the coals of the fire. Tom waited for a moment, then asked what had become of the men.

"They're dead," Kilian said shortly. Suddenly, he jerked his finger and pointed at the cottonwood tree. "There! Aim, quickly now."

Tom swung the pistol without thinking, squeezing off a dry shot automatically as the pistol came level. He looked with wonder at the pistol that seemed to have become an extension of his hand, then questioningly back at Kilian.

Kilian grinned. "That's what I mean. Gently, together. Like one. You just let the pistol come into your hand and everything else works like one. You got the idea. Now, you have to work with it."

"Why?" Tom asked. "I'm not a gunman."

Kilian looked significantly at the Spencer Tom had leaned against the tree. He sighed and shook his head.

"You are now," he said quietly. "The Hardestys will be coming and there is one thing about families like the Hardestys: They keep coming until they have no reason to come anymore."

Tom looked down at the Schofield and over at his Spencer. A wave of resentment swept through him, then sadness. What he had tried to escape by running from the Tennessee mountains had found him again. At that moment, he felt as if his life had been forged in iron and the mold broken. Only nineteen now, and the future had already been laid out for him by some mysterious force over which he had no control.

"It's like doing anything else," Kilian said softly, recognizing the indecision in the youth that he had once felt himself, the helplessness of knowing that one small disruption in time would change forever the world of another, and plans and hopes and dreams that one held for the moment could never be recovered, for there was no forgiveness in the world for those who stepped away from one sunlit path into the shadowed ways of another lit by a black sun where men held little regard for the present. It was an ancient world inhabited by desperate men who were governed by ancient laws of revenge and an archaic code of honor that had no place in a growing country.

"It is a trade. But it is a trade that does give you two paths to follow," Kilian continued. "It all depends upon the man and how he uses the gift that he's been given."

"This doesn't seem like a gift," Tom said. "It's like a curse."

"It's that too," Kilian said. "Because whatever you do

with the gift, there are some who will resent what you do for them and damn you for having it."

Tom stared long and hard into the coals of the dying fire, thinking about Kilian's words and recognizing the truth of what he had said.

At last, he stirred himself when the night birds began to sing and said, "Then, I reckon I'd better become familiar with what I need to know."

Kilian nodded. "We'll start tomorrow. Right now, I think it best if we get some sleep. We have a lot to do over the next few weeks."

Gently, he reached over and took the Schofield from Tom's grasp and slipped it into its holster. He wrapped the gunbelt around it and laid it on the blanket beside him. He took his own Navy and examined it carefully, before sliding down to rest his head on the saddle he was using as a pillow and pulling his blanket over him.

"Get some sleep," he said. "Things will be different in the morning."

Tom rose and went to his own bedroll and placed the Spencer within easy grasp as he covered himself. For a long while, he lay, looking at the stars, but this time noticing the black emptiness like guttered candles between the stars. As he drifted off to sleep, he felt as if he was being pulled into that emptiness, and knew that there was nothing he could do that would change the direction of his flight. Somewhere, a coyote howled and was answered by another, and crickets began to sing down by the creek between the deep grunts of bullfrogs as they tried to catch the fireflies flickering above the water and the grass. Bluebottles and dragonflies hovered along the water's edge, but by that time, Tom had fallen into a deep sleep.

4.

FOR some reason, when the sun appeared blood-red over the horizon, Tom awoke refreshed and sniffing the morning breeze, enjoying the freshness of the dew and the dank smell that rose up in a low fog from the creek. In time, the sun would burn off the fog, but for the moment, it seemed to Tom that the country spoke to him quietly, in whispers that one human voice would drown out for the rest of the day. He liked the morning and the morning sounds that came with it in the whistling of quail as they came single file down to the creek to drink, the trill of the meadowlarks as they rose from their nests in the thick grama grass, and the smoke gray of the sky turning slowly to a bright blue that would hurt the eyes if one stared at it too long. Even when he'd been working on the railroad, he'd liked to rise before the others and walk a mile out in the country away from the sound of men awakening and snorting and coughing the night away, and the clank of tools being readied for the day's work, and the ringing of the breakfast bell calling the men to their morning meal of hardtack and sorghum molasses and coffee thick enough to float a nail.

He lay in his bedroll for a long time, enjoying the morning rising, then reluctantly rolled out of his bed and pulled on his boots after shaking them to make certain no lizard or snake had crawled inside for warmth. His breath showed, and he knew that autumn was close on the heels of summer. He rose and walked to the campfire and dropped a handful of dried bark and leaves onto the gray coals, and stirred them with the toe of his boot until tiny flames licked along the curl of the leaves. Then he carefully laid twigs crosswise to catch the flame, and later, stout branches. Soon, a fire was flickering cheerfully, and he turned to making breakfast with beans and thin slices of rabbit that he used instead of bacon. He put the coffeepot on near the coals so that it would slowly steep without boiling over.

The smell of breakfast cooking roused Kilian, who sat up, wincing from the movement, but feeling the need within his rangy body to move after lying in healing for so long. He coughed and spat the night phlegm from his throat and looked around the clearing with bleary eyes.

"What's for breakfast?" he asked.

"Beans and rabbit," Tom answered.

Kilian sighed. "Sure am getting tired of those Mexican strawberries. I could use some real meat."

"I can go out after breakfast and fetch a deer or antelope," Tom said.

"Maybe later." Kilian coughed again and winced. "These nights are raising havoc with my old bones."

He reached for his boots and, with an effort, pulled them on. He stood slowly, swaying a minute until dark spots disappeared from in front of his eyes, then picked up his gunbelt and swung it around his hips. He had lost enough weight that the holstered pistol sagged lower than usual, and he swore softly as he tightened the belt another notch past usual.

"You maybe should rest some more before moving around," Tom suggested, turning the strips of rabbit in the skillet.

"Yeah, and men in hell should have ice water," Kilian said sourly. "I stay on that ground much longer and I'll wear my own grave into it. Besides, school begins as soon as we eat."

Tom nodded. "Don't overdo it. The way I figure, there isn't any hurry. Unless you think that we need to move camp. We been here a spell."

Kilian thought a moment, then said, "No, the Hardestys will wait a few weeks for Roy and Jim to return before they send out another pair. They usually hunt in pairs unless they figure they need to send more to get rid of a problem. The worst, though, is Spider Hardesty. He comes alone and is good, damn good. Fast and accurate."

"As fast as you?"

"I'd hate to try him," Kilian answered.

"That's good enough for me," Tom said. "Sounds like a good man to avoid."

"That's the key," Kilian said. "Avoid the trouble as long as you can, and when you know that there's no other way for it, be as fast and accurate as you can and don't wait on the niceties. Remember: the idea of a gunfight is to walk away alive."

Tom nodded and glanced over at Kilian's bedroll where the Schofield lay, wrapped in its own black gunbelt like a coiled snake. Cartridges gleamed dully from the loops in the belt, and the ivory handle of the pistol shone softly. A sinking feeling came into Tom's stomach and he took a sip of coffee, then flung the dregs from the cup with a swift movement.

"All right," he said resignedly. "Where do we start?"

*   *   *

The lessons began as they had ended the night before, after Kilian showed Tom how to wear the Schofield on his left hip, the butt canted forward. Tom objected as he had seen others wear their pistols on the right thigh, but Kilian told him that wearing the pistol on the left hip, the butt just forward of his hip bone, gave him constant access to the pistol whether he was standing, riding, or sitting down. It seemed awkward at first to Tom, but he quickly found that the pistol slid smoothly from the holster once Kilian carved a neat loop out of the leather that dropped the holster to the side, leaving the pistol canted forward.

For two days, Tom practiced letting the pistol come naturally to his hand over and over until his hand ached, before Kilian allowed him to load the pistol. Then came two more days of the same, drawing and holstering, drawing and holstering, so he could get used to the weight of the pistol as it slipped from its sheath. When he complained about the monotony of the practice, Kilian reminded him that he'd had to learn to crawl before he could walk, and walk before he could run, and that working with a pistol was much like growing from a babe to a young toddler. It took practice until the pistol would come naturally to hand, and that meant getting rid of the idea that the pistol was not a part of him.

At night, Tom would lie on his blanket, gently massaging his hand to work the ache and stiffness from his fingers. The muscles in his forearm felt stiff in the mornings, but limbered up quickly as he practiced drawing and drawing. Finally, Kilian decided that Tom was ready to begin working at shooting, but even this was not what Tom had expected.

The first time Tom tried drawing and shooting, the bullet missed the target, a slash that Kilian had blazed on the cottonwood tree. He had no idea where the bullet went, for he not only missed the slash but the whole tree as well.

"The trick," Kilian said dryly, "is to hit the mark with your first bullet. You have to remember that the other man is going to be drawing his pistol too. Whoever gets the first bullet in generally wins. You want that to be you. Now, take it a step at a time. Draw, then aim, then squeeze the trigger. Don't jerk at it like you just did. Squeeze it like you were milking a cow. The speed will come later once you're used to centering on the target. It's going to take time. No one's a natural shot. That's something for the dime novelists. Even Wild Bill had to practice that, and he still does each day."

"What does he use?" Tom asked.

"Navy Colts," Kilian answered

"Like you?"

"No, not like me. Better. But each day he practices by emptying his revolvers at a target, then cleaning and reloading them. He stays with the old cap-and-ball."

"So do you," Tom said.

"Yes, but the cartridge is the coming thing. You're young enough to get used to using cartridges. They load faster. Especially with that Schofield. You might as well get used to the new ways. Everything changes. Not always for the better, but you need to get used to the new ways, not the old. Now, try again. Draw and hold on your target for a second before you squeeze the trigger. The speed is already there. Now, you have to learn to combine speed with accuracy.

Tom nodded and began, but it took several hours before

he hit the slash for the first time. After that, the hits became more frequent than the misses, and after two weeks passed and they had almost exhausted the ammunition that had been in Hardesty's saddlebags, Tom was hitting the target constantly and the pistol had ceased to be a foreign extension of his hand.

The days spread into weeks as Kilian healed slowly. During that time, he kept up his teaching until he grew tired and had to lie down and rest. Then, he continued his lessons concerning using the pistol and what he had learned as a ranch hand and a deputy marshal. Once, Tom told him that he thought, as long as men carried guns, they were asking for trouble, and surprisingly, Kilian agreed, adding that he thought the day was coming when men would no longer need them. But, he argued, that time hadn't come yet and until it did come, a man was no better or worse for carrying one. It was how a man used a gun that mattered for the moment. Tom had no answer for that, but that night as he lay awake in his blankets, he pondered Kilian's words and he began to think as well about the long talks he and his father had had at night. The contradiction between the two bothered him, and he spent the rest of the night tossing restlessly upon his blankets, trying to reconcile both teachings.

The next morning, he appeared bleary-eyed and Kilian glanced at him, but wisely said nothing about their talk the night before. Instead, he commented upon how they were beginning to run low on supplies and that soon they'd have to move on. The lessons began again after breakfast, and that day Tom performed poorly, until Kilian called a halt to the lessons and sat down on his blankets, studying his student.

"Something's eating you," he said.

Tom nodded. "I got to thinking about what you said last night. You know, about the need for a man to carry a gun."

He shook his head. "I can see the need for a rifle, but about a pistol—I just don't know. It seems to me that someone carrying a pistol is just asking for trouble."

"That's one way of looking at it," Kilian said. "But remember what I also told you about how some men just don't give a damn about what another thinks. Those are the ones that you have to be careful with. You can walk away from most trouble and it won't follow you. But there'll come a time when some men will see that as a weakness and just follow you around until they push you into a corner and you'll have nowhere else to go. You saw that happen when the Hardestys came down upon us. The West is full of men like the Hardestys. And it won't make any difference if you carry a pistol or not. They'll always be there. Even when our time is over, there will still be men like the Hardestys. And they'll be using guns. Carrying a gun isn't what's important. What's important is knowing how and when to use it. I said it once and I'll say it again. A gun is only a tool. Just like a plow. It all depends upon the man."

Tom shook his head. "I still think that it would be better if all the guns were gone. Including yours. And mine."

"You're probably right," Kilian said. "But that time ain't come yet and I doubt if it ever will. You can read all you want from the Good Book, but if the other fellow isn't reading it, then the words don't matter none at all. You'd do good to remember that."

Kilian's words didn't ease Tom's thoughts, but he kept quiet about his misgivings to himself and settled down to the lessons the old gunfighter was set on giving him. He reasoned that it was best to know something rather than be ignorant and regret it later. Nothing said he had to use what he was learning, he told himself. And it was a way to pass the time while Kilian healed.

One night while they were sitting around the fire, enjoying a last cup of coffee, Kilian spoke.

"Well, I reckon that's about as much teaching as I can do. The rest will come from experience, and I hope to God you don't have to have that experience, although I reckon you will. It's time that we moved on. We've pushed our luck staying here as long as we have. The Hardestys will be out looking for Roy and Jim by now for they'll have figured something went wrong. Besides"—he grinned—"we're out of those Mexican strawberries, which don't hurt my feelings none, and almost out of coffee, which does. And I figure the two of us could use a good meal."

"Where are we going?" Tom asked.

Kilian shrugged. "I figure on going to the railhead. There's money to be made gambling there in the honest games if a player's good enough, and I usually win more than I lose."

"I don't gamble," Tom said.

"Sure you do," Kilian said. "You just haven't realized it yet. But you will. Maybe not with cards and dice, but you'll learn. Why don't you trail along with me?"

Tom stared into the fire for a long moment, then said, "I think I'd like that. But I've gotta find some work somewhere."

"You will. Given time," Kilian said. He stretched and yawned, then stood. "Right now, I think I'll head for the bedroll. We'll leave early in the morning."

Tom removed his gunbelt and dropped on his blankets. Unconsciously, he placed the Schofield unsheathed and close to his right hand. He lay staring at the night sky. The moon was full and bright orange, a hunter's moon.

5.

THEY broke camp in early morning before the fog had settled over the creek, and rode out on the prairie. Tom kept checking on Kilian as they made their way slowly over the brown rolling hills covered in places with late-blooming lance-leaf bluebells and false gromwell and the pink flowers of ironweed. Here and there, they rode through patches of goatsbeard, their horses scattering the puffballs in the light breeze. They spotted a few isolated herds of buffalo, and once a small herd of antelope in the distance. Meadowlarks sang and the sun was warm on their backs as they made their way northwest to cut the railroad and follow it down to the next railhead.

"I have nothing against your cooking," Kilian said, "but I sure would like to sit down at a table and enjoy a beef-steak an inch and a half thick and something besides those roots and berries you kept bringing back to camp."

"If wishes were horses, beggars would ride," Tom said.

"Another of your father's old sayings?"

Tom smiled. "Yep. We are all the sons of our fathers."

"Sometimes, I wish your father had been a horse trader instead of a preacher," Kilian said sourly. "I think I've had enough of his words to save me ten times over." He glanced at Tom. "We're going to have to get you outfitted once we get to a store somewhere. You're beginning to look like a bobtail."

Tom glanced down at his thin and ragged brown linen shirt and heavy blue cord breeches, both stained and ripped in places by now from wear. His mule-eared boots were run down at the heels and cracked, the uppers separated in places from the leather soles that he had laced backed together with strips of leather.

"I reckon I don't look much presentable," Tom said. "But these are going to have to do for a while until I can find some work."

Kilian made an impatient gesture with his hand, brushing aside Tom's comment. "I can't have a ragged scarecrow following me around. Not good for my image. 'Sides, we're partners now and partners care for each other."

"I can't take your money," Tom said.

"Not asking you to take it," Kilian said. "You pay me back when you can and I'm broke."

Tom thought a moment as they rode. He was saddled on the bay and the mule had been packed with Kilian's camp gear. The other two horses trailed by their reins tied to the mule's pack.

"I suppose that'd be all right. Long as you know that I'm going to be paying you back," Tom said at last.

"Well, let's see," Kilian said. "You found me and took care of me, so I figure I owe you as much as a doctor there.

And you provided food for our table—so to speak—so I reckon I owe you for that as well."

"We ate some of your food too," Tom interjected.

"Don't interrupt me when I'm calculating," Kilian said. "So the way I figure it, you were working for me when you should have been working for the railroad. So I figure I owe you for the wages you lost then."

Tom shook his head. "Nope. I don't figure that at all. I figure that was just doing what a man's supposed to do. Help his neighbor and all."

"That Bible teaching sure did stick with you, didn't it?" Kilian said, but he grinned to take any sting from his words, and Tom smiled back.

"You know, when I was still living with my pa, I thought that he didn't know much about what was happening in the world. He kept his head in those books and insisted that my brothers and I read them as well. But the more I been away from him, the smarter he seems to have become."

"Maybe," Kilian said.

By noon, they cut the shiny rails and turned west, following them until night. Tom was surprised at how much distance the crews had covered in laying rails. Heat waves from the railbed caused a shimmering that made the hills in the distance look like moving buffalo. Sometimes, Tom could squint an eye and the hills remained stationary for a while; then they began to move again. They made a small night camp a short distance from the tracks. Kilian knocked down a sage hen with a single shot from his Navy, and they prepared and spitted the hen over the coals of the fire Tom made while Kilian cleaned the hen. They drank the last of the coffee and turned in early. Kilian looked a little white behind his tan, and Tom knew that the day had been long for the gunfighter despite his claim that he was healed enough to ride. He walked a short distance from camp and found some gray-headed cornflower, and brought it back to make a tea for Kilian to drink.

At first, Kilian looked suspiciously at the tea, then sighed and drank it down, muttering that he might as well go poisoned by a friend as shot by someone who wasn't, and fell into a deep sleep. He awoke in the morning, fresh and clear-eyed. They ate the rest of the sage hen, then broke camp and continued their way west, following the rails.

By noon, they came to the railhead, where a tent camp had sprung up. Whores, like dark souls in want, called to them from the tents as they rode through the muddy streets. Tinny piano music came from makeshift saloons with canvas roofs spread over a framework of pine, and from somewhere a fiddle sawed its way through lively tunes. Curses and shouts and yells poured out of the saloons accompanied by the clink of bottles and glasses. They passed a bathhouse with tubs made from barrels.

Kilian rode slowly, his eyes shifting alertly from side to side, noting how the town had been laid out in a haphazard fashion, until they came to a few buildings already framed and sided with pine. A jail stood in the center of the town, but looked like it hadn't been used in some time, the door weathered gray and cracked. Two doors down from the jail was a bank, and next to it a small building housing a print shop. The recent edition of the *Walker Times* had been pinned to a bulletin board outside the front door. Across the street was a saddler, a hotel, a blacksmith shop next to a livery stable, and a store named Hawthorne Mercantile. Kilian swung his horse over to the mercantile store. Tom followed him. They dismounted and tied their horses off at a post that had been hammered in the ground next to a short covered boardwalk that extended along the front of the store.

"Looks like a lively place," Kilian said, gesturing down toward Tent City they had just passed through. A brief flurry of gunshots sounded, followed by someone screaming.

"Looks like a place to avoid if you don't want trouble," Tom said.

"These are troubling times," Kilian said, taking his saddlebags and one of the others off the horses.

He stepped up on the boardwalk and entered the store with Tom close on his heels. Inside, two women looked closely at bolts of cloth that the clerk had laid out on the counter for them. He looked up as Tom and Kilian entered, and told them to browse around and he would be with them in a moment. At the back of the store was a small desk and a set of cubbyholes labeled from A to Z that served as the town's post office.

Kilian made his way to a table where men's shirts and pants had been laid out. He picked up a couple of shirts, one blue and one white, and a pair of black cord pants and held them against Tom.

"I reckon these'll fit you passable enough," he said.

One of the women looked over, and Tom blushed from the way she took in his clothes.

Kilian motioned toward a curtained doorway. "I reckon you can go back there and change. Don't bother keeping those rags you got on. We'll let the storekeeper toss 'em."

Tom took the clothes and walked behind the curtain. When he came out again, the women were gone and Kilian had laid out boxes of cartridges for Tom's Schofield and Spencer, along with an ivory-handled razor and shaving tackle, a black scarf, a low-crowned black hat with a rawhide band, socks, and two pair of long underwear. He was eating a can of peaches as Tom stepped out from behind the curtain, and paused to nod approvingly.

"That's better," he said. He gestured toward another can that had been opened on the counter. "You want some?"

Tom nodded, and walked self-consciously to the counter and picked up the can of peaches. A new bowie knife was placed beside it. He raised an eyebrow at Kilian, who said, "It's yours."

Tom's mouth watered as he speared a peach and popped it into his mouth. Kilian grinned.

"Beats Mexican strawberries and sage hen, don't it?" he said.

"Sure does," Tom replied, and wolfed the remaining peaches down.

Kilian gestured at the goods on the counter. "Anything else you think you need?"

Tom shook his head, and Kilian nodded at the storekeeper. "Reckon that should about do it then."

"Yes, sir," the storekeeper said. He totaled everything up and looked at Kilian. "Mister, that's quite an order. I make it eighteen dollars and twenty cents."

Kilian nodded and laid a twenty-dollar gold piece on the counter. He picked up one of the saddlebags and dropped it on the counter. Tom noticed Kilian's own saddlebags were already filled. "You can pack his things in there." He wiped his mouth with the back of his hand. "There a decent place to stay in this town?"

The storekeeper paused. "Well, there's a hotel two doors down from here if you can find a room. Otherwise, I don't know. Walker's kind of new and we don't have much in the way of accommodation. You might be able to rent space in the stable loft, or else I can sell you a tent and you can pick your own place to pitch."

Kilian shook his head. "We'll try the hotel first. I've spent enough time on the ground to last me a spell."

They gathered the saddlebags and left, turning right and making their way to the hotel, which stood next to a small shop that had a small, hand-lettered sign advertising saddles and boots. Kilian nodded at it.

"We'll go in there and get you a new pair of boots once we get ourselves located."

"Thanks," Tom mumbled.

"Then we'll see about that bathhouse. I think the two of us need to wash some trail dust off."

They were in luck; the hotel had one room left with two beds, and Kilian paid the extra money that the hotel owner demanded to keep from double-renting the space. The hotel had its own bath, and for an extra dime, the owner had hot water hauled up to the bath for them. After bathing, they both stretched out on their beds and slept. Kilian dropped to sleep quickly, but Tom tossed and turned, unused to the softness of the mattress. But soon, he too fell into a deep and dreamless sleep, the first he had had since finding Kilian on the prairie.

• • •

A flurry of shots awoke Tom. Sweat covered him with a thin film, and for a moment, he was confused and disoriented by the roof over his head. Then, he remembered the hotel room and rolled up to sit on the edge of his bed. They had slept through the rest of the day to twilight. Kilian lay awake, watching, listening.

"Sounds like someone's having a good time," Tom said.

Kilian grunted. "Probably too good a time. Those were

angry shots, not happy shots. When someone's mad, the shots come closer together. You'll learn to tell the difference in time from a cowboy letting off a bit of steam to someone putting a bunch of holes in another."

He rose and carried his pistol to the small table in the room by the window off a balcony running along the front of the hotel. He took a small brush and a bottle from his saddlebags along with a linen cloth. He sat, breaking the Navy down and pulling the loads from the cylinder. He glanced up at Tom and nodded at the Schofield hanging in its holster from the bedpost.

"You clean your pistol?"

"Didn't use it yesterday," Tom said.

Kilian shook his head. "That's good enough for a rifle, but you need to get in the habit of cleaning your pistol every morning anyway. It's good for your hands to stay familiar with the pistol and you always know that it's ready. That's one less doubt that you have running through your mind if you get into trouble and have to use it quickly. Bring it here. I'll show you."

Tom took the Schofield and sat opposite Kilian, placing his pistol on the table. He watched as Kilian ran the brush through the Navy barrel and each chamber of the cylinder. He tore a small patch off the cloth, dampened it with oil, and ran it through the barrel and each chamber of the cylinder, then wiped down the outside of the Navy and put a couple of drops of oil in the trigger mechanism before reassembling the revolver. He carefully loaded the cylinder and replaced it, then took two more cylinders from small pouches attached to his gunbelt and cleaned and reloaded them as well.

"Normally, I'd shoot the cylinders free before cleaning them. That gives you a little daily practice to keep your eye

in as well. Besides, black powder has a habit of absorbing
moisture and it's best if you reload with fresh cartridges
each day. Lead has a tendency to foul the barrel, so you
need to keep it as clean as possible. But it's late now, and
I don't feel like riding out of town and back."

Kilian picked up the Schofield and shucked the cartridges from the cylinder. He began cleaning the pistol.

"A cartridge pistol doesn't need as much cleaning as a
percussion pistol, but the principle's the same. Shoot the
six cartridges through the barrel, then clean the pistol and
reload it. You should wipe down each cartridge with a little oil as well. That way, when you reload, you know that
the cartridges in the cylinder won't stick. Brass has a tendency to swell some between night and morning. It's always good to shuck them and reload again, even if you
don't shoot the cylinder empty. That way, you *know* your
pistol's ready. Same thing with your Spencer. Shuck the
cartridge from it and reload. Some people think that a pistol or rifle is only a tool like a farmer's plow or a set of
blacksmith tongs. But the truth is that a gun is part of you
that needs caring for each day. Sort of like washing and
shaving at sunup. You take care of your guns and you
know that they'll take care of you when you need them the
most."

"Pa always said that those who live by the sword will
die by the sword," Tom ventured.

Kilian's face became flat and serious. "There's a lot of
truth to that. But he's talking about men who go looking
for trouble. I don't, but it just seems to find me anyhow.
Out here, there are some men who are always looking for
trouble. I guess your pa'd say they had the devil in them.
Maybe they do. Carrying a pistol is not the same as looking for someone to use it on. But you can't trust others who

carry pistols to feel the same way as you. And it's those people that you need to be ready for. You can usually tell who they are. They have a mean and hungry look about them. You ever see the look a cat gets before it pounces on a mouse and how its eyes change after it gets done toying with it just before it kills and eats it?"

Tom nodded.

"Well, that's the same look some men get when they're hunting trouble. Usually, they're the young ones looking to build a reputation because they think that'll make them important. It doesn't. But they *feel* that it does. You'll see that look on some when we go down into Tent City tonight. There."

He handed the Schofield back to Sam, who loaded it.

"It'd be a good idea to wipe down the inside of your holster each day and rub a little oil inside it each day too."

"What makes a man like that? You know, the ones who are always looking for trouble?" he asked as he rose and brought his gunbelt back to the table. He used a small piece of the cloth to wipe down the inside of the holster, and was surprised at the dust the cloth brought out of it.

"A hunter?" Kilian frowned and thought a moment. "I reckon it's because there's something missing inside them. Something deep down. Like looking into a deep well at high noon and knowing there's water down there although you can't see it. But if the well's dry, you just know it without dropping the bucket into it." He shrugged. "That's the only way I know to explain it. You have to take the time to look at people instead of just noticing them. Most people walk around, knowing that others are around them, but if you ask them what a man was wearing who just walked by them, they can't tell you." He sighed. "But it don't make a bit of difference how many precautions you take. You'll always be surprised someday. Even the best get surprised, and you just have to accept that and do the best you can to try and keep it from happening. If you're not sure, just shuck your gun and hold it on the other person. There's something about looking down the bore of a pistol that just empties the sand from most. That's when you take his pistol from him. He'll hate you for it, but you'll be alive and he'll think twice before trying you again. That gives you an edge over him even if he tries to throw down on you later. And you want every edge you can get."

He slapped his hands on top of the table and rose.

"Well, that's about enough lecture for now. One more thing: Just because a man don't have a pistol on his hip or at his waist don't mean that he doesn't have one somewhere. Some men carry one in a shoulder holster. I know one who has a special leather pocket sewed just inside his coat and carries his pistol there. He makes a funny little gesture with his left hand just before he draws. John Wesley Hardin carries two pistols on his waist, but has a third in a shoulder holster. Hickok carries two in a red sash around his waist, butts forward, but he has a couple of derringers hidden in his coat as well. Doc Holliday keeps a knife on a string around his neck and tucked down the back of his coat where he can grab it when he needs it. Killed a man that way down in Texas. Gutted him when the man tried to pull on him while sitting at a card table. But Holliday just doesn't give a damn. He's dying of consumption. You need to remember, though, that some men always have a little surprise with them. But if you keep your eyes open, one pistol's all you need. It's just knowing how to carry it. The way I've showed you is as good as some and better than most. It's all a matter of learning instinct and

knowing that you'll do the right thing when you have to.
Now, let's go out and see if we can't earn a little money."

The night was different from the nights Tom had known
back in the hills of Tennessee. There, the nights seemed
humid, like walking through a curtain of water as a cotton
mist drifted into each hollow, filling it with a gray that was
home to superstitions. Here, the night seemed clear and
clean when they stepped out onto the street and turned toward Tent City. The moon was full and built shadows between the wooden buildings that made a man want to shy
away from them. Barrels in the alleys looked like men
crouching, and Tom felt a nervousness about the night slip
into him that made him jump sideways like he was
snakebit when a cat skittered across his path.

Walker was not roaring with nightlife, but the sounds
drifting up from Tent City made up for the cloistered quiet
where the citizens lived. But Tom suspected that behind
that quiet there were other sins being committed, more
subtle than those in Tent City, but just as potentially dangerous as the rip-roaring nightlife booming up from Tent
City. Briefly, Tom was reminded of the tales of Sodom and
Gomorrah.

Kilian was right. When they walked into the first saloon
in Tent City, labeled by a crude, hand-lettered sign in red
paint as Bull's Place, the hard-packed dirt floor had a large
dark splotch in the center of the room where someone had
been killed. But his death had been only a momentary
pause in the frantic living of the room as shrieking sounds
of laughter from the whore cubicles in the back rose above
the arguments and talk within the room. Blue cigar smoke
hung like a haze in the room. Rough-clad men sat on small

wooden kegs around makeshift tables where poker games were in play. A piano player wearing a bowler hat pounded away at a piano that had been out of tune since someone had punched bullet holes in it three tent cities before. The bar was three-men-deep, except around a slightly built man wearing a white shirt with the sleeves snapped down with garters at the elbows. He wore a black, small-brimmed, flat-crowned hat that had been carefully brushed, yet there were stains around the band that no amount of brushing would be able to remove. A black string tie that looked made out of a shoelace hung loosely around his neck. His thin hands held a glass of whiskey and a holstered gun was belted around his hips, slung low. His face was sallow and clean-shaven with hollowed cheeks. His eyes burned like hot, gray coals, and others around him kept sneaking curious looks his way.

"Looks like this is the place," Kilian murmured. He made a slight nod at the man. "That's a good one to remember. His name is Nat Brodie. A gunman from down around the Nations. He rode with Blue Duck for a while until Blue Duck got a little too wild and hung a couple of homesteaders and burnt their bodies."

"Looks like he might do something like that," Tom said softly.

Kilian nodded approvingly. "You're a quick study."

"Maybe we should go somewhere else."

Kilian grinned flatly. "No. A killing makes people reckless. They don't pay as close attention to their cards as usual and play recklessly. A careful man has another edge here."

A railroad worker cursed and threw his cards on the table and rose, pushing his way through the crowd to the bar, where he shouted for a drink. Kilian slid smoothly upon the man's seat and looked around the table.

"All right if I join you gentlemen?"

The others looked at him and dismissed him as a cowboy drifting through the town. The dealer shrugged and said, "No difference to me, cowboy. Your money's good as the others. If you got it," he added pointedly. A day-old black stubble stippled his jaw. His eyes were red-rimmed and emotionless. He wore a soiled blue shirt with the collar removed. His hands were long-fingered and white and the cards moved effortlessly in his hands.

Kilian reached inside his vest and removed a small sack and dropped it on the table in front of him. It clinked. He opened the sack and removed a small handful of gold coins. He took one and tossed it to the dealer. The dealer glanced at it, and took chips from a rack beside him and shoved them across the table to Kilian.

The dealer nodded. "Table stakes, cowboy. No credit or short on the pot."

"Reckon we can start with that," Kilian drawled.

"You dealing or talking?" the man opposite growled.

A wintery smile flickered across the first man's lips and disappeared.

"Draw poker," he said. His hands riffled the cards with a quick, economical motion and he slid the cards across to Kilian. "New man gets first cut and bet."

No one argued as Kilian pulled the cards to him and double-cut toward the dealer, stacking the bottom third on top of the first and the second on the bottom.

"A cautious man," the dealer said, gathering the cards to him. His hands moved quickly, and the pasteboards landed squarely in front of the others around the table. Tom watched from behind Kilian's left shoulder as Kilian gathered the cards to him and fanned them slightly, then put them in a neat pile in front of him. He took a chip from the stack and tossed it in the middle of the table.

"Reckon we'll open with a dollar," he said.

The man on his right raised him five dollars, and Kilian raised again without glancing at his cards. The dealer folded, his hooded eyes studying Kilian and his play. The others tossed in chips and the dealer called for cards. The man on Kilian's right took one, and Kilian picked up his cards, selecting two and tossing them into the deadwood pile next to the dealer's left. The dealer flipped two cards to him and moved on to the others. Kilian took a quick glance at them and silently added them to others lying on the table in front of him.

The man next to Kilian shoved ten dollars into the kitty. Kilian promptly raised him ten. One man stayed while the others folded their cards and flipped them to the dealer's left. The man glanced at Kilian's cards and then at Kilian, trying to read his face, but Kilian stared back calmly, waiting. The man held his cards cupped in his hand. He looked at them, studied the back of Kilian's cards lying on the table in front of him, and frowned. He picked up ten dollars' worth of chips, then hesitated before adding five dollars more.

"And another five," he said.

"Ten more," Kilian said, tossing in his bet.

The man pressed his lips together and reluctantly added ten dollars to the pile of chips in the center of the table.

"Call," he said.

Kilian used his left hand to flip his cards over. "Full house. Fours over eights," he said.

"You got the pair on the draw," the man said disgustedly. He laid his cards faceup on the table. He had drawn to an inside straight and missed it, but held an ace-high.

"Luck," Kilian said, raking in his chips.

"Maybe," the dealer said.

He gathered the rest of the chips to him and tossed a dollar into the center. "Ante up."

The others followed his lead, and the dealer shuffled the cards again with a quick snap of his wrist and flipped the cards around the table, beginning with the man on Kilian's left.

A young woman dressed in a red, low-cut dress that made her large breasts bunch and gather tantalizingly over black lace trim sidled up next to Tom and swung a hip into his thigh.

"You look lonely," she said. Powder grains hung in the fine creases of her face that shouldn't have been there in one so young, but her cheeks were hollow and her eyes were old and tired-looking from the life that she had been following for too long. A tiny scar marred her upper lip.

"Looks can be deceiving," Tom answered.

She tucked her hand through his arm. "Come on, let's dance," she said.

"Maybe later," Tom answered, slipping his arm away from her clutch.

Kilian glanced at him and the girl and shook his head. The girl pouted and flounced away. She didn't get far before a burly railroad worker wrapped a brawny arm around her middle and swung her into a foot-stomping dance. She winced as one of his feet crunched on her slippered toes, but she gamely wrapped a bare arm around his neck and smiled at him.

Tom turned his attention back to the table, and watched as the game continued with Kilian winning steadily. Then, he began studying the other men in the saloon. Most were railroad workers, drinking hard and fast. A line of men stood in the back of the room where the whores worked in their cubicles. They drank as they waited impatiently for their turns. He knew a couple, but they ignored his presence. He turned his attention to those in the rooms wearing guns and studied them carefully, remembering what Kilian had told him. Most of the men wore their guns high on the hips or slung low where the pistol grips came to their wrists. He focused on those, trying to read them as Kilian had told him. One was a young man about his own age whose face was flushed from too much whiskey. Tom made a mental note about him, then turned his attention to Brodie, who still stood alone at the bar, a solitary figure. No man stood next to him. He decided Brodie was just the kind of man that Kilian had been talking about—a killer working his way up to a reputation.

At that moment, Brodie's eyes flickered over to meet Tom's. Something murky moved in his eyes and he placed his glass deliberately on the bar and leaned back, resting his elbows on the planks laid across eight large beer kegs. A small smile came to his lips, but it was cold with no life in it at all. His eyes became cold and black like the rattlers that Tom used to kill and skin and trade to Perkins back in Tennessee. A coldness settled in Tom's stomach and made him want to look away, but he calmly met Brodie's stare.

"You want something?"

The words came softly, but cutting like a sharp knife through the noise of the saloon. Talk drifted away to silence and a wide path appeared between Brodie and Tom.

"Not particularly," Tom said.

Someone laughed and soft talk drifted around the room.

He heard someone say, "Brodie's found another." Short laughter followed the man's words and slipped away.

"Seems like you do," Brodie said. He slipped his elbows off the bar and took a step away.

Tom found himself moving toward Brodie, shortening the distance between them. He stopped within five feet of the man.

"I don't want any trouble," he said quietly.

Brodie's smiled turned cruel. "Then, you should just turn on around and walk out of here."

"Why?" Tom asked.

Brodie frowned uncertainly for a second; then his face turned hard and mean, lips curling down. His shoulders bunched, looking like vulture wings as they folded up around his ears.

"A man might take you staring at him wrongly," Brodie said.

"Some men might," Tom said easily. A strange calm came over him. He stood easily, relaxed as he watched the tension build up inside Brodie. Brodie's right shoulder lowered slightly, then froze as he stared at the Schofield in Tom's hand, centered on his belly. Brodie's hand opened and his half-drawn pistol slipped back into its holster.

Tom moved forward slowly.

"I told you I didn't want any trouble," he said quietly. He reached down and took Brodie's pistol from its holster and stepped back.

"I'll be damned!" someone whispered.

Brodie's eyes flamed madly. He licked his thin lips, staring at the Schofield still centered on his belly, his face white as a sun-bleached sheet.

"I think the best thing would be for you to leave," Tom said.

"My pistol," Brodie said thickly. He licked his thin lips. His shoulders twitched nervously.

"You can collect it from the bartender later," Tom answered. "When you get over being mad about nothing."

The muscles at the edge of Brodie's jaws worked furiously. Silently, he turned and stalked from the saloon, disappearing through the tent flap. Tom watched the door for a second, then holstered the Schofield and glanced at the other's pistol in his hand. A double-action, nickel-plated Remington-Rider pocket revolver converted to a .32-cartridge. The dovetailed cone front sight had been filed down to a nubbin to keep it from catching in the holster. It was a killer's pistol. Silently, he opened the loading gate and slid the cartridges out. He dropped them in his pocket and handed the pistol to the bartender.

"Give it to him when he comes back," he said conversationally.

"That one won't be coming back," the bartender said, taking the pistol. He turned and laid it by the bottles behind the bar. "You made him crawfish in front of too many."

Tom wanted to tell him that a man who puts that much time into his pistol wasn't going to leave it unclaimed, but he held his tongue.

"Let's go," Kilian said from behind him.

Tom glanced over his shoulder. "Thought you wanted to play a little poker," he said.

Kilian glanced over at the table. "Well, the night's young and we should study some of the other places. This one's played out for the moment."

Tom nodded silently and walked with Kilian out the door. He was surprised when Kilian turned toward the town.

"You did all right," Kilian said. "But Brodie will come

back when you least expect him. This time he won't figure you for an easy play."

"How do you know he'll be coming back?" Tom asked.

"Because he needs to," Kilian answered. "His kind always does. Come on. Let's see if the boot man is still open. We still need to get you some new boots."

They started back toward Walker. When they reached the border where Walker began, Kilian cleared his throat and said, "There is something you need to know as well. The days of men like me are numbered. This here railroad is going to bring a lot of people into the West who will want what they left behind. The West is beginning to shrink down and soon, the streets will be paved and people will have churches and lots of dry goods stores where there are saloons now. Those people are not going to take too kindly to men who make a living with a gun. Right now, there's a need for the right person to help bring that law civilized folks want in their towns. But people like Brodie back there are throwbacks to the old ways, and they are gonna want to try and keep the West the way it is right now. I'm not saying that's all bad, mind you. But you gotta learn to move with the times and recognize what's coming your way. Since the end of the War Between the States, the army has been coming to the West to push the Indians onto reservations. It won't be long and the citizens are gonna want to push people like me onto a reservation as well. In the meanwhile, though, there's a need for people like you. Not old rowdies like me. Think about that."

They walked through the door of the saddlemaker. A pleasant old man with a thick walrus mustache under a hooked nose looked up at them.

"What can I do for you?" he asked.

Kilian pointed at Tom's feet. "This young one needs a pair of boots. Can you make him a pair?"

The old man looked critically at Tom's feet and nodded. "He does indeed. I can have them ready for you tomorrow. I'll need a pattern, though."

Tom sat self-consciously as the old man drew an outline of his feet on brown paper.

"Now, how fancy you want them?" he asked when he'd finished.

"Low-heeled," Kilian said. "I have a hunch he'll be doing a mite of walking instead of riding."

The old man nodded. "Plain boots. Easy enough. Cost you ten dollars."

Kilian handed the old man a ten-dollar gold piece.

"My name's Jason Witherspoon," he said. "Most people just call me Jake."

"Good enough, Jake," Kilian said.

They left, and Kilian paused on the boardwalk outside the shop. He glanced around at the town.

"You know," he said quietly, "this wouldn't be a bad place for a person to settle down once the railhead moves on. Nice people. Stores and a church. Man couldn't ask for much more."

"You thinking about staying?" Tom asked.

Kilian shook his head. "Nope. But maybe someday. If I live that long."

He laughed and clapped Tom on the shoulder. "Come on. Let's have a glass and call it an evening."

6.

THE days passed with Tom going with Kilian out of town in the late morning to a bend in the creek that ran west of Walker. There, they had found a quiet place, protected from the casual passerby by a large stand of cottonwoods, where they would practice with their pistols. Kilian insisted that Tom work with both hands despite Tom's objection that he was right-handed.

"You never know when you might need to use your left hand instead of your right. Wearing your holster butt-forward on your left hip leaves the pistol available to either hand. With your left, you use a twist-draw and that gives you another edge. Remember: The more edges you have, the better off you are."

At first, it was awkward, and the first time Tom tried the twist draw with his left hand, he nearly blew Kilian's toe off when he pressed the trigger before the pistol was leveled. After that, Kilian was careful to keep a step behind Tom whenever Tom worked with his left hand.

When they began, Kilian made Tom fire fifty cartridges with each hand in practice. Later, when the Schofield seemed to become a part of him, they limited their practice to only twenty per day. Kilian would alternate, quietly correcting Tom when he hurried his shot, patiently taking him through the steps one by one until they seemed to blend into one movement, a natural function that Tom performed unconsciously, the pistol automatically coming up to level, cocked and ready.

They kept the same room in the hotel, and slowly began to make the room into a small nest. Books began to appear over the weeks when Kilian began to win steadily down in Tent City. Dickens, Trollope, Shakespeare, Sir Walter Scott, and Washington Irving. Tom read steadily the books that Kilian suggested after Kilian told him that words would help keep him alert.

"You need to exercise your mind as well as your hands," Kilian said. "Ain't nothing worse in a bad situation than a man who can't think quickly." He pointed at *Macbeth* lying on the table next to his bed. "Now, I don't expect you to know everything the first time out, but you work at it long enough and things begin to come to you. That's what I mean: Working things out keeps you thinking all the time."

Tom began with Washington Irving, and steadily worked his way through Dickens, liking the darkness in *Bleak House,* whose name appealed to him and, for a short while, made him lonesome for his father's cabin in Tennessee.

Nights they spent in Tent City, where Kilian was careful to keep his back as close to a wall as possible whenever he sat down to play a few hands of poker, always keeping to the advice that he had given Tom. He won, but not too much before he moved on to another game. Soon, men noticed his habit, but said nothing as he never left the table with someone penniless.

Tom followed him quietly, watching the boisterous men living life fast and careless, the cold ones who sat at the card tables, nimble fingers dealing cards, others who kept one hand close to the butt of their guns. He noticed those who favored shoulder holsters but hadn't had their coats cut to hide the telltale bulge.

One night while Kilian was playing in Daid's Place, rain began to pour down. Kilian was winning steadily and kept glancing at the rain, waiting for it to let up so he could leave. But rain continued to fall and, resigned, he continued to play.

Three men came in to watch, but for once, Kilian's instincts failed him as he concentrated on the cards. He knew the dealer was cheating, slipping seconds out from the deck whenever he thought the pot was big enough to warrant the chance of getting caught. Tom was at the back of the room, talking quietly to one of the railroad men who he remembered slightly from the time he had worked for the railroad.

Suddenly, two of the men stepped forward and pinned Kilian's arms to the table while the third shouted, "This man killed my brothers! He's a hired gun from Texas!" He drew his pistol as Kilian tried desperately to free his hands, and put three rounds into Kilian's chest.

The men stepped back as Kilian sat upright for a moment in his chair, then slowly toppled sideways and fell onto the floor.

"Reckon you've earned your money, Brodie," the shooter said. "And the Hardestys always pay their promises."

A quiet click of a drawn-back pistol hammer came from the corner of the room and the Hardestys and Brodie froze.

"He was my friend," Tom said quietly.

Brodie's face turned white and he tried to draw, but the room thundered with the sound of gunshots and within seconds the Hardestys and Brodie lay dead on the sawdust floor, their pistols still clutched in their hands. Brodie's face was nearly unrecognizable from the bullet that had taken him in the middle of his face. One of the Hardestys had his throat blown away, and the other had two bullet holes in his chest that could be covered with the ace of spades.

"Sweet Jesus!" someone whispered.

Tom stepped forward, glanced at the dead men, then went to Kilian's side. The gunman's breath was ragged and a bloody froth appeared on his lips. He tried to smile at Tom, but the smile slipped away.

"You . . . get . . . them?" he gasped.

Tom nodded.

Kilian sighed. "Watch . . . yourself . . . They'll . . . be coming . . . after you . . . now . . . Remember . . ."

But Tom never knew Kilian's last words as the gunman shuddered once, coughed out a gout of blood, and died in Tom's arms.

Wordlessly, Tom slipped an arm under the gunman's legs and rose. Without looking at anyone, he carried Kilian from the saloon. When the batwing doors swung closed, men crowded around the dead bodies on the floor, talking excitedly to any who would listen, all claiming to have seen Tom wait until the Hardestys and Brodie had drawn their pistols before he slipped his pistol so fast from the holster that a blink of the eye would have caused a person to miss his draw.

By morning, all the people in Tent City and Walker had heard the beginning of the legend of Tom Cade.

7.

FOR a week after Kilian was buried, Tom Cade wandered around the town and through Tent City, thinking about what he would do. Kilian had left him enough money that he didn't have to worry about taking a job, but a restlessness soon came upon him, and he began to feel the need to do something.

People gave him a wide berth in Tent City, and he heard their low voices in his wake as he made his way through the sprawling muddy streets. In Walker, the townspeople greeted him cordially, but he never received any invitations to have a drink or to come home with someone for supper. He felt their respect, but it was a respect for a man who had killed, even though the men he had killed were regarded by the citizens as "good riddance."

The cottonwood trees by the bend where he still went faithfully each day to practice began to turn yellow as summer started to slip into autumn. Practice was now routine,

yet he forced himself to concentrate on working harder
each day to hone the fine edges that Kilian had patiently
explained to him.

Twice, he visited Kilian's grave, but he felt nothing as
he stood beside the mound of dirt beneath which his friend
was buried, and soon decided that he preferred to remember the man as he knew him rather than the man lying in
the ground, and after that, avoided the cemetery.

One Sunday while he was walking by the church, he
heard singing, and impulsively walked between the horses
ground-hitched with flatirons clipped to their bridles and
climbed the steps. He opened the doors and stood in the
small vestibule for a moment, listening to the congregation
singing one of his father's favorite hymns.

"Come, let us gather by the riiiiver . . ."

A pang of nostalgia swept through him. He unbuckled
his gunbelt and hung it on a peg and removed his hat, placing it on top of the same peg. He stepped inside the church
and slid into the pew closest to him.

A pleasant-faced woman smiled at him and gently
nudged her children over to make room. She offered him
the hymnal, but he shook his head and raised his voice, a
rich baritone, joining in with the chorus.

Heads turned to see who was singing so beautifully in a
rich baritone. Their eyebrows rose in shock, and some of
the strength of the song trickled away as those in back recognized Tom Cade. The people in front glanced over their
shoulders, but could not see the reason, and when they
turned back, they saw the minister smiling, his curling
white hair backlit by the sun shining through the open win-
dows so that it looked like a rich halo. He wore a black suit
and shirt with a white Wesley tie tied neatly round his
neck.

At the end of the hymn, Tom took his seat beside the woman, who leaned over and whispered, "I'm Mrs. Rosie Shepherd. My husband, Aaron, and I have a small ranch just outside of town."

"Tom Cade," he said, smiling at her. The shoulders of those sitting in front of them stiffened, and for a moment, he was afraid that she would recognize his name and move away or ask him to leave, but she smiled and nodded toward the front of the church where the minister stood, waiting patiently for the hustle and bustle to die down before clearing his voice and beginning his sermon.

"In the past, I have spoken about sin here on earth. But today, I believe I will talk about the sin that once existed in heaven."

A startled murmur slipped through the congregation, but he ignored it and continued.

"You see, not every angel was a good angel, although we would like to think differently. There were some who desired to have God's power and rule the universe in His place. And so, a war broke out in heaven, led by that angel who God had created to be the most beautiful and to have dominion after Him: Lucifer.

"Now, some of the angels sided with Lucifer in his bid to unseat God from His heavenly throne, but God called upon the archangel Michael to lead the heavenly host in defense of His kingdom. And Michael became a warrior, the warrior that God needed to protect His creation from the clutches of Lucifer. Michael cast Lucifer out of heaven and . . ."

Tom found the minister's eyes resting on his as the minister spoke slowly and gravely about the fall of Lucifer from the powerful position that he had once held in heaven and how Lucifer established his own kingdom with those angels who had fallen with him.

". . . and so we must remember that once, even God had the need for a warrior to wield a mighty sword and serve as His left hand in the darkness that came down upon heaven."

The minister leaned forward, resting his forearms upon the pulpit, his piercing blue eyes sweeping over the congregation.

"There are those among us who are destined to serve man as Michael served God. It is not a pleasant task, but it is a task that must be fulfilled. Those men are the ones who are meant to protect the weak from the forces of evil and to serve as our left hand in times of need. We do not know who these people are, but often we fail to see the goodness that lies within those men who are forced to walk in the darkness to protect the good from the prevailing evil that walks this earth. Amen."

A murmur of amens echoed through the small church, followed by a shuffling of feet as people stood to leave. Tom rose and slipped back through the vestibule, pausing to collect his gunbelt and hat before walking down the steps. He turned his steps toward Tent City and walked slowly through the town, his mind working over the minister's words. He knew that the words had been directed toward him, but he still felt that he was walking through a darkness that cast a shadow even over the sun.

He walked past the last building in town, crossing the invisible line that seemed to separate Walker from Tent City. Even at this early hour, the sounds of carousing—the tinny pianos, the fiddles sawing, screams of laughter from women working in the saloons, the roar of men in pleasure and anger—created a din that surrounded him as he made his way slowly through the streets laid out in a haphazard manner by those who followed the railroad as it pushed its way west, picking up and moving to the new end of the line every month or so when the track had been laid far enough ahead that the workers could no longer walk to the city for their pleasure.

He walked past a saloon called Daid's Place, then paused, and retraced his steps. He stepped inside the saloon and moved instinctively to his right, keeping his back against the tent wall. His eyes flicked automatically to where Kilian had sprawled after being shot, then to the center of the room where the Hardestys and Brodie had died.

A few men recognized him and nudged others, who glanced at his face, then studied the drinks in their hands, pretending indifference. A man wearing a five-day-old black beard and trail-stained clothes stood at the end of the bar. He wore two pistols tied low on his thighs. Someone whispered to him. He turned to stare at Tom, then deliberately placed his drink on the bar and walked slowly on the balls of his feet to stand a few feet in front of Tom.

"You the kid who killed Brodie and Alan and Clem Hardesty?" he asked. His voice sounded as if a handful of gravel had been poured down his throat. A long white scar stretched from one ear to the corner of his mouth. His eyes were gray and hard.

"I knew Brodie, but didn't know the names of the others," Tom said.

"They were cousins of mine," the man said. "I'm Jack Hardesty. Some call me Texas Jack," he added with a hint of arrogance.

Tom shrugged. "A lot of cowboys coming up from Texas are called by that name."

A dull red flush began to climb up Hardesty's neck into his cheeks. His hands curled above the grips of his black-handled pistols.

"Seems to me that a man should take the trouble of learning the names of those he'd killed."

"I wasn't hunting trouble. Neither was my friend when they shot him without giving him a chance. I'm not hunting trouble now either. Why don't you go back to the bar and finish your drink?"

Hardesty glanced over his shoulder to where his drink stood waiting, then shook his head and looked back at Tom.

"Can't. Not now," he said, hunching his shoulders. "It's gone too far."

"Foolish thing to die for," Tom answered.

"You young—"

He reached for his pistols with both hands as he spoke. Tom stepped swiftly forward, drawing his pistol with one motion and striking Hardesty beside his head before the other man could finish his draw. His hands opened reflexively, he swayed for a second, then toppled forward.

Tom glanced at the crowd and said, "I wasn't looking for trouble. He brought it on himself."

"Mister," someone said, "when you took sides before, you took on the trouble as well."

Tom bent down and took the pistols from Hardesty's holsters. He slid them under his belt and turned to go.

"You stealing a man's pistols?" a voice asked from the crowd.

Tom turned slowly and looked at the faces staring back at him.

"He can have them when he decides to leave Walker.

Empty. But not until then. You tell him that when he comes
around."

He stepped through the tent flap and started on down
through Tent City, then changed his mind and turned back
toward the town, making his way up through the town to
the hotel and his room. He locked the door behind him,
leaving the key half-turned in the lock so it couldn't be
pushed through from the other side. He crossed to the table
beside the open window and took the pistols he had taken
from Hardesty and laid them on the table. A pair of .44-40-
caliber Colt single-action revolvers with seven-inch barrels. He placed his Schofield near at hand and sat, looking
at the Colts. He lifted one, studying its balance, frowning
as the handle turned back into his palm.

Butt-heavy, he thought. Recoil will bring the barrel up
even further. Not very steady for someone who needs to
know his pistols.

He sighed and looked out the window at the dusty
street. Walker had the makings of a good town once the
railhead moved on down the line. But something would
have to be done to keep Tent City away from the town itself so it wouldn't have the same problems of Abilene and
other towns that had grown the wrong way.

He leaned forward in his chair to look down the street
to the sheriff's office. He had met the sheriff once: Bill Jessup, who had built a reputation in other towns before turning to the bottle. Now, he was climbing down the ladder to
oblivion, taking jobs as sheriff or marshal in smaller and
smaller towns as his nerve began to slip more and more.
Even in Walker, he was seldom seen, making his rounds
sporadically, jumping at shadows, then running back to the
office for another bolster of Dutch courage from a whiskey
bottle.

A knock broke through his reverie. He slipped from his chair and picked up the Schofield, holding it loosely by his side as he went to open the door. He recognized the storekeeper. Two other men, dressed in black broadcloth suits, were with him. He raised his eyebrows in question as the storekeeper spoke.

"Mr. Cade? I'm John Hawthorne, the storekeeper. We never exchanged names when you and your, er, friend came in, but I'm a member of the town council. This"—he indicated the man to his left—"is Charles McCoy, the banker and mayor, and this"—he indicated the other—"is Bill Devlin, who owns the hotel and livery stable. He's a member of the council as well."

"What can I do for you?" Tom asked.

Hawthorne looked pointedly beyond Tom and said, "May we come in? We have a proposition we would like to talk over with you."

Tom stood for a moment, considering, then stepped aside and motioned for them to enter.

They stood awkwardly for a moment in the center of the room, until Tom sat on the bed and nodded at the chairs in the room. They took their seats gratefully, removing their hats.

McCoy was plump with white hair and shrewd blue eyes. His lips were thin and drawn in a line that would break in a humorless smile if the man smiled at all. Devlin was thin and dark, his face saturnine, his lips red as he continuously licked them nervously with the tip of his tongue. McCoy touched the cuffs of his shirt before speaking.

"You are younger than I thought, Mr. Cade," he said.

Tom shrugged. "Younger than you thought for what, Mr. McCoy?"

McCoy exchanged glances with Hawthorne and Devlin.

"Walker is growing," McCoy said. "The railroad is bringing in settlers, homesteaders, good people with family values. They will form the backbone of this community. Now"—he shifted his weight and leaned forward to lend emphasis to his words—"ranchers are bringing up cattle from Texas to ship back east on the railroad. This is already happening in some towns, and there's no reason for us to think that Walker will be any different. We will need someone who can keep the peace in Walker and not go off half-cocked when he faces some of those cowboys when they're liquored up."

"We need law and order," Hawthorne said. "Already, our women and children are afraid to walk the streets. We can't have that when other people come here with an idea toward settling down and making homes."

"You have a sheriff," Tom pointed out.

Devlin laughed. "Jessup is good for bringing in someone who's too drunk to resist. But let's face it: He's lost what he had before. He's just hanging on by his fingertips, hoping that he won't get shot."

"We propose to pension him off," McCoy said firmly.

"He may object," Tom said.

"He won't," Devlin said confidently. "He's barely going through the motions right now. If he says no, then we'll fire him and he'll have to move on to another town somewhere. If they'll have him," he added.

Tom shook his head. "I don't know anything about the law. You might be making a big mistake."

"We're willing to take the chance," Hawthorne said. "You have a knack for it. What you did with Brodie and Hardesty was right."

"It didn't work with Brodie," Tom reminded him.

McCoy shrugged. "Some things happen because they

were meant to happen. You're young. You'll make some mistakes. But we'll back you."

Tom rose and walked to the mirror and studied his reflection. A lawman? That seemed beyond the realm of all possibility.

"And the law is what we make it. You tell us what you think you'll need to do the job and you've got it," McCoy said.

"Why me?" Tom asked.

"Because you are the only decent man in town we have," Hawthorne said.

Tom gave him a grim smile. "Surely, there are other decent men in town."

Hawthorne looked down, suddenly embarrassed. McCoy's lips spread in a thin smile.

"You're the only decent man who is good with a gun," he said. "And we'll need a man like that to get this town under control before it becomes too wild to control."

"You could bring another man in," Tom said. "Someone with more experience."

"We don't want a gunman. We want someone with a sense of what's right and wrong," McCoy said.

"How do you know that I'm that man?"

"You went to church," Hawthorne said. "Gunmen have little need for going to church. That showed us your decency."

Tom laughed harshly. "Don't place too much on that. My father is a preacher back in Tennessee. Habit is hard to break."

"Some habits shouldn't be broken," McCoy said smoothly. "The plain and simple fact is that we need to have you right now. Tent City is about to get out of control. The railhead is not pushing forward as fast as it should. There's some Indian trouble and some financial trouble with the railroad people. It could take another four months or even six before those people down there pack up and move farther up the line. And even then, there will be some who will stay. We don't want Walker to go the way of other towns that have faced this same problem and later had to hire the best gunman they could get."

Tom nodded. "All right. Let me think about it."

McCoy rose. Hawthorne and Devlin followed.

"Don't take too long," McCoy said. "Time is very important right now."

Tom walked them to the door and closed it behind them. He returned to his chair beside the table and stared thoughtfully out into the street. A lawman. What would Kilian say if he knew that the lessons he had given to the boy who'd saved him were going to be used by a lawman?

Then he remembered that once Kilian had been a lawman, and that thought troubled him. He held no illusions about the goodness of the man; Kilian had been a gunfighter, and one who had made a name for himself by selling his gun on occasion to the highest bidder. Would he become another Kilian if he took the job? He sat at the window for long hours, staring into the night as he thought about lawmen who gave up enforcing the law to walk the thin line between law and lawlessness, and listened to a tiny voice inside him that whispered, Beware! Beware!

8.

THERE comes a time in a man's life when he must make a choice that will set the pace for the rest of his life. Sometimes, a man makes a wrong choice, and Tom awoke in the morning still troubled about the choice he was about to make. He felt overwhelmed, knowing what he was inside despite what others saw: a rawboned man who still had growing to do and things to learn. His education had been cut short with Kilian's death, and he wondered if he had what it would take to learn by himself what he needed to know. His youth kept him from worrying about what happened to most men who pinned on a star and took to bringing law and order to a town that was on the brink of exploding into a way station for the lawless, but he was also aware that once he put on the star, he would become a target for those reckless men who saw a man wearing a star as a man who would limit the wildness and freedom that they felt was due to them in the West.

Yet, he also knew that sometimes there was a need for men who were meant to protect those who could not protect themselves, and such men were hard to find when that need arose. Every man would become his prospective antagonist, which would mean that he would have few friends in the future.

Sighing, he swung his feet out of bed and washed and shaved, dressing himself as neatly as his meager wardrobe would allow. He buckled his gunbelt around his waist and drew the Schofield, checking its action.

He walked down the stairs and to the stable, where he saddled the bay that had been Kilian's and rode out to the bend in the creek beneath the golden cottonwoods to practice as he had been taught. But his mind was still troubled by the decision he was making. He would be living by the sword, and he remembered his father's words spoken in the little church back in Tennessee many times when a feud was threatening to explode between two families.

A grim smile came to his lips as he drew his pistol and fired over and over again, concentrating on letting the pistol come naturally to his hand, thumb cocking the hammer as it cleared the holster and squeezing the trigger the moment the pistol came level. The irony wasn't lost on him as he knew that he was beginning a feud with many men, and this time he would be forced to stand alone against many others who would feel a sense of honor to avenge the deaths of brothers and kinfolk who might be killed if they pushed Tom hard enough.

He practiced for an hour, then remounted the bay and walked it back to town. He pulled up in front of the general store and went in to find Hawthorne. The storekeeper was measuring cloth from a bolt of calico for a sun-bonneted woman with generous hips and thick waist. Her three children were clustered around a jar of peppermint sticks on the counter, eyes wide in hopes of a treat.

Hawthorne nodded at him as he came in through the door.

"Be right with you. Mr. Cade," he said.

For a second, he hesitated as the strange form of address registered with him; then he crossed to the counter and took three peppermint sticks from the jar, and handed one to each of the children. They hesitated, their eyes wide and hopeful as they looked at their mother for permission.

"Go ahead," Tom said. "My treat."

The woman considered Tom for a moment. Her face was weathered and seamed, a farmer's wife used to working beside her husband when the need arose. But it was a pleasant face with pale blue eyes that twinkled at him. Then, she nodded.

"Reckon one won't spoil their dinner none. Say your thanks," she said to the children.

A chorus of "thank you" rose as the children grabbed the peppermint sticks from Tom's hands before he could change his mind, and scampered outside to sit on the high boardwalk and rejoice in their good fortune.

"This is Mrs. Homstad," Hawthorne said as he carefully cut the cloth and wrapped it in brown paper. "She and her husband have a farm about five miles south of the town."

Tom removed his hat and nodded at her. "Pleased to meet you, ma'am," he said.

"This is Tom Cade," Hawthorne added as he handed the package to her.

A tiny frown appeared between her eyes. "I've heard about you."

"Don't believe everything you hear," Hawthorne said. "We're hoping to hire him to be the sheriff."

Mrs. Homstad considered him for a moment, then said, "We've been needing a good man around here for quite a spell. I'll let Jesse—he's my husband—know. You'll be welcome out at our place any time you're around. My name's Lila."

She gathered her packages and walked out.

Hawthorne smiled at Tom. "She makes the best fried chicken around. You'll be doing yourself a favor if you ride out there sometime around supper."

"I just might do that," Tom said.

"You've thought it over then," Hawthorne said. A smile wreathed his face as he came around the counter, hand outstretched.

"Yes. I have a few considerations, though," Tom said.

"I think we can work that out," Hawthorne said. He raised his voice. "Molly!"

A woman came from the back room. She wore a blue dress with a high collar. Her blond hair was streaked with gray, but her skin was smooth despite tiny wrinkles that appeared at the corners of her eyes.

"This is my wife," Hawthorne said. He motioned toward Tom. "Mr. Cade has decided to become our new sheriff."

Molly nodded at Tom. "John told me about you. You're younger than I expected."

Tom smiled. "That's what others say."

"I hope you know what you're doing," she said.

"Don't give him any doubts, Molly," Hawthorne said. "We're going over to see Charlie and Bill to work out his hiring."

Molly smiled. "Be careful," she said to Tom. "You're dealing with some shrewd people who squeeze every penny before they let it go."

Hawthorne shook his head as he slipped off his apron and

draped it over the counter. "You'd think a man's wife would be more supportive of him instead of the odd stranger who walks in," he complained. But Tom recognized the familiar humor behind his words, and smiled at him.

"Sometimes, a man needs reminding that he can't serve Mammon and God both," he said solemnly.

Molly's face beamed. "A man who reads his Bible. It would do others good if they followed his example more," she said, looking pointedly at her husband.

Hawthorne sighed. "I'll be back in an hour or two. Mind the front, will you please?"

"Of course," Molly said. She looked at Tom. "Welcome to Walker, Mr. Cade. Although I wish it was under better circumstances."

"So do I," Tom said dryly as he followed Hawthorne through the door.

He paused on the boardwalk, looking carefully up and down the street, beginning the habit that would stay with him in the days to come. He noted the loafers sitting in chairs outside the barbershop, the cowboy brushing down his horse by the livery stable, two women visiting outside the hotel while their children chased each other around them.

Hawthorne noticed his hesitation and nodded. "Good to be careful."

"I mean to be," Tom said quietly, stepping down off the boardwalk to follow Hawthorne across the street to the bank. A small trickle of sweat slid down his back as the sun rose. His boots made tiny puffs of dust rise in the street.

They stepped inside the bank. Two tellers were busy behind iron bars set into a walnut counter. Behind them, a door stood slightly ajar behind which McCoy worked on the books. To the right stood a huge safe with Houston & Dunn painted in flowing gold letters across the door.

"Come on," Hawthorne said.

He pushed a small swinging gate aside and held it for Tom. They walked into McCoy's office.

"Morning, Charlie," Hawthorne said.

McCoy looked up. For a second, he appeared annoyed at being interrupted in his work; then his expression cleared and he rose from behind his desk and came forward, hand outstretched.

"Since you're here, I guess you've decided to take the job," he said, pumping Tom's hand with enthusiasm.

"That depends upon a few things," Tom said.

A look of caution appeared in McCoy's eyes as he dropped Tom's hand and hooked his thumbs into the pockets of his paisley waistcoat. A heavy gold chain looped across his belly.

"Well, the job pays a hundred dollars a month and room and board at Devlin's hotel. As we told you before, you keep the peace. What more is there?"

"A hundred and fifty a month and expenses," Tom said calmly.

"What expenses?" McCoy asked quickly.

"Ammunition and the right to hire a deputy if I think we need one. A doctor if I need one and care for my horses. And a jailer. Someone to stay in the jail and take care of it. There'll probably be more once I see what I'm dealing with and what's needed."

McCoy stared at him in silence for a long moment. "You drive a hard bargain," he said.

"You came to me," Tom reminded him.

"He's right," Hawthorne said.

McCoy pursed his lips, then nodded. "All right. Let's get Bill in here and see to it."

"What about Jessup?" Tom asked.

"What about him?" McCoy answered carelessly. "After we swear you in, we'll go down and put him out to pasture. We'll give him a small pension. There's a small spread about ten miles out of town that the bank holds after the owner folded and went back East. He can live there." He shrugged. "It isn't much. Only fifty acres, but he can farm it or raise a few horses and graze a few cattle on it as long as he wants."

Tom nodded. "Sounds fair."

"Then, let's get Bill over here and get to it," McCoy said, clapping his hands together.

"What about a judge?" Tom asked as Hawthorne left to get Devlin.

"We got a circuit judge comes in once a month," McCoy said.

"What about in the meantime?"

McCoy shrugged. "Well, the sheriff fines people for small offenses. Disturbing the peace, drunk and disorderly, that sort of thing."

"What are the fines?"

"Whatever the sheriff levies," McCoy said impatiently. "The money goes into the town fund."

"And what's done with it?"

McCoy frowned. "Part of it goes to pay your salary. The rest for town improvements."

"What improvements?"

McCoy leaned back in his chair. "You have a lot of questions."

"Just trying to understand the situation."

"Very well. Right now, not much. Later, we hope to put together a voluntary fire department, pave the main street, build a train depot, and eventually get lighting in down the main street. But there hasn't been much revenue coming in lately," he said dryly. "Jessup has been, shall we say, a little lax in performing his duties."

Tom gave him a small smile. "So, I keep the peace and levy fines and feed the prisoners that need to be held over for the judge."

"That's about it," McCoy said, spreading his hands. "You pretty much have a broad power, but we do expect a little discretion to be used. Ma Lagerfield runs a diner and we usually let her cook for the prisoners. Devlin could from the hotel, but we thought it wouldn't be right to let him have that contract, being on the council and all. Right now, we're a small town. That will change once the railroad is in. We'll enact town ordinances as we see fit. Meanwhile, you take care of the law along with the judge when he arrives. Name's Isaac Wilkerson. He's a good man, but he's stretched thin in this area."

"All right," Tom said. "What about Tent City?"

"What about it?"

"Is that considered a part of Walker?"

"It is," McCoy said. "And the country around."

"How far?"

McCoy shrugged. "The next town is Dexter about thirty miles west, and Harper the same east. Harper's got a marshal, but Dexter has only a constable and not even a jail. Just a woodshed with a padlock on it that doesn't get much use. So, say about thirty miles in each direction. That would be about right. The army helps out, but Fort Hays is quite a distance from here and it has Indian problems to take care of, so don't expect much from them. The U.S. marshal has even more. Name is Pat Russell. You'll meet him when he comes through. Usually with prisoners."

Hawthorne and Devlin came in. Devlin shook Tom's hand and thanked him for taking the job. The ceremony was brief and Tom was sworn in as sheriff. Then, the four walked down to the sheriff's office, McCoy leading the way. They stepped inside, and Tom halted as the sour smell of vomit and urine struck him. He frowned at the careless sprawl of a man gone to seed. Old bridles lay in a jumbled heap in a corner. Yellowed wanted posters, their edges curling, hung on the walls. A scarred and battered rolltop desk had been pushed into a corner. Papers had been crammed into each drawer until they could no longer be shut. A gun rack hung on the wall holding two shotguns and a Henry repeating rifle.

Jessup sat in a swivel chair behind the desk. He looked up as they entered, his eyes bloodshot and red-rimmed. His jowls sagged and a salt-and-pepper stubble covered his cheeks. His hair was gray and oily and a bald spot shone in the dim light. His clothes were soiled, and salt-crusted creases ran down the front and sides of his shirt. His pistol belt hung on a peg behind him, the leather cracked and dry.

"Morning," he said huskily in a whiskey voice. He glanced from one to the other and sighed. "Reckon it isn't a good one." He nodded at Tom. "I see you've found someone to take my place. I can't say I ain't been expecting it for some time now."

"It's a young man's job, Bill," Devlin said. "Nothing personal, but you been making yourself scarce around town. People have to see the law to respect it."

Jessup laughed harshly. "You mean I've been neglecting my duties." He looked at Tom. "It's true. Won't deny it. But this is a job where a man gets old quick. It weighs on you night and day. Then there'll come a time when you know that there's someone out there who's quicker than you, and you'll wonder when he'll come to town, and every stranger who rides down that street could be that man. It makes you suspicious of everyone, and after a while, that begins to weigh on a man.

He looked down at his dirt-encrusted hands, the knuckles large and swollen.

"I've been at this job for twenty-two years," he said softly. "Sheriffing, I mean. And each year seems like five now." He looked up at Tom. "You'd be Tom Cade, I reckon."

Tom nodded.

Jessup chuckled. "Figured they'd get around to picking you after you took out Brodie. That took a fast man with a gun. These folks"—he nodded at the others—"picked up on that right away. Most townfolk. But they don't understand what that means. I sure hope you do."

"Yes, sir," Tom said. "I hope so too."

A gray eyebrow quirked and Jessup smiled, his teeth yellow-stained. "Maybe you do. Don't know much about you other than that. You rode with Sam Kilian for a while. He was a good man once before he took up the other side."

"He was still a good man," Tom said softly.

Jessup sighed, and reached up and unpinned the star sagging on his shirt. "Son, don't take it personal. I didn't mean nothing by that."

He laid the star on the desk in front of him, stared at it for a second, then sighed again and rose.

"Well, guess that's it," he said. He looked around the room. "You know, I've spent about four lifetimes in a room like this someplace or another. But they're all the same. So are the towns. Wonder what I'll do now."

McCoy made a gesture with his hand and said, "We're not firing you, Bill. You'll get a pension, a small one, but good enough to live on. And you can live at the old Wilson place outside of town, if you want. Raise a few horses and cattle. It's a living."

Jessup laughed. "Not much of a one, but better than I've been living for quite some time. I'll take you up on that."

"Glad to hear it," Tom said. "I'd like to come by sometime for advice, if you don't mind."

"Mind?" Jessup shook his head. "Nope, I won't mind. Don't expect I'll get much company out there. Folks remember what a man is until he's dead. Then, they forget him. I ain't leaving much good for them to remember here except a whiskey man."

He took his gunbelt from its peg and hung it over his shoulder. He picked up his battered and sweat-stained hat.

"I'll leave you to it," he said to Tom. "Now, if you don't mind, I'll just ride on out to the Wilson place and look it over. I'll gather my things later." He jerked his thumb over his shoulder. "I been sleeping in the back room. Afraid it's a bit messy right now."

He nodded at them and walked out of the office, leaving the door standing open. Tom watched him shuffle slowly down the street, his head bent, eyes intent on the ground in front of him. Behind him, Hawthorne heaved a sigh.

"Well, that went better than I expected," he said.

Devlin nodded. "It could have been worse, but I think Jessup was fully played out. In a way, I think he was relieved that you took over, Mr. Cade."

"Well," McCoy said, slapping his hands together. He reached over to the desk and picked up the sheriff's star. He handed it to Tom. "You're now the new sheriff. What are you going to do first?"

Tom glanced around the office and shook his head. "First thing is to find someone to clean this place up."

"I'll send the stable boy over," Devlin said.

"Then, I guess it's time for me to take a little walk around the town," Tom said.

9.

TOM made his way slowly around the town, stopping to talk to the bartenders and shopkeepers, getting a feel for what they wanted in the town. He received mixed opinions, several of which contradicted what McCoy had told him. Eyebrows were lifted when he walked into the stores and saloons with the star pinned on his shirt, but Tom was careful to keep his voice friendly. He met with one garrulous barkeep in the Sampler Emporium, but the rest of the town greeted him with guarded friendliness, unwilling to give him the benefit of their doubts until they saw where he stood.

He worked his way through the town and down to Tent City. The day was still young enough that many of the railroad men had yet to come in for their nightly carousing. Yet, enough workers were present that he knew word would be passed from one shift to another about Tom Cade being the new sheriff. Many of the railroad workers would remember him, and he was counting on their recollections of him and how he had always been a fair man in a dispute.

Most of the people in Tent City eyed him suspiciously when he came into the makeshift saloons. A couple of crib girls tried to entice him into the cubicles at the back of the Ace & Deuce, but Tom politely declined. Several men tried to buy him drinks, but Tom again politely declined as he worked his way slowly through the sprawling community. He studied the people as he went, trying to mark those with whom he might have trouble later, pausing to watch a couple of poker games, studying the dealers smoothly working old decks with trimmed edges and making a mental note of those he would ask to leave town. He saw a couple men dealing seconds, holding the top card up and deftly sliding the next card down to players, and knew that the decks were marked. But he simply noted them and continued his walk through Tent City, wanting to make his presence known, but most of all, wanting to familiarize himself with everything and make those in Tent City aware of him.

When he came to Daid's Place, where Kilian had been killed, he paused, then stepped inside the tent and stood to the right of the door, studying the people. Voices hesitated, then picked up boldly as they deliberately ignored him. He made his way to the makeshift bar and stood, waiting patiently until one of the bartenders came reluctantly down to him. The bartender had a hard look on his pockmarked face. He wore a stained apron and a string tie. He had a dirty towel thrown over his shoulder that he used to swipe down the bar and wipe out glasses. He was chunkily built and his hands were scarred, the knuckles broken repeatedly over the years. His black hair had been oiled down and smoothed until it shone like laquer in the dim light. He wore a small mustache above one lip, and when he smiled, two teeth were missing.

"New sheriff," the bartender observed. His words had a slight hiss to them. He nodded at the star. "A bit young for wearing that down here, I'd say."

"Perhaps," Tom said easily. "I'm Tom Cade. What's your name?"

"Willie," the man said. Then, his eyes narrowed fractionally. "There was a kid named Cade who shot a few people in here a couple weeks back. So they say. I wasn't here then. Would you be him?"

Tom smiled and glanced around the bar. "Anyone calling himself Texas Jack Hardesty still around?"

Willie shrugged. "Names ain't given much in here. But I haven't heard about nobody with that name. Like I said, though, I'm new."

"You see him, tell him he can collect his pistols at the sheriff's office," Tom said.

A cowboy at the bar turned and looked challengingly at Tom.

"You took a man's pistol from him?" he asked.

Tom nodded. "Seemed like the thing to do at the time."

"That ain't right, taking a man's pistol," the cowboy slurred. He placed the drink he'd been holding on the bar and stood away. "In fact, that ain't neighborly at all."

"Don't figure on being neighbors with everybody," Tom said.

The cowboy's face tightened. "I'd like to see you take my pistol," he said roughly.

He crouched, his hand stretched clawlike over the butt of his pistol riding low on his hip.

Willie inched away from the bar, his eyes narrow and watchful.

Tom sighed. With one movement, he drew his pistol and took a step forward, laying the barrel of his pistol alongside the cowboy's ear. The cowboy's eyes glazed, his hand gripped air; then he toppled forward facedown on the hard-packed dirt floor.

Tom glanced around, but no one showed any intention of coming to the cowboy's aid. He slipped the Schofield back into its holster and bent and took the cowboy's pistol. He pointed at two burly railroad men and said, "You two take him down to the jail. Keys are hanging on a peg. Lock him in one of the cells."

"We ain't doing nothing," one man complained.

"Sure we are," the other said quickly, then added in a low voice, "That's Tom Cade. He kilt Nat Brodie and two Hardestys. Used to hunt for the railroad. 'Member? That buffler dinner he brought in when we only had beans and bacon fer a week?"

The other's face turned a dirty white under his beard. Wordlessly, he picked up the cowboy's feet while the second man took the cowboy under the arms. Awkwardly, they stork-walked their burden from the tent.

Tom watched them go, then slid the cowboy's pistol in his belt. He beckoned to Willie. The bartender approached warily.

"Pass the word. No gunplay in Tent City. Folks can drink all they want as long as they don't go up into Walker. In some of the other saloons, I noticed a few gamblers helping the odds along. That stops too."

"This here's a railhead," Willie protested. "Workers have the right to let off a little steam."

"Keep the steam down here and not up in Walker. And no gunplay," Tom said, putting an edge to his voice. "Tent City may not be Walker, but bullets have a tendency of fly-

ing up in that direction. This is a judgment that's already
been made."

"And who made it?" Willie asked hostilely.

"I did," Tom said. "No gunplay. Pass the word."

Willie didn't like it, and Tom knew that others would
have something to say about the decision he had just made.
He would have some trouble but, he reasoned, it was better to have something laid down quickly. That might give
someone pause before drawing his gun and shooting up
someone or punching holes in the sky when he'd taken on
a load of whiskey and decided the night needed a little fire-
works to make it lively.

"I'll pass it," Willie said grudgingly. "But I don't think
the railroad folks are going to think much of it. The railroad
gets a piece of all the action here."

"I didn't know that," Tom said thoughtfully.

"There's a lot you probably don't know," Willie answered. "But you keep wearing that star, you'd better become a fast learner."

Tom nodded and turned to walk deliberately from the
saloon. He turned his steps toward Walker, and encountered the two railroad workers hurrying back to Tent City.
He paused as they came level to him.

"We done just what you said, Sheriff," one said. His
eyes batted nervously as he glanced at Tom's pistol.

"Thank you," Tom said politely. He took a silver dollar
from his pocket and handed it to the man. "Now, the two
of you go on back and have a drink on me."

The men looked at the silver dollar, then took it and
nodded their thanks. The bearded one grinned.

"We'll tote anyone you want on down to the jail for that
price," he said.

Tom laughed with them.

"Well," he said. "Let's hope that there aren't many more. That jail could get crowded in a hurry."

"Just as long as we ain't in it," the bearded one said. He pointed at himself "I'm Joe Watson and this here's Tim O'Reilly."

"We've met," Tom said, nodding at O'Reilly. "You drive a hammer on the railroad."

"Yep," O'Reilly said, pleased to have been remembered. "And I remember that you used to keep the pot filled for us. Eating hasn't been as good since you left." He nodded at the Schofield. "I heard you'd traded guns."

Tom shook his head. "I still have the Spencer. Just added one."

"Hope you're as good with that one as with the Spencer," O'Reilly said. "I have a hunch you're going to have to be."

"Well, let's hope you're wrong," Tom answered.

"Hope doesn't leave a man much in the way of things," Watson said.

"No," Tom said. "It doesn't."

He nodded at the two railroad workers and made his way back up the street to the jail, walking loose and easily, touching the brim of his hat to a couple of women going into Hawthorne's store.

When he walked into the jail, a young boy was furiously scrubbing the floor with a bucket of water and lye soap. The smell stung Tom's nose for a moment, but he could already see the result of the boy's work. The boy paused when Tom came in through the door and looked at him.

"I'm Bob Lismore. Mr. Devlin told me to come over and clean up," he said defensively, as if uncertain what Tom would say. He had long stringy hair the color of moldy hay, and wore a pair of overalls held up by a single suspender.

His face was long and narrow and pinched as if someone had squeezed his head between the heels of two hands.

"And I'd say you're doing a right fine job," Tom said approvingly. "I don't think any self-respecting hog would have taken up residence here the way it was before."

Lismore laughed. "Yeah. Yeah. I know. I smelt it the time I walked in. Most people just smell it walking by, but I work in the stables and after cleaning out the stalls, I gotta get close before I can smell anything anymore."

"It sure smells better now," Tom said.

"It's the lye," Lismore said seriously. "Stuff will burn a hole in you if you ain't careful."

"You be careful," Tom warned.

"You bet."

"How's the cowboy?"

Lismore shrugged. "He's still back there a-moaning about his head hurtin' an' all. You whacked him good."

Tom nodded. "You gotta whack someone, better to whack them good enough you don't have to do it a second time."

"Seen a man get his head cracked open like an egg once," Lismore said. "Fella did it used a hammer."

"Where was that?"

Lismore gave him a puzzled look. "Here in Walker. Ain't never been no place else where I could've seen it."

"What about your parents?"

Lismore shrugged and looked away. "Don't know. Don't remember them much," he mumbled. "Mr. Devlin, he took me in. Been working at the livery stable since I can remember."

"He been good to you?"

"Yes, sir. Real good. I don't want for nothing."

"I see." Tom thought for a moment, then said, "How

would you like to work here? We need a jailer, someone to keep things clean, feed the prisoners, that sort of thing."

Lismore's eyes lit up for a moment, then turned muddy brown again. "I dunno. Mr. Devlin may not want that."

"How old are you?"

"Seventeen," Lismore said.

"Old enough. I'll talk to Mr. Devlin, if you want," Tom said.

Lismore shrugged. "Okay."

"Do you want to work here?"

Lismore nodded.

"I'm tired of horses," he said. "But you don't know Mr. Devlin."

"I'll talk to him," Tom promised. "I think things will work out all right."

"I better get back to work," Lismore said. He paused and pointed toward the cells. "What about that cowboy? What you want to do with him?"

"Leave him there. Make sure he has water, but don't let him out until I tell you," Tom said.

"Okay, but I'll have to clean his cell sometime."

"When he's out of it. All right?"

"'Kay."

Lismore grabbed his mop and started scrubbing while Tom started sorting through the papers on the desk. He found a stack of unserved warrants, old wanted posters, unopened mail from the U.S. marshal that he opened from and set aside to answer later, and miscellaneous other letters from people wanting the sheriff to take action against neighbors, most of whom wanted him to deliver warrants against a rancher named Joe Griswald.

He paused, studying the letters, and then went through

the unserved warrants. Six of them named Griswald to be served.

He threw the old papers away and then leaned back in his desk, thinking.

"Bob? Who is Joe Griswald?"

Lismore paused in his mopping and frowned at Tom. "Mr. Griswald? He's the biggest rancher around here. His place is about twelve mile west of town."

"Seems like a lot of people don't like him," Tom said, gesturing toward the small pile of papers on his desk.

Lismore said, "I don't know much about that, Mr. Cade. He sells a lot of cattle to the army. But"—Lismore hesitated— "he ain't a very nice man."

"Why do you say that?"

"He don't treat people right. You'll see."

"Hey! Let me outta here!" the cowboy yelled.

Lismore returned to scrubbing the floor furiously as Tom rose and walked back to the cell. The cowboy stood by the cell door, rubbing his head and wincing. He looked at Tom.

"You didn't have to crack me on the head," he said accusingly.

"You were about to make a big mistake," Tom said.

"What was that? I don't remember."

"You tried to pull a gun on me down in Daid's Place," Tom answered.

The cowboy looked sheepish. "Well, I guess I'm sorry about that. That must've been the whiskey."

"Probably," Tom said.

"You gonna let me out?"

"It's going to cost you five dollars for disturbing the peace. You got five dollars?"

The cowboy looked at him incredulously. "Five dollars? I work for Mr. Griswald."

Tom shrugged. "The fine's still five dollars. You got it?"

"Yeah, I got it," the cowboy said sullenly. He dug his hand into the pocket of his trousers and pulled out the money and handed it through the bars to Tom. "There."

"All right," Tom said. "I'll get you a receipt. What's your name?"

"Ryan Sloan."

Tom opened the door and stood aside as the cowboy stepped out and walked to the desk. Tom sat and wrote out a receipt and handed it to him.

"What about my pistol?"

"You get it when you leave town," Tom said.

"What?!"

"That's it. You want to get liquored up, you leave your gun here. That goes from now on too. Any time you come to town to put on the tiger, you leave your gun here. You don't, I'll throw you back in jail and double your fine."

"That ain't right," Sloan protested.

"That's it. Take it or stay out of town."

Sloan glared at Tom for a long moment, then nodded. "Guess I don't have much choice."

"No, you don't," Tom said calmly, holding Sloan's eyes. "And you can tell the other hands out at Griswald's place that the same goes for them. They come in and plan on having a few drinks, they leave their pistols here. There's going to be a new town ordinance: no guns in Walker."

"What about Tent City?"

"That's part of Walker," Tom said.

"Since when?" Sloan demanded.

"Today."

"Give me my gun," Sloan said.

"You leaving town?"

"Yeah, I'm leaving town. But I'll be back. And others will come with me."

"Just as long as your guns stay here," Tom said. He took Sloan's pistol from the desk, unloaded it, and handed it to him.

Sloan stared at the pistol. "A gun ain't worth much unloaded."

"You can load it when you're out of town," Tom said.

"This ain't right."

Tom eyed him coldly. "It wasn't right for you to try and pull it on me. There are always consequences for things like that. Now, you have your pistol. Time for you to leave."

Sloan turned without a word and stalked out of the office, slamming the door behind him.

Tom looked over at Lismore.

"That's an unhappy man," Lismore said. "You'll have trouble from him, I expect."

"Probably," Tom said. "He won't be the last."

He rose and put on his hat. "You finish up here, then clean out that room in the back. You'll sleep there once I clear it up with Mr. Devlin."

Lismore's face brightened and he nodded. "Hope it works out. But I dunno."

Tom left the office and watched as Sloan stalked down the street toward Tent City. He debated about following him, then thought better of it and walked across the street to the hotel. He found Devlin working on some papers in his office behind the counter.

Devlin looked up in surprise as Tom knocked and entered.

"What can I do for you?" he asked.

"I need a jailer. I talked with McCoy and we agreed that I could hire one."

"What's that got to do with me?" Devlin said. "If you need my okay, you have it."

"Good," Tom said. "I want to hire Bob Lismore."

Devlin put his pen on his desk and slowly leaned back. "Lismore? Why him? Isn't he a bit young for the job?"

Tom shrugged. "Maybe. But he'll grow fast."

"Why do you want him? He's just a swamper."

"He's a hard worker," Tom said.

Devlin frowned and pulled at his lower lip with thumb and forefinger. "You don't know anything about him. He's a bit slow-witted. Doesn't have any family."

"All he'll have to do is keep the office and jail clean and fetch food for the prisoners. That shouldn't be too hard for him," Tom said. "Besides, he'd like to do it."

"He said that?"

"Yes. And I can use him."

"I don't know," Devlin said, hesitating.

"What's the problem?"

Devlin pressed his lips together. "I just don't want him to get into something that might not be good for him. He's had a hard life. His father killed his mother, you know."

"No, I didn't," Tom said. "He did tell me that he saw a man kill someone with a hammer once."

Devlin nodded reluctantly. "Yes. That's what happened. Then his father used a shotgun and blew off his own head. Bob was in the house. Just a kid when it happened. He doesn't remember much about it."

"Why did his father do that?"

Devlin shrugged. "No one knows. I took him in and raised him the best I could. But he didn't take to schooling. You know how kids can be. The others kept teasing him until I put him to work in the stable. He sort of stays away from everyone now. Just does his work and sleeps in the loft."

"I thought I'd let him have Jessup's old room in back of the office."

Devlin's eyebrows raised. "Why are you doing this?"

"I need a jailer."

"You could get someone better qualified."

"Who? There's not much to choose from in Walker. The boy will do fine. At least, I can trust him."

Devlin nodded slowly. "You can trust him. I just wonder if the job might not be too much for him."

"It's little more than swamping out the stables. The only difference is that he's dealing with men instead of horses."

"Men can harm him."

Tom smiled. "So can horses. But he's learned to avoid those who can harm him or to approach them in a certain way that's different from others. The same thing with this. He'll learn who he can come close to and who he can't. There's not much difference between horses and men in that regard. Or, for that matter," he added, "between any animal and man. Each animal can be dangerous in its own regard and man has all of their traits. Bob will learn—if he already hasn't."

"In the stable he won't be killed," Devlin said.

Tom gave him a curious smile. "And why should that interest you? Is there something about Bob that I should know?"

Devlin flushed and cast his eyes down at the papers on the table in front of him. Tiny muscles worked at the corners of his jaws and his eyes blinked rapidly.

"No," he mumbled. "No, reckon there isn't. Go ahead and tell him that as far as I'm concerned, he can work for you. If it turns out that he doesn't like it, then he can still come back to his old job."

Tom nodded. "I'll tell him." He paused, then continued. "But it doesn't sound like you need a swamper much."

Tiny dots of sweat appeared on Devlin's forehead. He drew a deep breath and leaned back in his chair, his eyes steady upon Tom's eyes, challenging him to go deeper.

"I need help where I can get it. But I like Bob and I'll do what I can to help him go further. He hasn't had much of a life around here. Folks don't take much to him on account of his parents—or what his father did." Devlin's eyes flickered as if they wanted to turn away, but he wouldn't let them. "But he's still a boy who's growing and needs some direction to help him along the way."

"You think being a swamper in the stable is going to do that?" Tom asked.

Devlin shook his head. "The best I can do. That's all there's to it. He ain't as swift as some—I blame what happened in the home for that—but he tries and he learns well enough if someone is patient enough with him. You going to be patient enough with him? Excuse me for saying the obvious, but you're pretty young for that. You're only three or four years older than Bob."

Tom rubbed his finger alongside his nose, then hitched his gunbelt, settling the Schofield's butt just below his left hip bone. He nibbled on the inside of his lower lip while he thought on Devlin's words, hearing his father's admonitions in them when he'd messed up an order or forgot it, or dreamed away the moment. There had been strength in his father's words—he recognized that now and suddenly *knew* that he recognized it—and for one sweeping moment, a regret ran through him as strong as spring rains racing along Plum Creek.

"Yes," he said quietly, "I think I can."

Devlin studied him carefully. "Then," he said, "you are

one extraordinary young man. All right. I said it once, I'll say it again: You can have him if he wants to work for you."

"Appreciate that," Tom said. He straightened. "Well, I think it's time to stop back at the jail and tell Bob to set up his new room, then take another walk around town. You know"—he paused—"if McCoy's right and the cattle drives come up from Texas through here or stop here, then I'm going to need a deputy. Not a shooter, but a solid man who will walk up to a man and stop him from doing—whatever."

Devlin nodded. "McCoy is a bit more visioned than the rest of us. Sometimes, I have my doubts, but there's a good chance that he's right on this one. If he's right, then I'll get you what you want."

Tom grinned. "Even if McCoy and Hawthorne argue about the expense?"

Devlin smiled thinly. "Despite what you may think, Mr. Cade, I do want a—shall we say—'sense' of peace around Walker? Not enough to discourage the trail herds from coming up north, but enough to keep the farmers and home-steaders happy to stay here as well. You'll be walking a tight rail, Mr. Cade. We need the trail herds in order to get the money to build Walker, but we need the settlers coming in to give us stability down the line. For the moment, we have to live with both, and that takes a clever man to know which line to cross at the time. And there *will* be lines to cross. Don't forget that for a minute!" he added sharply.

Tom grinned suddenly, his eyes sparkling. "Oh," he said, "I think I understand you. Probably for the first time. Don't worry. I'll do the best I can. But"—he leaned forward, pressing his hands upon the desk, until his face was inches from Devlin's—"don't you make the mistake of try-ing to cross the lines that you just drew."

Devlin flushed, his face turning as red as an October beet. "You threatening me?"

"Nope," Tom said, straightening. "Just reading the word as it's going to be."

He turned and walked to the door, pausing with his hand on the doorknob. He looked over his shoulder at Devlin, and from somewhere deep within him came the words that would govern his walk through life. Later, he would wonder where they came from, but the answer would slip away from his grasp and he would remember his flesh pebbling when he uttered the words.

"We all have to remember that life is a poker game dealt by the Lord," he said quietly.

Then, he opened the door and walked out, closing the door gently behind him.

He paused, and his eyes began to adjust to the bright sunlight. Few people moved along Walker's main street, but from Tent City came the roar of laughter, screams, shouts, threats, all punctuated by the sound of shots as men tried to put out the sun.

He drew a deep breath and walked purposefully across the street to the jail. He opened the door, stepping inside. His nostrils dilated as he cautiously smelled the interior, then relaxed. Bob sat on a chair, hands on knees, beside the small corridor leading to the five jails. He looked up anxiously as Tom entered.

"Is everything all right, Mr. Cade?" he asked.

Tom looked around, noting that Bob had not only cleaned the floor, but waxed it and the mahogany railing separating the jail from the office. Everywhere, surfaces gleamed from polish or scrubbing. Tom crossed to the crock sitting on a wooden stand and lifted the lid. The water was clean and fresh, and the tin cup attached to a peg on the wall beside it had been scoured until it shone bright and shiny as a new dime.

"Yes," he said, noting the gleam of oil on the Winchesters and Greeners in the gun rack behind the desk, "yes, everything is just right."

He turned and nodded at Bob, whose face was wreathed in a smile.

"In fact, everything is so all right, that I think you need to stay on permanently. And," he added as a frown flickered across Bob's face, "so does Mr. Devlin. He also okayed a raise in your wages," he added impulsively, promising himself that he would make up the difference if the others would disagree.

Bob's face broke out into a sunlit grin that burst through the room.

"Thanks, Mr. Cade. I—uh—mean—thanks!" He gulped.

He leaped from his chair and grabbed Tom's hand, pumping it energetically.

"Well," Tom said, embarrassed by Bob's display, "you'd better rustle over to the stable and gather your belongings. If you're the jailer, you're going to have to live in the back."

He pointed at the room where Jessup had lived. Bob gave him a puzzled look, then hope beamed on his face.

"You mean, I get my own private room?" he asked hopefully.

"Yes. That's your room. I need you here," Tom said. "I don't want to have to go looking for you."

"You won't, Mr. Cade!" Bob shouted gleefully as he ran out the door.

Tom sighed and glanced back at the cells, then shook his head, drew a deep breath, and walked purposefully out of the jail, turning his steps toward Tent City.

10

L AUGHTER seemed to slip away when Tom crossed the invisible line separating Walker from Tent City and began his walk into the various saloons. He knew instinctively that word had spread about his arrest of the Texas cowboy, and now hard faces turned in his direction, considering him. He studied the men carefully, noticing how their hands occasionally twitched near their holstered pistols, but no man made a move toward drawing one. He felt a small glow of satisfaction, then quickly chastised himself for that feeling. He was determined not to become another Brodie, and although he wore a lawman's star, he also knew that in some instances, it was only the star that separated one outlaw from another. He needed to remember his place in Walker: to uphold the law and not become a gunman protected by it.

He walked into Daid's and nodded at Willie working the bar. Willie frowned and gave a slight nod in return.

"You! Sheriff!"

Tom turned slowly to stare at a young rowdy, face flushed with anger. He was broad-shouldered with a narrow waist. His eyes were bright blue, his blond hair carefully combed. He wore a flat-topped hat with a silver band around it, a blue shirt with silver buttons down each side of his chest, and a matching silk scarf around his neck. He wore tight-fitting buckskin chaps with silver conchos down each leg. His gunbelt and holster were black and fine-tooled. His hand quivered above the curve of the ivory-handled pistol in the holster.

"Yes?" Tom asked calmly.

"I hear you arrested Ryan Sloan!" the cowboy said.

"That's right. He paid his fine and left town," Tom said.

A puzzled look appeared on the cowboy's face. "Fine? For what?"

Tom nodded at the cowboy's waist. "For carrying a gun in Walker."

"For carrying a gun?" The cowboy's face twisted in rage.

"It's against the law," Tom said quietly. "And I'm going to have to ask you for yours if you plan on remaining in town."

"Since when did carrying a gun become against the law?" the cowboy demanded.

"Since today," Tom said. He looked slowly around the room. "I'm serving notice here as well as everywhere else in Walker that we have a new law: no guns allowed in town. You may deposit them with the jailer and go about your business and reclaim them when you leave."

"This ain't Walker! It's Tent City!" someone shouted.

Tom located the speaker at the back of the crowd, and allowed a small smile to play across his face.

"Tent City is within the jurisdiction of Walker. Now, I notice a lot of you are carrying guns. You may keep them if you leave. Otherwise, walk on down and leave them with the jailer. I'll be telling the rest of the people in Tent City as well. Printed notice will go up as soon as we can arrange it. In the meantime, all of you are being told of the new law."

"I'll be damned if I'll give up my gun!" the young cowboy said furiously.

An older man slipped up beside him and said, "You're going to make quite a name for yourself. But it'll be a name they'll carve over your grave."

"Huh? What the hell you talking about?" the young cowboy snapped.

"That's Tom Cade," the older man said quietly. "And I've seen you shoot. You couldn't hit the floor if you was standing on it."

The cowboy's face blanched and a sick look sagged his features. The older man unbuckled his gunbelt and draped it over his shoulder as he turned to face Tom.

"Understand that Kilian was a friend of yours," he said.

"That's right," Tom answered.

The man nodded. "He was a good man. I'm planning on staying a while in town, Sheriff. If it's all right with you, I'll just take my gun on down to the jail."

"Go ahead," Tom said. "And I appreciate it muchly."

The old man nodded again and turned to leave. "By the way, my name's Fred Wilson. I work for Joe Griswald too." He nudged the young cowboy. "I was you, Dan, I'd let it go."

"I ain't giving up my gun!" Dan said hotly.

Wilson shrugged. "Young fools become dead fools when there's no need for it. But you decide. The ground's full of them. One more won't matter much, I reckon. Now, me, well, I'm a practical man. And I got to work for a living, and that's kind of hard to do when you got a bunch of holes shot in you. You got as much chance of beating him as pigs have of flying. And I ain't waiting around for them to grow wings."

He turned and left, and Tom focused his attention on the young cowboy.

"He's right, Dan. There isn't any reason for you to chance going in the ground because you think you're the faster man. None at all. It's an easy choice for you to make. Just take your gun on down to the jail, stay in town, and have a couple of drinks, or leave. No sense in chancing this."

Dan glanced around at the men giving them a wide berth. Their faces were feral and lean, taut and watchful, like a pack of wolves waiting for a hamstrung steer to drop before they moved in for the kill.

"Be damned if I will!" Dan said hotly.

But Tom saw what the words cost him as Dan's face suddenly grew wet with sweat. Impulsively, Tom started walking forward and Dan's eyes widened.

"You! Stop right there!" he yelled.

His hand grabbed for his pistol, but before he could lift it from its holster, Tom's hand flashed in the dim light and the Schofield was leveled at Dan's belly. Dan froze, his face becoming almost green as he stared at the pistol. At this distance, the Schofield would make a big hole in his belly if he continued. Slowly, he let his hand relax and drop to his side.

"All right," Tom said softly. "You made your choice. Now, unbuckle your gunbelt and put it on the bar."

Numbly, Dan's fingers fumbled at his belt. Then he dropped the holstered pistol on the bar.

"Now, go outside, find your pony, and leave. Don't come back to town. I'm posting you out of Walker and Tent City for thirty days. That should give you some time to cool off. I'll tell Wilson he can pick up your gun here and take it out to Griswald's place for you. But the next time I see you, that pistol better not be around your waist."

The young cowboy turned and walked quickly from the saloon. Men sighed and talk picked up as Tom turned to Willie and pushed the gunbelt toward the bartender.

"This is getting to be a habit," Willie said, taking the gunbelt and stowing it beneath the bar.

"Hope it ends soon," Tom said. "You can help there. Let the people know they have to deposit their guns at the jail and pick them up on their way out of town."

"It might be easier letting people know they can leave them with the bartender," Willie answered.

Tom shook his head. "Nope. Too much chance that they will get in an argument, put on their guns, and settle it then. This way, they have to walk up to the jail to get them. Might give them time to think things over a bit."

Willie nodded thoughtfully. "Good idea. *If* you can make it stick," he added emphatically.

Tom smiled. "Too true. But we'll see."

"One thing," Willie said, his face curious. "Why did you let that cowboy go?"

"He'd lost enough," Tom said.

Willie suddenly stretched out his hand. Surprised, Tom took it.

"I think we have a sheriff," Willie said.

Tom smiled and gave him a hearty handshake, then turned and left.

Word of what had happened spread rapidly through Tent City, and by the time Tom got to the last saloon, where the crib girls worked in the back, pistols were piled at the end of the bar. Wisely, Tom said nothing, but nodded at the faces turned toward him when he entered. He walked through to the end of the bar, glanced at the pistols, then made his way out of the saloon.

He turned his steps back toward the town, and suddenly became aware of the muted silence that hung over Tent City, and a happy warmth spread through him.

When he reached the main street through Walker, he paused, staring around him, feeling for the first time a sense of contentment and happiness. But beneath the contentment lay a brooding sense that the moment would not last long.

11.

THE next morning, Tom rose early and went down to the creek to practice. While he was reloading his pistol, Fred Wilson rode up on a sorrel and hooked a leg over the pommel while he built a cigarette.

"Heard the shooting," he said conversationally. "Thought I'd ride over and see what was happening."

"Good to have company," Tom said. He slid the last cartridge in the chamber and slipped the Schofield back into his holster. He leaned against the cottonwood tree and looked up at the cowboy.

"A bit off your range, aren't you?" he asked.

Wilson smiled and put the cigarette in his mouth. He popped a match head with his thumbnail and lit the cigarette, and drew the smoke in gratefully, holding it deep in his lungs before letting it trickle out.

"A ways," he said. "But I have a ways to go too. I was given my wages this morning."

Tom raised an eyebrow. "What happened?"

"Seems like Joe Griswald didn't like what happened to Dan," he said. "Figured that I should have sided with him. But he figures that with all of his riders. Wants them to think, then gets mad at them for doing a little figuring on their own. Hell, he even takes on the cook, and that can be a dangerous thing for a man to do. I remember once down on the Brazos when the men got to complaining about the cook and he took it a little personal. Put a bunch of Doctor Scaggs' Oil in his next flapjack batter. There wasn't a bush that didn't have a cowboy behind it with his pants down around his ankles and a-moaning about the bellyache."

"I guess I don't understand," Tom said. "Why would siding with Dan have made any difference to Griswald?"

"You don't know?"

Tom shook his head.

"Dan is Griswald's son. His only son. And he doesn't think anything that boy decides is wrong. He dotes on that boy something fierce. But he ain't doing the boy any good. Still," Fred added, pinching the cigarette out between thumb and forefinger, "he figures that his riders need to follow that boy's lead. But that boy ain't got the sense God gave a jackrabbit, and following him is like hopping from one spot to another and getting nowheres. Besides, I figure the slaves were freed a long time ago and I have no intention of wearing shackles to wipe the nose of someone bent on being buzzard bait."

"Why didn't you yesterday?" Tom asked.

Fred smiled. "There comes a time when a young cub has to leave the pack and go out on his own. Dan's been stretching the rope tying him to the Box G for a long time now. Someday, he'll kill a man or do something that'll get his old man mad, and I don't want to be caught in the back-lash of that."

He swung his leg around and settled into the stirrups. "But there are a lot of men working for Griswald who don't mind playing nursemaid to the boy. Especially the foreman. Name's Bodeen and he's handy with a gun or fists. Likes to stomp a man when he gets him down. You watch yourself. Bracing young Griswald like you did, you'll have a run-in with Bodeen. Or with a new man that Griswald took on. Calls himself Texas Jack Hardesty."

He gave Tom a shrewd look. "I think I heard something about you having a run-in with him a day or two ago."

Tom nodded.

"Well, you'll probably have another. It looked like Bodeen and Hardesty were getting along pretty well. They might have rode together in the past." He shook his head. "I have a hunch you're going to have your hands full with those two right soon."

"Where you going now?" Tom asked.

Fred shrugged. "I reckon I'll stick around for a bit. Maybe sign on with an outfit going through or drift down to Texas with one." He grinned. "Or maybe I'll get lucky and find a whore willing to take me and my manly beauty on permanent loan."

He touched a forefinger to his hat and gigged the sorrel and rode off as Tom raised a hand in farewell.

He watched Wilson until he rounded the bend in the creek and disappeared. Then, he turned back to stare at one of the cottonwoods he'd been using as a target. He stared at it thoughtfully for a long moment, thinking about what Wilson had told him.

Bodeen. And Hardesty.

Trouble was coming. He could feel it start to surround

him like a malignant wind just before a thunderstorm broke. For a brief moment, he wished Kilian was still with him, then pushed the moment aside and concentrated on the cottonwood. When the time came, he'd better be ready.

With one smooth motion, the Schofield appeared in his hand. He fired as it came up level. Bark leaped off the tree. Deliberately, he thumbed the hammer, placing the next five shots in the same spot. He frowned. So far, he'd been lucky in his brief run as the sheriff. But he remembered the words of his father the time he'd spoken out from his pulpit against a feuding family.

"Good intentions will not save a man who comes down to that level where he decides to use a gun to settle a dispute. Violence begets violence, and it is a weak man who gives in to the urge to do another harm. The meek will inherit the earth."

You may have been right, Pa, he thought. But there does come a time when the meek may need a helping hand. Even God had a need for St. Michael once. And I sure hope that when that time comes, I do the right thing.

He reloaded the Schofield and replaced it in his holster. He ran a finger along the neat cuts that Kilian had made in the holster.

I sure wish Kilian was here, he thought.

He walked to his horse, tied a short distance away, and mounted. He turned the bay's head toward town and nudged the horse with his heels. The trouble might be in deciding which folks needed saving. But in the meantime, he had a town to manage, and a sheriff too long away gave the wrong people a chance to play.

He lifted the bay into a trot and rode back to town.

• • •

The smell of carbolic acid struck him as soon as he walked into the jail. He glanced around appreciatively. Bob had outdone himself. The office was spotless, and even the iron bars of the cells gleamed from a light coating of oil that Bob had rubbed on them. Papers were neatly stacked on his desk, which gleamed with a fresh polish. A long plank of wood had been nailed to one wall and holstered pistols hung from it, each with the owner's name on a small tag attached to the buckle. The stove had a coffeepot on it, and three tin cups were on a small shelf to the left of the stove. A crock stood on a small wooden stand next to the cells with a dipper hanging on a nail above the crock. The water inside was fresh and cool when he drank from it.

He walked to the room behind the office and found that Bob had moved in. The cot was neatly made and clothes hung from pegs on the wall. A small tintype of a woman stood beside a Bible on a small table next to the cot. He guessed it was a picture of Bob's mother.

He went back into the office and hung his hat on a hat rack behind his desk. He sat and glanced at the pile of papers. Bob had gone through and winnowed out the outdated wanted posters. Beside the papers was a small pile of mail that had apparently come in while he'd been down to the creek. He started to open the mail as Bob walked in through the door.

"Morning, Mr. Cade," Bob said. His clothes had been freshly laundered and his hair combed.

"Good morning, Bob," Tom said. He motioned at the office. "You've done a good job. Better than I expected."

A large smile appeared on Bob's face. He pointed at the plank where the pistols hung.

"I hope you don't mind, but I had to figure something to do with all those pistols when the men started bringing them in. Sure was surprised, but then I heard that you'd told people about not carrying guns in town. It kept me pretty busy for a while."

Tom nodded. "You did right. I'm sorry that I didn't tell you to get something ready. I should have let you know first. I'll do that in the future."

Bob shook his head. "That's all right, Mr. Cade. I'm used to making do at the last minute."

"Good," Tom said. "Did anyone give you any trouble?"

"No, sir," Bob answered. "A couple of cowboys from the Box G complained a little when they came back to claim their pistols, but nothing much."

"Who were they? Did you know them?"

Bob made a face. "Jimmy Woodson and someone named Drago."

"Did they ride out?"

"As far as I know," Bob said. His face showed sudden concern. "Was I supposed to see if they ride out after they get their pistols?"

"It's a small thing," Tom said. He rose. "Well, I'd better make early rounds."

Bob grinned. "I'll be here, Mr. Cade, if you need me."

Tom settled his hat on his head and walked down to the bank. McCoy was in his office, the door slightly ajar so he could keep an eye on the two tellers as he worked on a ledger. He looked up, his face mirroring his annoyance as Tom came unannounced into his office.

"Morning," Tom said, settling into a straight-backed chair across the desk from McCoy. He noticed that the chair was lower than McCoy's and grinned, knowing that it was deliberate on the part of the banker to keep visitors at a disadvantage.

"What can I do for you?" McCoy asked.

"Just wanted to let you know that I need to have some posters printed up and placed around town."

"Posters? For what?" McCoy drummed his fingers impatiently on the ledger, reminding Tom that he was a busy man.

"Warning people that they won't be carrying guns in town," Tom said.

"I thought you already did that," McCoy answered. "Seems to me that has already been taken care of."

Tom shrugged. "The railroad is about to move on to another railhead, but some of Tent City will stay. You said yourself that you were expecting Walker to become a town that settlers would want to come to and there's always the possibility that trail herds would come up from Texas. A couple of Texas cattlemen, Goodnight and Chisolm, have already brought a herd up. I think you'll find others making the same trip soon and they'll be looking for different towns to drive their herds to. A town can only handle so many herds at a time until they're sold and sent back East. That means a lot of strangers coming through, and I can't be out warning everyone who rides in and plans on spending some time. I want posters up at both ends of town and on some of the buildings in town so there can be no misunderstanding about carrying guns in town."

McCoy settled back in his chair, studying Tom. He thumbed his upper lip thoughtfully, then said, "You certain that's such a good idea? Keeping men from wearing guns? These are hard times and a man has a right to protect himself." He held up a hand as Tom started to speak. "I know we told you to do what you had to do to keep the town safe, but you must remember that Walker isn't Chicago or St. Louis or New York City. We're a small town out in a harsh country."

Tom smiled. "I thought you were predicting that Walker was going to grow. If that's the case and you want the town safe, then guns have to go. As long as a man carries a gun, he'll be thinking about using it when he gets into an argument. If he doesn't have it, he won't think about using it. You're right about needing a gun outside of town. That's common sense. But in town, there's no need to carry one. The town wasn't made to be a shooting range. Besides, if you post a warning that guns are to be checked in, then that'll help people realize that guns aren't the answer to all problems." He shrugged. "It's the first step, as I see it, to setting up the type of town you and Hawthorne and Devlin said you wanted."

McCoy raised his hands in surrender. "All right. Have the posters printed. We'll try it your way. But," he emphasized, "you're the one who's going to have to enforce it. And I don't know what you're going to do if Griswald decides that he wants to come into town with his men and they're all carrying guns."

Tom rose as he said, "I'll ask them politely to check their guns at the jail and pick them up on their way out of town."

"And if they don't?"

"I guess I'll cross that stream when I come to it," Tom answered. "There's no sense worrying about something until it happens. A man can get old festering about something that may or may not happen."

"It'll happen," McCoy said grimly. "Count on it. Especially after what you did yesterday with young Griswald."

"Maybe," Tom said.

He left, and turned into the newspaper office. A bell jangled when he opened it, and a man wearing an ink-stained apron and green eyeshade looked up. He had unruly white hair and a mustache that hung down in twin curls on either side of his mouth. His eyes looked merrily at Tom, then his lips broke open in a wide smile.

"Howdy. I was wondering when you'd get around to me," he said. "I'm Frank Parsons."

He wiped his hands on a rag smelling of kerosene and extended it to Tom, who took it firmly.

"When I heard the others had made you the town sheriff, I got to wondering how you'd work out. I had doubts," Parsons added. "But you handled yourself well down in Tent City when young Griswald tried to brace you. I wouldn't have given a plugged nickel for your life if you had killed him."

Tom shook his head. "Don't make more of it than it was. I didn't know who it was at the time."

"Would it have made any difference if you had?" Parsons asked, his eyes shrewd behind his thick wire-framed glasses.

"Nope," Tom said, leaning a hip against the journalist's desk. "When a man's wrong, he's wrong. Doesn't make any difference who he is. A man has to live by what he believes is right. You can't have it both ways."

"Sounds like you had a good teacher," Parsons said.

"My father is a preacher back in Tennessee," Tom said.

"Ah, that explains it," Parsons said. "I heard you went to church the other day. That set pretty well with some of the folks here."

"And you?"

Parsons laughed. "Well, let's just say that I don't believe God is only up there in that little house. If He's anywhere, He's out watching over the earth. And I don't particularly agree with everything that the preacher has to say about what's right and what's not right. The Bible's only a book, as far as I'm concerned. Mind you, that doesn't mean there isn't some good reading in it. I just don't believe it has all the answers in it."

Tom smiled. "Probably not. But I think it'll do until something else comes along. A man who follows it at least knows where he's standing. It's as good a place to start as any, and a man has to have somewhere to begin."

"Refreshing," Parsons said. "A sheriff who thinks with his head instead of his gun."

"And that," Tom said, "is what brings me to you. I want you to print up a couple dozen posters to hang around town warning people of the new ordinance about not carrying guns in town."

Parsons's shaggy eyebrows rose. "You clear this with McCoy and the others?"

"Yes," Tom answered. "People coming into town need to check their guns at the jail. They can pick them up on their way out of town."

"That's pretty raw for a place like this," Parsons said doubtfully.

"But it's a start in keeping men from perishing by the sword," Tom said.

"I don't know," Parsons said. "I think if a man wants to kill someone, he'll do it one way or another."

"Well, I can't help that," Tom said, "but we make certain that there's one way it won't be done."

"And that's your start?"

"I hope so. There's some men who'd be alive today if they wouldn't have had a gun to rely upon," Tom said.

"I know," Parsons said dryly. "You put some of them up in Boot Hill already."

"My point," Tom said. "I don't want to put any more up there if I can help it."

Parsons sighed. "Well, I'll print your posters for you. But I don't think that's going to keep some men from taking up residence up there. Maybe even you."

"That's possible," Tom said. "I can't keep what's going to happen from happening. But I might be able to discourage it some."

"There's that," Parsons said. "I'll have the posters ready for you by tomorrow. That soon enough?"

Tom allowed how that would be fine, and left the printer to his work. He stepped out into the sunshine and squinted as he studied the town. Across from him, Fred Wilson sat in a chair, leaning back against the hotel wall. He had made a tiny noose out of a piece of latigo and was idly practicing roping the toe of his boot. Tom started across the street, then paused as a buckboard rattled by. He touched the brim of his hat at Mrs. Homstad and smiled as her children looked shyly at him.

"Morning," she called. "We're still looking forward to you coming out to visit, Mr. Cade."

"I'll be out real soon," Tom said. "Just been a little too busy."

She smiled pleasantly at him as she pulled up beside Hawthorne's store and climbed down out of the wagon. She took a flatiron out of the buckboard and hooked it to the bit of the horse, then helped her children out of the wagon.

"Tell Hawthorne that each is to get a stick of peppermint and put it on my tab," Tom called.

"You're spoiling them. They'll come to expect that every time we come to town," she said. But her face showed her pleasure as the children's faces lit up with hope, and Tom knew that she'd let them have a peppermint stick before they left town.

He continued across the street to Wilson, who grinned as he came up to him.

"She's right, you know," the cowboy said. "Those kids will get to expecting a treat each time they come into town."

"There's nothing wrong with that," Tom answered. "I don't expect they get much in that way."

"Times are hard and money don't go far these days," Wilson said soberly, the lines in his tanned face settling. Tom looked into his washed-out blue eyes, studying him for a moment.

"How are you fixed?" Tom asked.

Wilson tossed the loop over the toe of his boot, then flicked it off.

"I'm getting along for now," he said. Then, he added, "Saw Bodeen and that Hardesty fellow ride into town while you were in talking with Parsons. Both of them looked like cats with bellies full of mice."

Tom looked casually up and down the street, noting where horses stood hitched to railings and posts.

"You happen to notice where they went?"

"Yep. They went on down to Tent City. They were packing," he added.

He tossed the loop one more time around the toe of his boot and flipped it off. He coiled it and stood, slipping it into his pocket.

"Thought I might wander on down and see what's happening," he said, pulling the brim of his hat lower over his eyes. "You watch yourself. Griswald don't take kindly to people who buck him."

"You said that before," Tom said.

"Yeah, but some things are worth repeating to keep

them from getting lost in the works," Wilson said. He waved his hand casually. "You going on down?"

Tom debated for a moment, then nodded. "Pa always said that it was best to meet the unpleasant head-on instead of letting it fester and making things worse. They'll want to get a few whiskeys before doing anything. They won't be expecting me this early."

Wilson shook his head. "I wouldn't bet on that. That Bodeen is hard iron and got a mean streak running clean through him. I don't know about Hardesty 'cept you took him down in front of people and now he's got to face up if he wants to ride the line again. That makes him dangerous."

He paused, thinking, then said, "You want help?"

Tom shook his head. "Sometime. But now, I'd better handle it myself"

"You're bucking two of them."

"Yeah. But I'm pure in heart," Tom said lightly.

He loosened the Schofield in its holster and turned to walk down to Tent City. A trickle of sweat began to run down his back, but the day appeared brighter at the moment and people and buildings appeared sharply outlined. He felt a lightness in his stomach, and unconsciously moved on the balls of his feet like a cat, his muscles loosening as he crossed the deadline. He noted the loafers watching him, and knew that word had quickly spread among the saloons and gambling tents. He nibbled the inside of his lower lip, considering, then took a deep breath and walked into Daid's Place, stepping to the side. Smoke filled the room, drifting in slow tendrils near the ceiling. His nose twitched at the sour smell of spilled beer and whiskey and bodies long overdue for a bath. He quickly noted the crowd, larger than normal for this time of day, then saw Hardesty standing at the bar with a drink in front of him. A large, beefy man with sloping shoulders straining the seams of his clean blue shirt stood next to him, his left hand cupping a drink, the right resting casually on the butt of his pistol, a Starr double-action .44 with a heavy pull on the trigger, but if Tom didn't miss his guess, Bodeen had filed the sear down to ease the pull. His hands looked too big to handle the Starr with ease.

Hardesty saw him and gave him a wolfish smile.

"Well, if it isn't the little sheriff. Come to try and take my gun again?" he challenged. His eyes were bright, and Tom knew he had already had a few drinks.

"Took it once," Tom said calmly. "And I warned you about carrying in the town. Goes for your friend too."

The man slowly turned muddy brown eyes toward Tom.

"You'd be Bodeen, I reckon," Tom said.

The man nodded. "Most folks call me Mr. Bodeen."

"The posters won't be up until this afternoon so you might not have heard, but guns are to be checked at the sheriff's office when you come into town. You can pick them up again when you leave," Tom said, keeping bis voice firm, but courteous, letting Bodeen decide how to take his words.

Bodeen's face remained impassive. "I heard. Also heard that you killed a couple of men."

"A necessity," Tom said. "They had their chances to walk away from it all. But they decided to make an issue out of something that's a small matter."

"A man's gun isn't a small matter," Bodeen said.

"A man's life isn't either," Tom answered. "But a man's got free will. He was given that at the beginning. Trouble is, most people seem to forget that they are supposed to use that to make right choices."

Bodeen's eyes flickered to the star on Tom's pearl-gray shirt. "You sound more like a preacher than a sheriff," he said.

Tom shrugged. "There's not much difference between them. Both want to keep the peace. Killing a man's a waste of time. Doesn't really seem to make a difference to some men who've forgotten that men are supposed to live, not die."

A puzzled look crossed Bodeen's face, then disappeared. Tom was deliberately avoiding the argument that would lead normal men into drawing their guns. A vague disquiet began to gnaw at Bodeen, but he quickly suppressed it, focusing his attention on the man behind the star.

"Like you said, it's a choice that some men make. Especially when they pin a star on their chest."

"Sometimes, there's a need for a man to do that. Especially when some men want to run roughshod over others," Tom answered. "Now, I'm going to have to ask the two of you to unbuckle your guns and lay them on the bar and step back."

"We under arrest?" Hardesty asked smugly.

He stepped away from the bar, crouching slightly, his hand inches away from his gun butt. But Tom kept his eyes on Bodeen, recognizing him as the more dangerous.

"If you want it that way, I'll oblige you," Tom said. "But it seems plain foolish to me for a man to make much ado over nothing that matters little in the long run."

Uncertainty flickered over Hardesty's face. He touched his tongue to his suddenly dry lips and felt sweat begin to bead on his forehead.

"You two came in looking for trouble," Tom said. "Why?"

"You shucked Mr. Griswald's son and drove him out of town," Bodeen said. He took a step away from the bar to stand next to Hardesty. Hardesty slipped nervously, automatically, away from him.

"You can still leave town," Tom said mildly. "No shame in that. I'll forget what you said."

Bodeen smiled for the first time, his lips pulling back from his large, yellow teeth. But Hardesty knew that he had just been offered a way out, and although he wished he could take it, he knew he wouldn't be able to walk away from a second meeting with Tom, especially with Bodeen at his side.

"Can't," Bodeen said. "I take Mr. Griswald's money."

"You can make a living other ways," Tom said. "Dying's not one of them, though. Last chance. Give up your guns or get out of Walker."

Bodeen's smile broadened. Tom shook his head and glanced at Hardesty before focusing his attention on Bodeen. He felt loose and supple, and a great calm slipped down over him.

"When you feel ready then," he said.

The words had scarcely left his mouth when Bodeen's hand flashed down to his pistol. Everyone in the saloon saw him grasp the pistol and start to lift it from its holster, but then he staggered backward as if something had struck him a huge blow in his chest. At the same time, Hardesty, caught unaware for an instant by Bodeen's sudden move, made an impulsive grab for his gun. It was the last move he ever made as his head snapped backward as hard as if kicked by a mule. Then Bodeen staggered backward twice more, buckling at the waist and knees. Blood blossomed like a bright rose on his shirt, and dribbled down onto the floor as his hand forgot about lifting the pistol from its holster. Slowly, he leaned forward until his forehead touched the floor. He hesitated for a second, then fell onto his side, pinning the pistol under his huge frame.

"Sweet Lord!" someone whispered in the hushed silence. "How did he do that?"

Over the years, the story of Tom Cade and what happened that morning in Daid's Place would spread over campfires wherever cowboys gathered to talk, and the number of people who claimed to have seen it would grow, until the story moved into one of the legends of the West about a young man who had magic in his hands.

Tom holstered the Schofield and looked around the room. He saw Wilson standing quietly in the corner of the bar near to him and nodded at him. Wilson's face was composed, eyes watchful, and he moved slightly so that Tom could see the pistol as he placed it back under his shirt.

"I was a bit worried. Don't know why," Wilson said dryly.

The room remained silent while Tom turned and walked out. He made his way back up the street toward the main street running through Walker. As he passed the church, he noticed the door was open, and impulsively, he entered, removing his hat. He saw the preacher sweeping the floor and stood for a moment, indecisive.

The preacher looked up, noticed him, and leaned the broom against one of the pews. The room felt cool and pleasant to Tom, and he felt the tension in his shoulders begin to slip away from him as a great and sad emptiness began to engulf him.

"I heard shooting," the preacher said casually, taking a bandanna from his pocket and blotting his face gently.

"Two men are dead," Tom said. "I'd like them to have a Christian burial. If the town won't pay for it, I will."

The preacher nodded for a moment, then came down, extending his hand as he approached Tom.

"I saw you in church last Sunday. I think it's time we introduced ourselves. I'm Isaac Hancock," he said.

"Tom Cade." He took Hancock's hand and felt the gentle power in it despite the white hair and years of the preacher.

"I know," Hancock said. He released Tom's hand and stood back. "You kill those men?"

Tom nodded. "I didn't want to. I tried to get them to listen to reason, but they wouldn't. Bodeen and a man calling himself Hardesty."

"How do you feel about that?" Hancock asked.

"Badly."

"I knew about Bodeen, although he never came in here," Hancock said. "I don't know this Hardesty."

"Both worked for Joe Griswald."

"Did you have to kill them?"

Tom shrugged and shook his head regretfully. "At the moment, it seemed a good thing to do. But I can't help feeling that if I had handled it better, there wouldn't have been a need to do that."

Hancock sighed and rubbed his cheek. "I can understand that. But I wonder if it wasn't meant to be. It might be part of God's plan to destroy the decay that came into man after his fall and bring order into His world."

"You sound like my pa. He was a preacher back in Tennessee," Tom said.

Hancock smiled gently. "It sounds like your father was a good man."

"He was," Tom answered. "Better than I knew at the time. I remember one thing that he told me: All men's deaths diminish me. I guess that's what I'm feeling. Like I've taken something away from myself."

Hancock placed his hand upon Tom's shoulder.

"All men come into the world with a winding sheet already wrapped around them and seeking their graves. In the time that passes before they find their graves, that is the time in which they make their mark in the world. The choice is theirs; we can do nothing about that. All we can do is to look inside ourselves and try to understand what is right. There are times, however, when we do not have those moments in which we can deliberate upon our actions. We have to trust to those instincts which have been instilled within us by the times and our fathers and mothers. But we cannot be our fathers or mothers. We can only be what we are and what we have been prepared for."

He squeezed Tom's shoulder gently. "I think you have been well prepared for that, although you may not have known it at the time. But as time passes, you will come to understand that, I think, and you will know what role you have been destined to play. Some men never learn that. I think that you already know, but haven't realized it yet. Give yourself that time and come to understand yourself." His hand dropped away from Tom's shoulder. "In the meantime, it just may be that you are doing God's work here in Walker. We have needed a strong and good man for quite some time now."

"Thank you, Mr. Hancock," Tom said. "I'll try to remember that."

"You will," Hancock said, moving back to his broom. "You will. In time. One more thing," he added. "Joe Griswald will take this personally. You'll have trouble with him." A small, wry smile crept onto his face. "He doesn't come to our services either."

Tom turned and left the church, pausing in the bright light to settle his hat on his brow and let his eyes become accustomed to the brightness of the day that seemed to bathe the town in rays of golden sunlight.

Slowly, he stepped down the church stairs and walked up through the town to the jail. For the first time, he noticed how it sat, gray and ugly stone in the middle of wooden buildings. He stepped up onto the wooden walk in front of the jail and turned to look back over the town. He thought about Hancock's words, but they did little to dispel the emptiness within him.

"It can be a good little town," he said softly to himself. "Maybe this is what I'm meant to do. I sure wish I knew."

He opened the door and stepped inside and into the loneliness of himself.

12.

THE solemn beat of a bass drum brought Tom out of his office as a small funeral procession marched slowly down the street. He noted the Reverend Hancock following a buckboard wagon bearing two coffins, and behind him came an iron-gray-haired man slightly in front of a sullen young man who kept his eyes on the ground in front of him. Tom recognized Dan Griswald, and assumed that the older man was his father, Joe Griswald. At least, he looked as if he was the most successful rancher in the parts. He wore a white shirt with a black string tie, a pearl-gray Stetson, corded pants, and a black tooled-leather gun-belt holding an ivory-handled pistol. He wore Mexican spurs with large rowels and jingle bobs that tinkled as he walked. Dan was dressed all in black with a long red scarf tied at the side of his neck, the tails trailing down his left breast.

Behind him came twenty-some cowboys, all dressed

out in their Saturday night dance-hall clothes. He noticed Ryan Sloan in the bunch. A few curious stragglers from Tent City ambled along in the rear. All wore sidearms.

"Looks like Griswald came in loaded for bear," said a voice at his side.

Tom glanced at Fred Wilson standing hip-shot beside him, carefully rolling a cigarette from a packet of Bull Durham. He popped a kitchen match with his thumbnail and lit the cigarette. He blew out a cloud of dirty gray smoke.

"I didn't think Bodeen and Hardesty were that popular," Tom ventured.

"They ain't," Wilson answered dryly. "But you ride for Griswald. you ain't got much choice but to follow his lead. 'Course you ain't made that too hard for those cowboys to think otherwise. Given your no-guns order. There's some who'd just as soon ride nekkid through the town as go around without a pistol. Though most of 'em would have a hard time hitting a hill if they was standing in front of it."

Tom remained silent, watching the procession make its way to the cemetery on the outskirts of town.

"They'll be back through town hell-bent on drinking Bodeen and Hardesty's souls to heaven or hell. Although," Fred added, "I doubt if St. Peter's going to swing the Pearly Gates wide open for either one of them. Principles have to be followed even in the hereafter."

"Well, they'll have to do their drinking without their guns," Tom said.

Wilson glanced at him and drew deeply upon his cigarette, letting the smoke out between his teeth in a light hiss.

"There ain't an inch of give in you, is there," he said. "You remind me of a horse I once tried to break who just couldn't be rode. Bit a chunk out of my butt for my trouble."

"I have doubts, but not with this," Tom said. "You want a star?"

Wilson gave him a sour grin. He took a last pull on his cigarette and flipped it into the dust of the street.

"I'm not much use with a gun," he said.

"Neither are most of them," Tom said, nodding in the direction of the funeral procession.

"I'm not worried about that," Wilson said. "What I am worried about is them bullets that don't have a name on them buzzing around. They don't care who they hit."

"I could use the help," Tom said.

"Yeah. And people in hell want a pail of ice water. But"—he sighed again—"I reckon there comes a time when someone needs to try to take a pail of water down to them now and then. All right."

He smiled crookedly.

"'Sides, might be that some of those boys will be taking second thoughts they see me alongside you."

Tom nodded. "Best thing is to avoid gunplay if we can. I know it doesn't look like it now, but I'm not given to shooting people."

Wilson frowned. "Well, I have to admit that it sure seems like you been throwing a wide loop lately. How many has it been?"

"Too many," Tom said soberly. "Come on. Let's get you that star. They won't be up at the cemetery that long. Back home, it was easier to reason with a sober man than one who had a bit of home-still in his belly and feeling he wants to tree a bear."

They walked into the sheriff's office, and after a bit of hunting, Tom found a deputy's badge in a drawer in his desk. Bob watched as Tom handed the badge to Wilson, then said, "You want I should go along with you too, Mr. Cade?"

Tom shook his head. "No, Bob. Any more than two might make them want to fight instead of remaining peaceable," he added when he saw the boy's face fall. On an impulse, he took a second star out of the desk and handed it to the boy. "But I think you'd probably better wear this so people will know you're the jailer."

The boy's face lit up as Tom had them hold up their right hands and swear to uphold the peace in Walker, repeating the same oath he had taken when McCoy had sworn him in.

"All right," he said grimly after they'd pinned the stars on their chests. "Bob, you stay away from guns unless I tell you differently. People coming in to check their guns will take it far easier if they see you are unarmed. Fred, where's your gun?"

Wilson walked to the board holding gunbelts, and took down a worn leather belt and holster holding an old Navy Colt .36 that had been converted to cartridges. He buckled it around his waist and drew it, spinning the cylinder to check the loads.

"You had another, I think," Tom said. "At least, I remember seeing you with one down at Daid's in Tent City."

"I borrowed that one from behind the bar," he said. "But I'd like a shotgun. Folks see a shotgun up close think again before starting the dance. I saw that happen over in Abilene once," he added as Tom raised his eyebrows. "A mob was threatening to lynch a fellow who had gotten liquored up before he came into town shooting and accidently killed the undertaker. The barber had to lay the undertaker out, and he wasn't happy about that. But that mob broke right up when the marshal came down on them, holding that shotgun. Sobered some of them up who had been hitting the Who-flung-John to get a little Dutch courage."

"All right," Tom said, taking a Greener from the rack behind his desk. He found a small sack holding ten-gauge shells and handed both to Wilson. "I'm willing to try anything if we can avoid a shoot-out. Nobody wins one of those."

Wilson broke the Greener open and loaded it, slipping extra shells under his gunbelt.

"They're coming back," Bob said, glancing out the window. "And they're all wearing guns yet."

Tom took a deep breath. "All right. Let's go do it."

Wilson wiped his forehead on the sleeve of his shirt and nodded.

"Watch Griswald," he said. "I don't think no one 'cept his boy will open up until he does. And I'll be watching the boy," he added grimly.

They stepped outside. Tom left the office door open in case they had to beat a hasty retreat, although he knew the chances of getting back into the office if shooting started were slim. He took his place in the middle of the street as Griswald came walking down toward him.

Tom watched the angry face of the rancher as he came nearer, then held up his hand to stop him. Griswald came to a halt, his son on his right hand, Ryan Sloan on the other.

"You boys need to check your guns in the office," Tom said calmly, keeping his eyes on Griswald. "You all know the rules by now."

Griswald's cold black eyes shifted to rest on Wilson.

"What are you doing buying into this, Wilson?" he asked. "You rode for the Box G."

"Don't ride for it no more," Wilson said easily, holding

the shotgun pointing at the feet of the crowd, the butt clamped tightly under his arm. "A man's gotta work at something. Reckon this is as good as chasing cows, and I don't have to ride no fence line."

"You're just asking for trouble along with this two-bit star," Dan said.

"Shut up, Dan," his father said. "You let him take your gun and now we've got a couple of boys dead. You had your chance to finish it when you could."

"Maybe. But Dan's alive 'cause I took Tom's side," Wilson said. "May happen that some of your other boys will be too."

The crowd behind Griswald shifted a bit as some started to step aside, but stopped as Wilson lifted the Greener a little.

"You sent Bodeen and Hardesty into town to take me down," Tom said, keeping his eyes steady on Griswald. "They had their chance to live things peaceable. Same chance that you have right now. Check your guns."

"I'll be damned if I will!" Dan blurted.

"You'll be dead if you don't," Tom said. "We've had enough shooting in Walker. We don't need anymore. But the law's the law. I'm not telling you again. Check your guns or drop them in the street."

Griswald's face turned the color of old liver as anger flooded through him. He tightened his jaw, grinding his teeth as Tom stared calmly at him.

"You'll be the first to go," Tom said. "Someone else makes a mistake of pulling a gun, I'll shoot you first anyway. Your choice. Now, checking time's done. Unbuckle your guns and drop them in the street and go on about your business. You can collect them when you leave town. Two at a time," he added.

"He means it, Mr. Griswald," Sloan said. His hand went to the buckle of his gunbelt and hovered there, waiting.

Tom saw the uncertainty cross Griswald's face and took two rapid steps toward him, closing the distance between them. Griswald's eyebrows twitched. Slowly, he reached down and unbuckled his gunbelt and reached out to hand it to Tom.

"Drop it there," Tom said.

He hesitated, then his hand opened and the holstered pistol fell into the dust of the street. Sloan's pistol followed.

"Pa!" Dan said.

"Do what he says!" Griswald snapped. "All of you! Else draw your wages and ride on!"

Guns began to drop into the street. Dan stood defiantly, his hand hovering over the butt of his gun. Tom shifted his eyes to him and said, "You had your chance once before. Don't be a fool this time!"

Sullenly, Dan unbuckled his belt and let his gun drop. He glared at Wilson, then turned to his father.

"You let him do this to us? We have him outnumbered."

"Shut up," his father said.

Dan turned furiously to Tom. "You walk tall with that gun. How about taking it off?"

Tom looked into Dan's eyes, holding them for a long moment, then said, "All of you, move to the other side of the street away from your guns." He raised his voice. "Bob, come on out."

Bob stepped out of the office. His eyes shone with excitement. "Yes, sir?"

"Collect the guns and take them into the office."

Bob scurried down into the street and gathered the guns as the cowboys and Griswald moved across the street and bunched together, wary eyes glittering in anticipation. Dan stood still, arms crossed defiantly.

When all the guns had been collected, Tom unbuckled his gunbelt and handed it to Wilson.

"Keep the shotgun on them. Anyone tries to interfere, shoot them," he said.

"Watch him," Wilson said quietly. "He's good in a fight."

Tom smiled at Dan.

"All right. You wanted it. Come and get it," he said.

With a roar, Dan charged, swinging wildly. Tom slipped aside and threw a straight left that flattened Dan's lip against his teeth. Blood poured from the cut and as Dan stood, confused, Tom threw a right, high and hard, that caught him on his cheek.

Dan fell to the ground and rolled twice, expecting Tom to come in with his boots, but Tom stood quietly, waiting until Dan climbed to his feet. Dan shook his head, then came in slower, swinging both fists as fast as he could. Tom slipped through them, but one caught him on the side of his head. His eyes went fuzzy for a second and he stepped back and away, weaving from side to side to avoid Dan's punches as he shook his head to clear it. Dan threw a punch to Tom's midsection, but he blocked it with an elbow. His hand caught Dan's left and, spinning on his toes, he pulled the arm across and threw Dan with a hiplock. Tom moved in, but Dan raised his feet and lashed out with his spurs, trying to rooster him. Tom leaped back. Dan rolled and came up off the ground. This time, Tom moved in and nailed him with a left that spatted on his nose with a wicked sound. Blood smeared across Dan's face, but he hit hard with both hands, and Tom felt the smoky taste in his mouth that he had felt during the fights he'd had in

Tennessee. He ignored the danger and walked in, both fists snapping left-right combinations that rocked Dan back on his heels.

Dan swung a right toward Tom's belly, but Tom went in under it, hooked Dan with a left in the belly, then rolled his hips and dug a right in the same spot, just under the breastbone. Dan grunted and his knees started to buckle. He dove straight into Tom, wrapping his arms around Tom's midsection. They tumbled to the ground, but Tom threw an elbow that snapped against Dan's broken nose. He cupped his right hand and struck Dan under the chin, raking up with the heel of his hand. Dan's head snapped back and Tom heaved with his knees, throwing Dan away from him.

He rolled to his feet and moved to the side, waiting for Dan to rise. Then, Tom slipped in, weaving to miss the wide haymakers that Dan threw. One caught Tom alongside the head, but he managed to slip away from it and hit Dan with both fists hard in the face.

They circled, studying each other. When Dan lunged, Tom feinted with his left and smashed a right into his belly that made Dan gag. A second later, Tom dug again with his right, then came up hard with a left uppercut that straightened Dan. Tom smashed both hands to the body, then swung a right from his heels, spinning from the hips. The blow caught Dan on the chin, driving him back. He caught himself and stared at Tom from under lowered brows. He tried to throw a left, but Tom blocked it with his right, snapped his right fist into the battered features, and hit him in the solar plexus with his left. Dan's knees sagged, and Tom spread his legs and snapped left-right combinations hard against Dan's face, splitting the skin on Dan's cheekbones. Setting himself, he threw a right, high and hard, that caught Dan on the chin. He swayed, then fell forward into the dust of the street. He rolled over and tried to rise, but the fight was gone from him and he collapsed back into the dust of the street, sprawled out.

"'Nough," he mumbled through battered lips.

"Get up!" Griswald shouted from the side of the street. "Goddamn you, get up!"

Dan shook his head.

"'Nough," he mumbled again.

"I think your boy's finished," Wilson drawled. "If I were you, I'd take him down the street to the sawbones and get him patched up."

Heart pounding, Tom took his gunbelt from Wilson and buckled it around his waist, fumbling with swollen fingers. He walked stiff-legged back to the sheriff's office and leaned against a post, panting with exertion.

"All right," he said, gasping. He took a deep breath and straightened. "You've had your say. Now, pick up your boy, Griswald, and get out of town. The Box G is posted until further notice. Send your cook in for supplies, but one of your cowboys comes in, he'll spend the night in jail and be sent packing. When your cook comes in, he can collect all your guns and bring them to you."

"You can't do that!" Griswald said furiously.

"It's done," Tom said. "Fred, get them off the street and out of town."

He turned and walked into the sheriff's office. He felt tired and sore. He worked his fingers to keep the stiffness from them as he walked to a pitcher and basin sitting on a scarred walnut table. He filled the basin with cold water and gently bathed his face with a wet towel. Then, he lowered his hands into the basin and soaked them, working his fingers as the stiffness slowly disappeared.

He heard horses galloping down the street. Moments

later, Wilson came in and leaned the shotgun against the desk. He sat in the chair, studying Tom.

"You look like you been stomped by a mule," he said.

"Feel like it too," Tom said. He dried his hands on another towel. "How's Griswald's boy?"

"Looks worse. Griswald wouldn't take him to the sawbones. Had a cowboy throw him on his horse and took him home. You mean that about posting the Box G out of town?"

"Yes. They need time to cool off."

"How long you figure on giving them?"

Tom shrugged, then winced as stiff muscles protested.

"Two, maybe three weeks," he said. "Then, I'll ride out and tell them the posting's been lifted."

Wilson frowned. "Might be better if I do it."

Tom shook his head. "No, I'll do it. Better if it comes from me. In the meantime, I want you to do a little patrolling the streets and down to Tent City. I want everyone to know that you're a deputy. Take the shotgun with you. They know you as a cowboy right now, but they see that shotgun and the star, they'll take you seriously if you have to give any warnings."

Wilson nodded and rose. "Makes sense. What are you going to do?"

"Rest a minute or two, then go down and tell McCoy that I've hired a deputy and get you on the payroll."

Wilson grinned. "I imagine that tightwad will throw a fit. He's used to holding money, not giving it out."

"What about me?" Bob asked.

"I want you to be here in case Fred has to bring a rowdy in. You're running the jail."

Bob nodded, his face pleased. "I'm in charge?"

"You're in charge," Tom answered.

He flexed his fingers, then suddenly slipped the Schofield from its holster, cocking it. His hand ached, but he was satisfied that his fingers were working even if they were still stiff. He slipped the Schofield back into its holster and continued working his fingers.

"A bit stiff?" Wilson asked.

"A bit," Tom said. "But it'll wear off."

"I'd better get to making the rounds," Wilson said. "News of this fight will travel fast, and it might be good if they see the law's still around before any arguments start getting out of hand."

"Good thinking," Tom said. He sighed and reached for his hat, settling it gingerly over the lumps on his forehead. "Meanwhile, I'd better get down to McCoy."

"Thought you were going to rest," Wilson said.

"Changed my mind," Tom answered. "I want him to know the law's still working the town with you."

They stepped out of the office onto the boardwalk together. Tom squinted against the hard sunlight, then sighed and turned to walk down to the bank while Wilson slowly walked down toward Tent City.

Tom walked into the bank and made his way back to the banker's office. McCoy looked up as Tom entered.

"Yeah, I can see the rumors were right," he said dryly. "If he looks worse than you, he'll be a sorry sight."

"Had to be done," Tom said. He sat carefully in the chair opposite the banker and rested his hands on the arms of the chair. "Thought you should know that I hired Fred Wilson on as a deputy."

McCoy's eyes narrowed. "Wilson? Who used to ride with the Box G?"

Tom nodded.

"You think that's a good move? Hiring a Box G rider?"

"He doesn't ride for them anymore. And he's a good man. I want him."

McCoy sighed and rubbed his hand around his jaw. "Well, we promised you a deputy. You want him, you can have him."

"He gets seventy-five a month and found," Tom said.

"That's higher than any deputy gets!" McCoy protested.

"I don't want anybody working cheaper," Tom said. "You want good men, you pay for them. Going cheap isn't going to get this job done."

"All right," McCoy said irritably. "I'll okay it with the others."

"Thanks," Tom said. He rose and looked down at McCoy. "One more thing: Who owns the Lismore place now?"

McCoy's eyebrows went up. "The Lismore place? Why bring that up?"

"I want to know," Tom said.

"McCoy shrugged. "Devlin owns it. He bought the note after Lismore killed his wife and himself. Came in two days after we buried them and bought the note outright."

"What's he doing with it?"

"He's got a squatter working the land along with his. Man by the name of Homstad."

"Thanks," Tom said.

He left and stood for a moment outside the bank, staring thoughtfully across the street, thinking. Then, he stepped down off the walk and crossed the street to the hotel.

13

DEVLIN grinned as Tom walked unannounced into his office.

"Well, I guess I heard rightly," he said. "How are you feeling?"

Tom gave him a brief smile as he removed his hat and settled into an easy chair. He sighed, stretching out his legs.

"Like I'm fifty," he said.

Devlin laughed. "That goes with the job, I reckon. What made you do it?"

"Seemed the right thing to do at the time. A man can get too used to using a gun and others get to expecting it. This way, they don't know what to expect."

"Or fear what they don't know," Devlin said thoughtfully.

"Right," Tom said. "The unexpected can happen at any time. That gives me an edge now."

"You took a risk," Devlin said pointedly. "That could have backfired on you. Dan Griswald's beaten a few men."

"Because of his name or because he's good?"

"Point taken," Devlin said. "The Griswald name is a powerful incentive in these parts. Joe Griswald carved his empire out of the area when nothing was here but Indians. He fought them to keep what he wanted, and he's been the law in the area long before Walker was first settled. Some men tried to rustle some of his stock, and he caught them and hung them from the nearest tree every time. Once, he had to chase a man down into the Territories. But he caught him. Brought him all the way back to his ranch before he strung him up. The lesson stuck. Since then, people left the Box G pretty much alone, with the exception of a few squatters who tried to settle on what he considers his land."

"What he considers his land?" Tom asked. "Or what he owns?"

Devlin smiled. "Griswald keeps grazing rights to a lot of land that he doesn't have title to. We still have a lot of open range and it belongs to whoever can control it. McCoy wants to settle land around the Box G and keep Griswald in bounds that way. But each settler he sent out there was either burned out or shot out. Word spread pretty quickly, and now squatters who come in are warned away from his land."

"What about the Homstads?" Tom asked idly. "They on Griswald land?"

"No. They came early enough to settle outside it. Land's going fast, though. Won't be long and some of that free range is going to come up for settling. Then, we'll have to see what happens."

"I see," Tom said thoughtfully. "So, McCoy has his own plan about the territory. I'd think that he'd want to keep Griswald happy. He has to be one of the largest depositors around."

"He banks in St. Louis," Devlin said. "But McCoy honors all his drafts. Has to. Otherwise, Griswald would probably come into town and settle up with McCoy. He uses a bullwhip when he wants to do that. A cowboy got crossways with Griswald about a year ago, and Griswald rode into town and whipped him from one end of the town to the other. That was before the railroad came in, but I think he'd still do that if he wanted to. That makes me wonder why he let you get away with what you did. That doesn't sound like Griswald."

"I told him I'd shoot him first despite whoever drew first," Tom said. "That didn't leave him much option."

"Unless he could beat you."

"Unless he could beat me," Tom echoed. "There's always that chance. Sooner or later, someone will come along who's better. Kilian told me that. And Pa always said that you need to be right before you start throwing your weight around."

"And that's another reason why you worked this morning the way you did, right?"

"Yes. The gun should always be the last resort. And even then, I'm not certain that it is the last resort," he added. "It seems to me that there should always be another way."

"You've killed a few men since you came to Walker," Devlin pointed out.

"Only because I thought it was needed at the moment. But I keep wondering if there wasn't another way that I could've handled it. That's the problem with shooting someone. You'll never know if you couldn't have solved the problem another way."

"Hard to settle a problem that way when someone's drawing a gun on you. A man's entitled to defend himself.

And you have a responsibility to the town not to get your-self killed. A dead sheriff is useless."

"Any dead man is useless," Tom said. "Tell me some-thing: Why did you buy the Lismore place?"

The smile slipped from Devlin's face. He leaned back in his chair, regarding Tom suspiciously.

"What brought that up?"

Tom shrugged. "Been wondering about that. You taking in the young boy and raising him. Buying his father's place and putting Homstad on it to keep it up. Why?"

"I don't think that's any of your business."

"Maybe not. I'm just trying to get a handle on the area. The more I know, the better I'll be at my job. What made Lismore kill his wife? What was her name? Alma?"

"Edith," Devlin corrected automatically. Then, his face reddened and he pressed his lips together tightly.

"Edith. I understand that Lismore discovered that his wife was having an affair with someone else and that's why he killed her and himself."

"Some people have wagging tongues," Devlin said. "But, yes, that's what I hear happened."

"And a couple of days later, you buy the land."

"What do you mean by that?"

"That?" Tom waved his hand. "An observation."

Devlin eyed him narrowly. "Something else, I think."

Tom ignored the implied question and smiled easily at Devlin. "You think there's any truth to Lismore's thinking when he killed Edith?"

Devlin's eyes shifted away from Tom.

"I don't pay much attention to rumors."

"That why you brought the boy in and raised him and kept someone else from getting his father's place?"

"The boy needed a home and the Lismore place was a sound investment," Devlin said.

"You acted pretty quickly," Tom said.

"Opportunity knocks just once," Devlin said. "You wait around trying to think about it and you miss out on it."

"I can understand that if all you did was buy the place," Tom said. "But why take in the boy? You're not married, seem to already have a lot on your plate. Raising a boy is a big responsibility for a busy man without any help from a wife."

Devlin flinched. He swung his eyes around to face Tom.

"You got something to say, say it," he said.

"The boy's yours, isn't he?" Tom asked.

Devlin tried to hold Tom's eyes, but couldn't. He stared down at his hands resting on the desk in front of him. His face sagged and he slowly shook his head.

"How'd you figure that?"

"The boy likes you and you took a big interest in his well-being when I came to ask you if he could work for you. The kind of interest a father would take in his son. Then I found out that you had bought the place right after Lismore killed Edith. I figure you did that because you wanted to save the place for your son for when he got old enough to handle it."

"We were in love," Devlin said lowly. "I didn't plan it that way. It just happened."

"That's the way it goes," Tom answered, suddenly flashing back on Eula, remembering the way she came to him down at Plum Creek. He remembered the moments, and how time seemed to slip away from them when they were together for the short while, and the happiness he had until her father tried to force a shotgun wedding. He pressed the pads of his fingers against his eyes for a moment, pushing the memory away.

He rose, and Devlin looked up at him.

"You going to tell the boy?"

"He isn't a boy anymore," Tom said. "He's young, true, but he isn't a boy. He might not be ready to take over Lismore's place, but he will be soon enough. He's learning more each day."

"You going to tell him?"

"No," Tom said. "I reckon that's your job. But the longer you wait, the harder it's going to get. For both you and him."

He turned and left the room, gently closing the office door behind him. He paused, drawing slow deep breaths, then turned and climbed slowly to his room, feeling the soreness in his muscles and the weight of the town upon his shoulders.

14

THREE weeks passed and the Box G riders stayed away from town. The cook came in the day after Griswald left with his men, and silently collected the guns that the cowboys had left in the street and took them back to the ranch with him along with enough supplies to last a month. Meanwhile, the town turned to a restless peace, and Tom had the feeling that he was walking into a powder keg each time he made a round through Tent City. Sullen glares followed him from saloon to saloon, but no trouble erupted. Occasionally, a stranger would take exception to checking his guns at the sheriff's office, but someone would always mention, "That's Tom Cade," and a strange look would come over the man's face and his guns would be quickly checked.

At the end of the third week, Tom decided to ride out to the Box G and deliver word that the posting had been lifted and the Box G riders would be allowed in town as long as they left their guns at the ranch or checked them in at the sheriff's office. He saddled the bay and left in early morning light, pausing only at the cottonwood, where he practiced briefly before heading toward the Box G.

When he came to the fence line separating the Box G from the lands worked by Homstad, he saw a rider mending fence. He rode down slowly, recognizing Dan Griswald wearing heavy leather gloves as he tightened barb wire. Tom was surprised to see the younger Griswald riding fence, a job normally left to the cowboy who was the youngest and had the least experience. Many cowboys would refuse to ride fence, holding such duty to be beneath them.

Tom reined in beside Griswald and looked down at him. The young man's face still bore signs of the beating he had taken and he moved stiffly, as if his muscles were protesting all movement.

"Good morning," Tom said.

Griswald straightened with a wince and stared harshly at Tom. He nodded curtly and turned, wincing as he picked up a pulley and rope to tighten the wire before nailing it to the post.

"I rode out to tell the Box G that they're welcome back in town if they leave their guns behind," Tom said genially.

"Why tell me?" Dan growled.

"You're Box G," Tom answered.

Dan gave a short, hard laugh, the sound harsh and jeering.

"I work for it," he said. "Like any other cowboy. You want to tell the Box G, you better ride on up and tell Pa. He's the Box G. Him and no other."

Dan jerked hard on the tail end of the rope wrapped around the pulley, and gasped, straightening against the pain that shot through his back.

Tom frowned. "What's the matter?"

"You should know," Dan growled, tenderly touching his back.

"That was three weeks ago," Tom said.

"Not according to Pa," Dan snapped. "He makes sure I remember it each day."

Tom gave him a puzzled look. "I don't understand."

"Pa likes to use his whip," Dan said. "And he doesn't like a Griswald to be beaten."

Tom shook his head. "I'm sorry. But you could have avoided it, if you wanted."

Dan spat and glared vengefully at Tom. "I'm not finished yet. My time will come."

"Leave it alone," Tom said evenly.

"I owe you," Dan said bitterly.

"You owe yourself," Tom said.

He gigged the bay and rode away, heading along the fence line to the road leading through the fence and winding up into the hills. In the distance, he could see the ranch house setting on a small knoll. The barn and corrals were on the left, along with the bunkhouse and cookhouse. Tom turned the bay onto the road and lifted him into a trot, riding easily, his hand resting on the pommel near his pistol.

A cowboy saw him coming and turned to walk rapidly to the house. By the time Tom reached the house, Griswald was standing out on the porch. Several cowboys angled out from the house, their hands on their pistols.

"You took a big chance coming out here," Griswald said when Tom halted the bay in front of him.

"Maybe. But I figure you're too smart to do anything on your own land," Tom said.

Griswald grunted. "What do you want?"

"Just thought I'd make a courtesy call and tell you that I'm lifting the posting on the Box G."

"All right," Griswald said.

"Just leave your guns here or check them in at the sheriff's office when you come into town," Tom added. "There's no sense in making more trouble."

Griswald remained silent for a long moment, then gave a curt nod. "You had your say. Now, leave."

"I'll leave," Tom said. He glanced at the cowboys scattered off to his right. "Any of your boys feel lucky, you'll be the first I shoot, Griswald."

Griswald stared at him as Tom backed the bay away until only a lucky pistol shot would hit him, then turned the bay's head and slapped his heels against the bay's side, lifting him into a sharp gallop. He rode hard down the road toward the fence, then reined the bay down to a trot. He relaxed in the saddle, thinking as he rode across the brown prairie. He knew that the trouble with Griswald and his riders wasn't over yet, but the time wasn't right. Still, he would need to be on his guard.

As he rode into town, lost in his thoughts, he saw the stagecoach pull up in front of Hawthorne's store. A young woman dressed in blue stepped down from the stagecoach, sunlight highlighting her auburn hair. She paused, turned, and looked up the street as Tom rode to the hitching post by the sheriff's office. Her eyes were brown and soft, her mouth generous, and he felt his heart lurch in his chest.

"Amy!"

She turned, smiling as Hawthorne bustled out of his store and hugged her.

Tom dismounted, tying the bay to the post, then crossed the street and mounted the steps to Hawthorne's store. He took off his hat as Hawthorne turned, holding the young woman by the arm.

"Tom, I'd like you to meet my niece, Amy Hawthorne.

She'll be staying with us for a while. Amy, this is Tom Cade, our sheriff," he said.

"I'm pleased to meet you," Amy said.

Tom felt his face growing red as he clumsily took her hand.

"Yes, ma'am," he said. "I mean, well, my pleasure."

She smiled, her cheeks curving into dimples, and Tom was certain that he had never seen a woman as lovely.

"I hope that you won't be a stranger, Sheriff," she said.

"I won't," Tom answered.

She glanced down at her hand, and Tom suddenly realized that he was still holding it. He dropped it and stood awkwardly, turning his hat in his hands.

"Sorry," he mumbled. "I guess I didn't realize, er, well."

She laughed as Hawthorne clapped Tom on the shoulder, his laughter ringing through the street.

"I think you've already made a conquest, Amy," he said.

She cocked her head to one side, studying Tom. "I'm not certain yet," she said.

"Well," Tom said, "I'll leave you two. I've got some business to do."

"What?" Hawthorne asked, his eyes twinkling merrily.

"You know, er, business," Tom said, stumbling over the words. "I need to take a turn down in Tent City and make certain that Bob's okay."

"He's in the office," Hawthorne said helpfully. "That's across the street, Tom."

Tom could hardly pull his eyes away from Amy, she was so pretty. It felt like he was being pulled into a warm pit. Tiny beads of sweat lingered on her upper lip, one right at the edge of a dimple. But she didn't seem bothered by the heat.

"Uh, yes," Tom said. "Maybe I might see you later?"

"That could be, Tom," Hawthorne said.

Tom nodded at both, then turned on his heel and crossed back over the street. He opened the door and walked inside, closing it behind him and leaning against it. He felt hot and feverish and sweat was slick on his face.

"You damn fool," he said.

"Who?" Bob asked from the jail.

"Me. And don't ask why," he said grimly.

Bob popped his head around the corner, took one look at Tom's face, and tactfully withdrew as Tom glowered at him.

Tom tossed his hat on the hook behind his desk and sat, shuffling through the papers that had been laid out for him. But the action was only action; his eyes never registered the print, nor did the faces on the new wanted posters mean anything to him.

He sat for an hour, staring blindly at the papers, feeling profoundly embarrassed. The feeling went down into the pit of his stomach like he had put too much pepper on his steak. He didn't remember his mother, but he remembered Eula, and this feeling was far different than what he had felt for her. He lost all sense of what he thought life had been about. The sheriff's star disappeared from his mind, and the Schofield felt awkward and heavy on his hip.

In a flash, he realized it was Amy that was bothering him; it was as if lightning had struck, burning his old notions about women to a crisp instantly.

Growling, he rose, grabbed his hat, and stormed from the office, turning his steps toward Tent City, his boot heels thudding hard upon the boardwalk, hoping that there would be someone down there upon whom he could vent his feelings and work the strangeness from him.

Willie was polishing glasses in Daid's Place when Tom pushed his way in. Willie noticed immediately that something was bothering Tom; his face was flushed and a strange light shone from his eyes. Willie didn't know what it was, but he had seen men like that before, as if they were being driven by a mule.

"Want a drink?" he asked casually as Tom came up to the bar.

Tom glanced at the bottle next to Willie's elbow and shook his head.

"That looks stronger than a horse's kick," he said owly.

"I've got a little soda pop around here somewhere," Willie said, bending over to glance beneath the bar. "Ain't cold, but it might go some to ease your stomach. You look like you just ate a bunch of figs laced with alum."

"I'll take one," Tom said. He thumbed his hat back from his forehead.

Willie pulled the cork and set the soda bottle on the bar, wiping up a little spill that leaked over the top.

"Saw a couple of men come in today from the trail," he said casually as Tom took a long swallow. "They were packing iron," he added casually.

Tom put the bottle down on the bar and sighed. "You get any names?"

"Johnson. Figured them to be brothers or cousins. They looked alike. Mean and ornery. One has a knife scar across his nose like someone decided to flay it open one time back. He was the small one and looked the meanest. Like he'd just as soon munch on a railroad spike as a sausage. The tall one looked like he'd just swallowed some green persimmon juice. Both had black hair and short beards. They had a thirst in them. A fish couldn't have drunk water as fast as they pulled on the bottle."

He paused, eyeing Tom from under bushy eyebrows. "They sorta sounded like you with that long drawl you get when you feel someone's biting your tail."

"Johnson."

Willie nodded.

Tom sighed, remembering the threat Eula's father had made the evening he came to the Cade cabin. Toadknock and Peapod. Two of the feuding Johnsons who took any affront to their family with relish. It looked like the Tennessee hills had followed him and found him.

"You know where they might be now?" he asked.

Willie shrugged. "In Tent City somewheres. You might try the cribs. Both looked like they were in a rut and wanted a little rooting around for a spell while conditions were slack and they had a choice. Ain't much action until late afternoon, you know, and some of them whores get a little itchy before then. The Johnsons more than likely will be whittling down their need right now."

"Thanks," Tom said. "I'd better take care of things before they get a chance to get out of hand."

"You could stick around a bit and let them whores tire 'em out. A contented man is easier to work with than a randy one whose bean is still wagging."

"No, best to get at it," Tom said. He tugged his hat brim down over his eyes and motioned at the soda bottle. "Much obliged for the drink."

Willie waved the thanks away. "Don't mention it. Ain't got much call for that stuff 'cept when a young hand comes in who hasn't started on the Who-flung-John yet."

Tom made his way down to the cribs. The bartender looked up when he walked in, then down, pretending to be busy scrubbing a nonexistent spot from the planked bar. Tom paused, letting his eyes adjust to the deliberate darkness that let the whores appear younger than they were. He walked over to the bartender and rapped his knuckles on the bar. Reluctantly, the bartender looked up.

"Hullo, Sheriff," he grumbled.

"I'm looking for a pair of new riders. One having a scar across his nose. The other looks like he has a sour stomach," Tom said.

"Can't say I've seen 'em. 'Course, I've been pretty busy," the bartender said.

Tom looked slowly around the room, noting the customers. One sat nursing a beer while squeezing his temples with one hand. He looked as if someone had pickaxed each temple. Another played a game of solitaire, ignoring the room as he waited patiently for someone with money to join in a game. They were the only ones, but Tom could hear muffled laughter coming from the cribs in the back. He turned back to the bartender and stared hard at him.

The bartender tried to ignore him, but time seemed to pass too slow. Finally, he looked up reluctantly.

"Try again," Tom said dryly.

"I said—"

"I heard. And I don't want to hear it again. Who's in the back?" He nodded toward the cribs.

The bartender shrugged. "Don't rightly know."

"You're making me very unhappy," Tom said warningly.

"Now look here, Sheriff!" the bartender started, but before he could finish, Tom reached out, grabbed a handful of hair, and slammed him face-first onto the bar before he could react.

"Guhdum! Yuh bwoke muh node!" the bartender said as blood gushed down the front of his shirt.

"Now, all I ask for is a bit of respect," Tom said pleasantly.

The bartender grabbed the dirty towel in front of him and held it to his nose as blood continued to pour from it.

"Yuh sumbith," the bartender mumbled, his voice muffled by the towel.

Before the bartender could say anything else, Tom slipped the Schofield from its holster and banged the bartender above the ear with the gun barrel. The bartender fell to the floor behind the bar with a thud.

Tom turned to eye the other two men in the room. The man playing solitaire played a black ten on a red jack. "The two you want are in the back. Third crib. Three women."

Tom walked to the back, ignoring the closed curtains of the first two cribs. He paused in front of the third one, then swept the curtain back with his hand.

The two Johnsons looked up in surprise. Toadknock had his coveralls down to his knees, while Peapod lay drunk and naked in the corner with a fat henna-haired woman sprawled on top of him. Their pistols and Toadknock's rifle were in the corner of the room.

"Hello, Toad. Pea," Tom said casually. "What brings you to Walker?"

"Well, if it ain't young Cade," Toadknock said, pushing himself away from the two women. He stood and pulled his coveralls up, slipping the suspenders over his shoulders. He smiled, revealing mossy teeth beneath his black and scraggly beard. "You remember Eula, I 'spect"

"I remember," Tom said shortly. He nodded at the Johnsons' guns. "You boys have a problem, though. Guns have to be checked at the sheriff's office."

"And I see yer wearin' the star," Peapod said, trying to squirm out from under the fat woman.

"I am," Tom said quietly. "Now, you Johnsons take your guns up and check them with the jailer. Or else ride on out of Walker. Choice is yours."

Toadknock laughed. "Damned if I'll run from a preacher's kid. You know your old man's dead, I 'spect."

A cold chill ran through Tom.

"No," he said. "I didn't. How'd it happen?"

"He got in the way of a bullet," Peapod said, staggering to his feet. "Toad was shootin' at a tinker when the preacher tried to stop him. But the bullet stopped the preacher. I 'spect your brother's written you a letter that you ain't got. But now, there's no reason for you to have to read it, is there?"

"I see," Tom said slowly. "So, what brings you boys to Walker?"

They exchanged glances, then Peapod started to slip over toward their guns.

"Nope," Tom said, tapping his fingernail against the Schofield's handle. "You get much closer, I'm going to have to figure that you're being a bit unfriendly."

Toadknock wiped his hands down the sides of his coveralls and nodded at Peapod.

"Well," Peapod said, "reckon you know why we're here."

"No, I don't," Tom said. He watched them carefully. Peapod caught his concentration and pulled up short.

"Matter of Johnson honor," Peapod said. Suddenly, he turned red in the face and shook a dirty finger at Tom. "You plowed a little corn with Eula, didn't you? And then you got her with child and ran out on her."

"That's a lie," Tom said calmly.

"You calling our cousin a liar?" Toadknock asked, his voice low and dangerous. "Seems like you got all the say, what with your pistol there and our'n over there."

"I wasn't the first one with Eula," Tom said calmly. "And it doesn't take much of a farmer to figure out when a heifer's due after she's been with a bull. With Eula and me, it just didn't add up. And I think you know that."

"Don't make no matter what we think. Or what happened. You didn't do right with Eula and that ain't something that no Johnson's gonna fergit," Peapod said angrily.

"What happened between Eula and myself is our business," Tom said. "That's in the past and should remain in the past. You bringing such things here doesn't change that one bit."

"It damn will change," Toadknock said.

"You two have worn out your welcome," Tom said. "Get dressed and ride on back to Tennessee. There's nothing here for you."

"Free country," Peapod said.

"Not that free," Tom answered. "Get dressed and leave town. You've been warned. I see you on the streets of Walker, I'll arrest you. And tell Eula and her father not to send any more of their kin around. This is senseless."

"A preacher's kid," Toadknock sneered.

"I said what I had to. Now"—he gestured at their clothes—"get your things together and leave."

He drew the tattered curtains together and backed away, keeping his eyes on the curtains. He was halfway across the room when the curtains swept aside and the Johnsons stormed out, guns in hand. He hadn't expected that, and cursed himself as he pulled the Schofield from its holster, thumbing the hammer as he brought it up. Peapod shot first, the bullet taking Tom in the left shoulder and spinning him around, saving his life as Toadknock fired where he had been. Tom crashed into a table and rolled, coming to his knee. He fired, hitting Peapod in the middle. Peapod folded and fell to the floor. Toadknock fired again, and the bullet slammed high into Tom's chest, knocking him backward. He fired again and Toadknock's head jerked back as if poleaxed. With an effort, Peapod pushed himself up and fired and missed, but Tom steadied his pistol, and the next bullet took Peapod in the throat. Then, he fired again, hitting Peapod in the chest.

The room was a dim haze of black powder smoke. Tom tried to rise, but fell back on his side as a small crowd burst through the door. Then, he heard Wilson's shotgun and a warning for all to get back. Again, he tried to rise. The room spun and went dark and he felt himself falling forward into darkness.

15.

VOICES kept murmuring in the twilight as he slipped in and out of darkness. In the night of his unconscious, he kept seeing figures slipping and falling in front of him. Kilian was there, then his father.

And the goat.

His father, Micah, used to keep a goat in the fenced backyard to keep the weeds down. Apple trees were planted back there, and at the foot of the split-rail-fenced yard, there was a toolshed. His father like to store the kindling down there to keep mice and bugs away from the cabin, and when Tom was a yonker, one of his chores was to gather the kindling in the morning for the stove and fireplace.

The goat hated Tom and Tom hated the goat. Each time he was sent to get kindling, Tom would peek out the back door and try to find out where the goat was, and calculate his chances of getting down to the woodpile and back without being knocked rump over noggin by the goat. The goat usually won—unless Tom could make it to one of the apple trees and bawl loud enough for his father to come out and hold the goat so Tom could safely make the journey to the cabin with his load of kindling.

One day, Tom peeked out and couldn't find the goat. Warily, he stepped out the back door of the cabin and glanced around. Still no goat. Taking a deep breath, he sprinted down to the pile of kindling, gathered an armful, and turned to race back to the cabin, only to find the goat standing between him and the door and staring at him through malevolent yellow eyes and, Tom was certain, gleefully. It dug a hoof into the ground, sounded a triumphant trumpet, and charged, head-down, straight at Tom. By now, however, Tom had had enough. He dropped the kindling, grabbed a stove-length oak branch, and banged the goat right on the boss of his horns above his eyes.

The goat stopped, staggered, shook its head, and looked blearily at Tom.

"You—you—goat!" he screamed, and whacked the goat again between the eyes.

The goat made a bleating sound that still seemed defiant to Tom, and he took to beating that goat as hard as he could with the oak branch.

The back door banged open and his father ran down the steps, shouting at Tom as he came.

"Tom! Tom! Stop that! Stop that now!"

He grabbed Tom and held him close as Tom sobbed out his rage and relief. The goat staggered around the yard, shaking its head, then went back to nibbling at the ragweed threatening to come through the fence and into the yard.

"Tom, what made you hit that goat?" his father asked as he helped him carry the firewood into the house.

"He kept coming after me. He's like—like—the devil!" Tom said.

Micah remained silent for a moment, thinking, then said, "There's going to be a lot of times when you can get your way by beating someone or something, Tom, but the best way is to make friends with that person. A man or a goat is the same; you got to earn their respect before you can have a friend. Otherwise, you'll always have an enemy, but he'll hide his feelings from you and strike when your back is turned."

"That goat did that a bunch of times," Tom said, sniffling his fear away. "I can't tell you how many times he's hit me when my back was turned. I told you about that too, but you said that I had to deal with it. Well, I did! I bonked him good!"

"Yes," Micah said, "but have you solved the problem?"

Tom felt something cold pressing against his lips and wiping his face. The images of his father and the goat flickered away. He opened his eyes, squinting against the bright sunlight pouring in through the raised shade in his room. The window had been opened and a cool breeze blew in through it.

He looked down and saw that he was tucked beneath a sheet, a heavy bandage wrapped around his chest and shoulder. For a brief moment, he was confused, then a voice welcomed him back to the living.

"Well, I'd say it was about time that you opened your eyes."

He turned his head and looked at Wilson sitting in a chair by the window, his shotgun resting over his legs.

"Aren't—"

His voice cracked. He swallowed and tried again.

"Aren't you supposed to be on rounds?" Tom asked.

"Been on them. Been doing yours too for the past four days and, frankly, I'm a bit bushed."

"Four days!"

"Yep. Not one of them balls went through you and the doc had to dig around for both. He got 'em out, though, and you can thank whoever's been looking over you that he managed to do that. The one in your chest was tricky; an inch more to the right and you'd be knocking on the Gates and begging for admittance. Who were those men?"

Tom sighed. "From Tennessee. The Johnsons. They came out to kill me."

"Why?" a puzzled Wilson asked.

"A misunderstanding," Tom said.

"You guilty of that misunderstanding or not?" Wilson asked.

"Both," Tom said shortly. "But not like they think. Thought. You have to remember that in the hills, problems and disagreements are settled between families. Usually the hard way."

"Uh-huh. Feuds. Heard about some of them," Wilson said. "Same thing here out West. You kill a man's pard, he'll feel obligated to return the favor. Like you did with Kilian. And he might have a pard and, well, the whole thing eventually gets out of hand."

"You got it," Tom said. "Can I have a glass of water?"

Wilson rose and poured a glass, handing it to Tom.

"You reckon we'll be seeing more of those Johnsons?"

"I reckon," Tom answered. He drank slowly, savoring the coolness as the water slid down his throat.

"And Hardestys too, I'm figuring."

Tom sighed. "I wouldn't be surprised."

"You got an adventurer's spirit, that's certain," Wilson said. "Or else, just plain dumb bad luck. Seems to me the more you get around to rectifying a problem, the more complicated you make it."

"Maybe I should take up a new line of work," Tom said, trying to push himself up into a sitting position.

"I think some people been trying to tell you that all along. But there are some people just like mules. You got to hit 'em in the head to get their attention 'fore you can do anything at all with them. Now, what are you fixing to do?"

"Get up. If I can," Tom said. "I wouldn't want an old man like you to have to do all the work around here. I'd never hear the end of it. Probably won't now," he added.

"By God, if you ain't the stubborn one," Wilson said. "Here you got a chancet to lie in bed with a good-looking woman hovering over you, and you saying you want to get up so you can get shot again. If that don't beat all. You ain't got a lick of horse sense."

"Wait a minute. What was that about a woman?" Tom demanded.

"Well, it ain't the Virgin I'm talking about, but she's pretty enough to give any other a run for their money. Of course," he added, "given that most of the other single women around here are whores down in Tent City, ain't saying much."

"Who?"

"Well, I don't rightly know all their names—"

"No, you meathead!" Tom said, exasperated. "Who was the woman looking in on me?"

Wilson grinned and cradled the shotgun in his arms. "Well now, I might have to give that some thought. What with you arguing all the time and thinking I'm just like a stump around here, sitting and making certain no one comes crawling in through the window to finish the job those Johnsons started and doing your share of the work in addition to my own. I reckon I'm due a raise."

"When pigs fly," Tom said. "What woman?"

Wilson tugged at his ear and grinned down at Tom. "That

niece of Hawthorne's. She's been up here ever day, sitting with you, changing your bandages and bedsheets and all."

"All?"

Wilson grinned and pulled at his ear. "Well, you wouldn't want to sleep in dirty sheets, would you? And you had to be washed and someone had to do it and that someone wasn't going to be me. I don't care to know about your shortcomings, and I sure have no intention of playing nurse to a man foolish enough to get holes shot in him."

Tom's face turned as red as a radish as he thought about Amy's hands washing him. Wilson laughed at his look of mortification.

"Most men wouldn't mind the thought of a pretty girl washing them all over," he said. "But I reckon each man must have his Achilles' heel. I reckon I just found out yours."

"Haven't you got something you should be doing? Like keeping peace in the town?"

"Oh, this town's right peaceful when they saw how hard it was to get you killed," Wilson said easily. "Before you got yourself shot, betting was five to three and pick 'em on you getting killed. But now, there ain't much action going down against you at all. Why, no one's even taking a potshot at a stray dog or cat for fear of bringing down the wrath of Cade."

"Strange," Tom mused.

"Not so strange, I reckon," Wilson said. "A man gets a reputation as a fast gun, well, people know that he won't be around for that long 'cause there's always someone faster. But someone who manages to come away after being shot full of holes is a miracle. And there's enough superstition in this world that no one wants to mess around with a miracle. That's like messing around with a rattler when you could just as easily go around him and tend to your own business."

A knock came at the door, and Wilson shifted the shot-gun around so the barrels were centered on the middle.

"Who's there?" he called.

"McCoy and Hancock. The preacher," a voice called back.

Wilson looked at Tom. "You want to talk to them or rest a mite first?"

Tom sighed. "Might as well get it over with," he said.

Wilson crossed to the door and unlocked it, stepping back as he swung it open. He kept the Greener dead center on the middle of the doorway. When McCoy saw that, he went white.

"Jesus! Wilson, point that thing somewhere else. It's apt to go off!"

Wilson lowered the shotgun. "I reckon I might be doing some a favor," he grumbled. "Bankers and lawyers." He looked over at Tom. "You reckon this world would be a bit better off if we started eliminating some? The way they take on when they get a chance at someone's land is some-thing terrifying."

"We did the same thing with the Indians," Tom re-minded him.

"I had an Indian once promise to cut off my balls if I came south again," Wilson said seriously.

"What happened?"

"I stayed north. Didn't know if the Indian was serious or not, but I reckon it's best not to take a Comanche or Kiowa too lightly. Then, there's them Cheyenne Dog Soldiers. They can get pretty persnickety too. Besides, I'm sort of at-tached to my balls and ain't willing to give them up yet."

"Are you through?" McCoy asked, obviously annoyed.

"I reckon," Wilson said, and sat back down in the chair near the window, resting the Greener across his legs. He grinned at Tom. "Don't take no wooden nickels," he said.

"What can I do for you?" Tom asked, pulling the sheet up to his shoulders and tucking it around his chest.

"Well, it's the matter of what happened down in Tent City a few days back," McCoy said. "I understand you knew those two?"

Tom nodded. "I knew them. They were from back in Tennessee."

"And"—McCoy looked a little embarrassed—"if I understand right, they came out here looking for you."

Tom's eyes narrowed. "That's right."

"Well?" McCoy asked, spreading his hands.

"Well, what?" Tom asked.

"Was this a personal thing or . . ." He hesitated.

"They were carrying guns," Tom said tiredly. "I told them to check their guns at the sheriff's office. They decided they wanted to argue the point."

"I heard," McCoy said, trying to put it delicately, "that there was a lady's reputation at stake."

Tom remained silent, watching a fly buzz in the slanted light coming in through the open window.

"Well?" McCoy prompted.

Tom turned to him, his jaw set hard. "That's personal."

"Well, we can't have you using the sheriff's office to settle personal grudges," McCoy said.

"I didn't," Tom said. "I told them to pack up and get out of town. That we didn't need their sort here."

"I see." McCoy furrowed his brow, clasping his hands behind his back. "But then you killed them."

"Yes," Tom answered. "I killed them just as quickly as I could. They were shooting at me, in case you have forgotten. The Johnsons are a feuding family back in Tennessee. In fact"—he glanced at the reverend—"just before the fracas broke out, they told me that my father, a preacher, had been killed while trying to stop a shooting."

Hancock's face looked concerned. "I'm sorry about your loss," he said.

"Thank you," Tom said quietly. "He was a good man."

"Yes, yes," McCoy said, waving his hands. "But I need to know what happened. There's been talk."

"There'll always be talk!" Tom snapped. "Whenever there's a shooting, there's always going to be talk. And there's always going to be shooting whenever a town wants cleaning up. You know that. Now, here you are, in my room, questioning me about doing my duty."

"There's been a lot of killing lately," McCoy said coolly.

"Regrettably so," Tom said. "But none of it my choice."

McCoy remained quiet for a short time, then said, "There's been talk among some of the citizens that you might be a little, shall we say, overzealous in your job? Since you took over, it seems like we've had one burial in Boot Hill after another."

"I see," Tom said slowly. "So, now that the town's a bit quieter, suddenly it's too quiet? Is that it?"

"There's a good chance that Walker could become a shipping point for some of those Texas herds that are starting to come up," McCoy said. "A man named Yates has already brought two herds north and others are starting to follow his lead. Now, there are a lot of towns that they can slip off to, but if they come straight on through to Walker, that will help the town's economy."

"I think that maybe you are being a little unreasonable now, Mr. McCoy," Hancock said sternly. "For the first time in the past five years, the citizens of Walker are able to walk the streets relatively safe, thanks to this young man. I would like to remind you that you can't serve God and Mammon."

"Thank you, Reverend," McCoy said, annoyed. "But that isn't the question here."

"No, I think that it is the question," Hancock said quietly. "You are not so upset that Mr. Cade might be misusing his office as you are about the possibility that some Texas cattlemen might take their herds to some other town where the laws are more relaxed. When we said we needed a new lawman, it was because we didn't want to be terrorized by cowboys anymore. Or have you forgotten that?"

McCoy looked perturbed. "Reverend, it's not that we are ungrateful for what this young man has done, but it is the manner in which he has continued to do it. We can't have him using the office of sheriff to settle old feuds."

"Get out," Tom said quietly.

McCoy's mouth opened and closed like a fish gulping water. "What—what'd you say?"

"You heard me," Tom said. He looked over at Wilson. "Fred, escort Mr. McCoy to the door, please."

"My pleasure," Wilson said grimly, climbing to his feet. He waved the Greener at McCoy. "You heard the man. Git!"

"Now, see here!" McCoy began, but Wilson nudged him gently in the stomach with the Greener, pushing him back. McCoy backed away rapidly until he reached the door. He paused and shook a fat finger at Tom and Wilson.

"The two of you haven't heard the last of this! I promise you!"

"I reckon I'm just going to have to assist you through that door," Wilson said, cocking the hammers of the Greener.

The door opened and slammed shut. McCoy's heels could be heard clattering down the stairs. Wilson chuckled as he lowered the hammers.

"Well, won't say that was the right thing to do, but I won't say it didn't make me feel good too." He glanced at

Hancock. "So, I reckon that'd come under your canopy of sin, wouldn't it, Reverend?"

Hancock smiled and shook his head. "There are some men whom even God would like to kick in the pants." He looked over at Tom. "He was not speaking for the council or the town, Mr. Cade. He came on his own."

"I figured that," Tom said, shifting his weight on the pillows to ease a nagging pain in his shoulder. "That is, I figured the Texas business was going to come up sooner or later, but I sure didn't expect to be accused of shooting someone behind the protection of the badge."

"We cannot ever forget or avoid our past," Hancock said. "Even when we begin a new life, the past keeps coming back to us one way or the other despite what we do to avoid it. You're a good man, Mr. Cade. You may be the sheriff, but that doesn't mean that you haven't had a life before you became our sheriff. Now, there is a little problem that we need to resolve. We had to bury those men, but none of us knew their names to put over them."

"Toadknock and Peapod Johnson," Tom said wearily. "From Tennessee around Plum Creek Hollow. You can write there and someone will read the letter to the Johnsons eventually."

"Er, yes. But which was which?"

"They're dead now. It doesn't matter," Tom said. "Call one by one name and the other by the other and let God or the Devil sort them out."

Hancock frowned. "That's not very Christian," he said.

"Neither were they," Tom answered.

He closed his eyes and drifted away into sleep, aware of the disturbance that came over Hancock as he left, closing the door softly behind him.

16

TOM healed rapidly, thanks to Wilson and Lismore's attention, but none was as welcome as that he received from Amy Hawthorne, who took to ordering Tom's deputies around, sending them scurrying for this and that until they began to complain that they were more errand boys than deputies.

The first time she came, Tom felt embarrassed and clutched the bedsheets desperately to his chin while she tried to pull them down to dress his wounds. Finally, after a bit of coaxing, he gingerly lowered the sheets, but held them firmly at his stomach, aware that his face was blushing as scarlet as a painted Indian.

She pretended not to notice as she wiped his face and chest with a wet washcloth and wrapped clean bandages around his wounds. Then she spoon-fed him broth that she'd made, making certain that he ate every spoonful. Later, he promised himself, after she left, he'd send Wilson out to get him a piece of beefsteak to satisfy the gnawing hunger in his belly.

After a week, Tom rose and dressed himself, buckling his gunbelt awkwardly around his stomach. He was surprised to see that he'd lost weight and had to draw two more notches through the buckle before the Schofield would rest where it was supposed to on his hip. He tried pulling the pistol quickly from the holster, and was dismayed at the twinges he felt in his shoulder and how the pistol seemed to drag instead of leap from its holster.

When Amy entered the room and saw him dressed and about, she became quiet and glanced at the pistol on his hip as if she was seeing a darkness within him for the first time. But she tried to behave lightly.

"What are you doing out of bed?" she said, scolding him gently. "You want to rip open those wounds?"

"They're pretty well healed by now," Tom said. He rubbed his shoulder gingerly. "Besides, I stay in that bed any longer, I'd wear a hole clean through the mattress."

"A couple more days wouldn't hurt you," she said, hands on hips.

"Maybe, but I do have a job to do and Fred's been pulling double duty long enough. He looked fair wasted the last time he was up here. And I think the boy's been doing more than he's supposed to be doing as well. It's time I started pulling some weight around here."

"Men!" She sniffed and looked at him as if she was miffed. "You can't tell them anything, even if it's for their own good."

"No, ma'am. I expect that's correct," Tom said. "But sometimes, I think a woman just needs to listen to a man too."

"Why, Tom Cade! I've never been so insulted in my life!" she said.

But he could see that she really wasn't, and suddenly, he was standing next to her, looking down at her eyes, big and brown, and suddenly nervous. He took a deep breath, smelling a faint hint of lemon verbena.

"Thank you for all you've done," he said.

"You're welcome," she said. She took a deep breath, but she did not move away from him.

So he bent and kissed her gently on her lips, feeling the softness of them beneath his own. She held the kiss for a second, then moved back, laughing shakily, touching her hair with the tips of her fingers as she tried to make light of what had just happened between them.

For an instant, Tom wondered if he had overstepped a line that he never knew had been drawn, and started to stammer an apology, but Amy held up her hand, stopping him.

"If I hadn't wanted you to kiss me, I would have stopped you," she said.

He made a move toward her, but she skipped away, shaking a finger in admonition at him.

"Uh-uh. Now, behave yourself. There are still the proprieties that have to be observed."

"Why did you let me kiss you?"

She smiled. "Because I wondered what it would be like."

"And what was it like?"

"More than I expected."

Tom stepped to the window and looked down into the street, trying to work his way through the confusion that was racing in him.

"Isn't this rather sudden?" he asked.

She laughed, the sound tinkling in the closeness of the room.

"Yes, I suppose it is," she said.

"Well, then—"

"But you have to admit that you were thinking about this the first time you saw me with my uncle. Things just speeded up a bit after you were wounded, that's all."

"Then you feel the same way?" Tom asked, holding his breath.

She smiled, and he was certain that she would never look lovelier than she looked at the moment, standing in the path of the sun shining through the open window on the other side of the room, dust motes dancing around her like tiny bits of silver, auburn lights glinting from her hair.

"Yes," she said simply.

He tried to tell her that a sheriff's life was uncertain and that to pretend otherwise was to deceive each other. But then he discovered that he was telling her about his childhood in Tennessee, about his father, his brothers, what the seasons were like, and how he liked the fall best of all when the apples hung heavily upon the trees and ripe and heavy plums bent the limbs of the bushes along the creek. He heard the nostalgia in his voice, and knew that he couldn't go home again. Then, he heard the sadness in his voice, and saw that sadness reflected in her face.

They began walking together in the cool of the evening and became regulars in church. They danced together at church socials and went on church picnics together. Once, she went with him down to the bend of the creek to watch him practice among the old cottonwoods, but only once. She told him that when she saw the intensity in him and the look that came over his face, she was frightened.

For a couple of days, that morning hung between them like a dark blanket, but soon she realized that their world would have to be kept as far apart as possible from the other world, even though she knew that the other world would occasionally intrude upon the one that they built for themselves.

People began to talk about them and smile knowingly when they passed them on the street. At first, Tom was a bit embarrassed about the attention they were getting, but when they sat together on a swing on the back porch of her uncle's store and the scent of flowers was heavy in the air, he got over his embarrassment quickly.

Meanwhile, the town remained quiet. When Tom walked through Tent City, people stepped politely aside. Guns were checked regularly at the sheriff's office, and peace seemed to have come at last to Walker as the railroad moved its head another twenty miles down the track. Many of those in Tent City chose to follow the railroad, but some elected to stay, having discovered in Walker a tranquillity that had not existed in other railhead towns.

Griswald's riders came into town in pairs, but behaved quietly. Many did not even bother to wear their guns to town, electing to leave them back on the Box G to avoid having to wait to check their weapons in at the sheriff's office. But some cowboys would stare insolently at Tom when they encountered him in town, and a couple of times, he had to arrest some who had taken on a load of whiskey and decided they had enough of what was needed to take the sheriff down a peg. These men Tom quickly dropped by laying the barrel of his gun alongside their ears, contributing greatly to the hangovers suffered the next morning.

But an uneasiness began to grow within Tom, an awareness that something was coming like the gathering of a storm. He didn't have long to wait. Two weeks after word of their engagement appeared in the paper, Joe Griswald rode into town as mad as if a wolf had bitten a chunk out of his side.

17.

TOM was catching up on the bookwork, listing the fines that he had gathered from those who had been drunk and disorderly, when Joe Griswald stormed into his office, seething. He carried a whip tightly coiled in his right hand. His pistol was belted around his waist. His face was a mottled red, his eyes angry and snapping with anger. He leaned over the desk, shaking the whip in Tom's face.

"Goddamnit! I want him arrested! You hear me? I want him arrested!"

Tom leaned back from Griswald's anger and studied him coolly. He nodded at the pistol and said, "You forget something, Griswald?"

"I ain't staying here that long! But I want him arrested!"

"Right now, you're the one in danger of being arrested," Tom said. He nodded at Bob, standing in the doorway to the cells. "Hand it over. Then we'll talk. But not until then."

Griswald stood erect, trembling with anger. For a moment, Tom was afraid that he would erupt. But after a long moment, Griswald swore and furiously unbuckled his gun and flung it at Bob, who ducked as he caught it.

"Take it, then! Damnit, I came in to lodge a complaint against a horse thief!"

Tom nodded. "Very well. Sit down. We'll talk about it."

He motioned to a chair opposite his desk. Frustrated, Griswald dropped onto it, leaning forward on his elbows.

Tom drew a sheet of paper to him and took up a pen, dipping it into the inkwell. He looked at Griswald.

"All right. You said someone stole a horse from you. Explain."

"It was my prize stallion!" Griswald sputtered. "And that little whelp helped himself to him like he was an ordinary plug!"

"You know who took your stallion?"

"That's what I've been trying to tell you! It was Dan! He stole Hector."

"Description of the horse?"

Griswald rolled his eyes. "For Chrissake! Everyone around knows what Hector looks like! Black with a white star on his face. Sixteen good hands."

"No other markings?"

"No! Now, you going to do something?"

Tom stared at him until Griswald leaned back in his chair and looked away.

"I'll do something," Tom said. "But are you certain you want to bring the law into this? He's your son. I go after him and your horse, I'll have to arrest him and charge him. You know what that can mean."

"A man's gotta face up to the consequences!" Griswald snapped. "Don't matter none if he's my son or not!"

"All right," Tom said. "Do you have any idea about which way he was headed?"

"South, I'd reckon," Griswald said. He crossed his legs and began to slap his boot with his whip. "He hasn't got enough gizzard to go north. The Sioux are in arms up there and it's worth a man's hair to go that direction. East, maybe, but I doubt it. No, it'd have to be south. He might try to tuck into one of those herds coming north. Or that I understand are coming north. You going to bring my horse back to me?"

"I'll bring him back," Tom said. "What about your son?"

Griswald's face tightened. He lifted the whip and shook it slightly. "Yes, bring him back too. I'll deal with him then."

"No," Tom said. "The law will deal with him. Not you. I told you that making this complaint brings his actions into my jurisdiction. He now is the law's problem, not yours."

Griswald rose. "Until I get that stallion back, he's still my problem as well," he said.

He motioned at Bob, still holding his pistol. "Gimme that gun back!"

"Are you officially leaving Walker?" Tom asked.

Griswald said, "There's nothing more for me here. And I gotta ranch to run."

"Give him his pistol," Tom said.

Bob handed it to him. Griswald snatched it out of his hand and stormed out, buckling it around his waist. He climbed onto his buckskin and yanked its head around, roweling its sides cruelly. The horse leaped forward, breaking into a gallop as they headed out of town.

"That ain't a good man," Bob said. "You see the way he treated that horse. I think he must've swallowed a gob of barbed wire."

Tom glanced down at the warrant on his desk. He

touched it with his fingers. "Somehow, I think I'd rather be his horse than his son," he said.

He gathered his hat. "You're in charge," he said to Bob. "Make certain you tell Fred what's happening. I'll be back as soon as I can."

Then, he walked out of the office, heading across the street to the hotel. He was packing a saddlebag when a knock came at the door. He opened it to see Hancock and Amy. He nodded at them.

"Reverend. Amy."

"We heard, Thomas," Amy said. "Are you really going after Griswald's boy?"

"That's my job," Tom said.

"Son, sometimes there's a higher law that needs to be obeyed," Hancock said.

Tom buckled the flap on his saddlebag and sighed.

"Right now, all I've got is a citizen who's made a complaint about someone stealing his horse. A very valuable horse."

"But Dan's his son! His child!" Amy said.

"I know," Tom said quietly.

Hancock pressed Tom's shoulder gently. "You must do what is right," he said. "It isn't your fault that the father has forsaken his son."

"That's comforting," Tom said. He lifted the saddlebags from the bed and picked up his Spencer.

"Be careful," Amy said.

"I plan to," Tom said.

He walked down to the livery stable and saddled the bay. Within an hour, he was riding south, weaving his way back and forth in a giant serpentine to catch a trail. He found several that he debated following, but decided against them, playing a hunch that Griswald's stallion would leave a deeper track than those he had found.

The bay's hooves powdered the grama grass as it loped across the dry prairie. He rode around a patch of soapweed, and found a large area covered with golden sunflowers among some prairie dropseed. The sun stretched across the sky, blue and cloudless, yet Tom kept the bay moving, casting about for some track that might have been made by a stallion sixteen hands tall.

He found a small patch of water in the bottom of a buffalo wallow, and paused to let the bay drink. Many prints were around the edge of the water, but the ground was soft here and he didn't trust that the prints registered true.

When the bay raised its head, he touched it gently with his spurs, riding around the wallow, scanning the ground where the prints would be truer. Still, nothing. He rode a short distance to where a small stand of cottonwoods stood in the middle of long bluestem grass, and pulled up to think.

He had found no tracks that he felt could have been made by the Griswald stallion. Maybe he had misjudged or Griswald had misjudged the direction that Dan could have taken. He sighed and stepped down from the bay, loosening the girth to give the horse a breather. He tied the horse away from a small patch of late-blooming gray death camas, then walked around the small stand to stretch his legs.

Strange, he thought, that a father would take to his son in such a way. But it was a harsh land and Griswald had to have been a harsh man to build a sizable ranch out here before the railroad came. Maybe even before Walker was settled. It took a harsh and unpleasant man to hold onto his stock and land where the law was seldom seen. Maybe Griswald was trying to raise his son to be like him, knowing that when he died, if his son had not been made into a hard man, the Box G would soon be engulfed with home-steaders and squatters, and rustlers would drain the ranch of its stock.

He leaned against one of the cottonwoods, staring idly over the prairie to the south. Suddenly, he frowned and straightened, concentrating on a small gathering of purple-rose ironweed that stood at an odd angle, almost as if the stalks had been brushed or stepped on by a large animal.

Slowly, he walked out to the ironweed, carefully study-ing the ground in front of him. When he came near the ironweed, he noted a deep hoofprint, finely defined, and squatted on his heels as he studied it.

He knew the chances of that print having been made by Griswald's stallion were slim, but something felt right to him. The more he studied it, the more certain he became that the stallion Hector had made it.

Rising, he dusted his hands together, staring off into the distance. The hills seemed to roll on continually, like brown sea waves. Yet, he knew that distance was deceptive and the hills could as easily hide a number of Kiowa warriors as they could one man with a Sharps rifle. The thought did not settle well with him, but he knew that he had to follow the trail until he knew if his hunch was right or wrong.

He walked back to the cottonwoods and unsaddled the bay, staking it out so it could graze. He made a small camp and settled down to rest. Now that he had a trail to follow, it would be best on a fresh horse. He built a small fire and made a pot of coffee. He sipped a cup while eating some dried beef and hardtack. Then he moved the pot back off the coals and settled on the blanket to clean the Schofield and Spencer before taking a short nap.

The next morning, he rose early, drank a cup of coffee left over from the night before, then broke camp and headed south, following the trail carefully. The horse had been fresh-shod and moved with a long, pacing gait, and its rider kept it heading due south as if he wanted to put as many miles behind him as possible. Tom became more and more certain that he had found the right trail.

After two hours, he found the remains of a hasty camp between two yucca plants. The rider had kept the horse hobbled and on a short picket. Tom reined in and studied the ground carefully before climbing down from his saddle. He knelt beside the small fire and gently touched the coals. They were warm, but the rider who had made them could be twenty miles away if he had risen for an early start.

And, Tom reflected, given Griswald's temper, Dan probably would have been an early riser.

He remounted and pointed the bay's head south, lifting it into an easy lope. Whoever was on the horse he was following was riding him hard. Eventually, Tom would catch up with him as the horse tired. He settled back in the saddle and relaxed, letting the bay pick its own way along the trail.

By noon, the sun was beating down like a smithy's hammer upon the prairie anvil. Sweat darkened the bay's skin along his neck. Tom removed his hat and wiped it out with a bandanna. He reined in and stepped down, taking his canteen with him. He soaked the bandanna with water and swabbed out the bay's mouth before taking a small drink for himself. He had seen no water for the better part of three hours, and did not know if any water holes lay south or if they might have been dried out over the summer. Until he found water, it was wise to conserve it.

He led the bay to rest it as he stayed on the trail, noting how the stallion's stride was becoming shorter as the miles passed. If this was Griswald's horse, then Dan was beginning to push the stallion hard. Yet, they were far enough away from Walker and the Box G that he should have been relaxing a bit. Or, Tom thought, at least change direction and try to hide his back trail. Heading south for so long suggested that he was afraid of being followed and of what *might* be following him. Fear was keeping him flying south as fast as he could manage.

Tonight, Tom would play a hunch and ride after dark, holding the bearing as well as he could to close the distance when the rider in front would have to stop. He glanced up at the sun and sighed. A few hours of daylight yet. He stepped up into the saddle and rode south.

• • •

Two hours after dark had settled in, Tom spotted a flickering fire in the distance. He reined in, considering, then decided that he would make a dry camp and wait until false dawn before riding into the camp. He hoped that he would be able to surprise whoever was in the camp, although he was certain by now that the rider was Dan Griswald.

He pulled up in a small grove green with willow and cottonwood and a small seep that had kept the buffalo grass green despite the heat.

His bay was tired, and after he had unsaddled and picketed it, the horse rolled with a slow heave of relief in the dusty grass before it began to crop the green grass.

Tom stretched out full length beside the tiny seep and drank thirstily, then rinsed his canteen and filled it with the cool water that was missing the alkali bite he had been expecting. As the night lengthened, he listened to the rustle of the dry leaves in the trees as a hot breeze blew across the prairie.

Impatiently, he waited for false dawn, watching the fire slowly burn down to embers and the embers slowly disappear. Twice, he rose to move closer to check on the fire, but forced himself to settle down and wait. He watched the full moon move across the sky, bathing the prairie in a cold, white light. The sky seemed different tonight, the stars colder and closer and the darkness between them deeper.

He must have dozed off for an hour or two as a gunshot brought him to his feet, pistol in hand. He waited, alert. Another shot came, followed closely by a third. But they were off in the distance to the south. He frowned, wondering.

At last, false dawn came slowly, the gray pushing the night away. Tom rose, saddled the bay, and mounted, riding in a slow detour to bring him into the camp from the south. He resisted the urge to clamp spurs to the bay and gallop the short distance to where he had last seen the fire, but kept the bay moving around the hills.

He came in from the south, riding slowly, watching. A short distance from the camp, he heard a whimpering and reined in. He dismounted, following the sound, and discovered a wolf dead, red tongue lolling out, while her pup pushed at her dugs, whimpering from hunger. He reached down and picked the pup up by the scruff of its neck.

"Sorry, boy, but I'm afraid she's dead," he whispered.

The pup whined and scrambled to get away, but Tom held it close, humming musically to it. When it quieted, he put it next to its mother.

"I'll be back, boy," he said softly.

He slipped the Schofield from its holster and moved quietly into the camp. The black stallion stood hobbled at the end of its picket rope, eyes rolling nervously at Tom's appearance. Dan Griswald lay in his blankets, feet toward the dying coals. Tom whistled softly. The black stomped its feet. Dan rolled rapidly from his blanket, pistol in hand.

"Don't!" Tom shouted.

But Dan was already aiming at him. Tom took a wide step to the left as Dan fired. He heard the wet slap of the bullet and the bay grunt behind him. Dan swung his pistol toward Tom. Automatically, Tom thumbed the hammer on his pistol. The shot staggered Dan as it struck him in the right shoulder. Desperately, he tried to shift the pistol to his left hand.

"Leave it alone, Dan!" Tom said sharply.

Dan ignored him, raising the pistol, rage and pain twisting his features. He fired, and Tom felt the bullet whisper past his ear.

His pistol bucked twice in his hand. Dan staggered back as each shot caught him in the chest. He sprawled on the earth, rolled over, tried to rise, but his muscles refused to obey. He screamed once, then shuddered and died, blood spilling from his mouth.

A great weariness came over Tom as he stepped over the fire and knelt beside the boy.

"You stupid fool," he said softly. "Why couldn't you let it be?"

He rose and walked back to the bay. The horse had been hit hard, and Tom looked down at it in pity. He lifted the Schofield and shot it, then stood for a long moment, staring down at the horse, feeling empty inside.

Slowly, he made his way back to the wolf and found the pup nudging its mother's neck, whimpering again. He picked it up and the pup snuggled against his chest, its tiny tongue licking his neck.

"I reckon I'll call you Sam," he said. "The last man I knew with that name was a good one. It should be passed on."

The pup whimpered and wiggled in his arms. He carried the pup back to the camp and sat beside a clump of skeletonweed, smelling the pink flowers, feeling the loss of a son he had wanted to save from his father.

18

THREE days later, a weary Tom Cade rode slowly into Walker, the black stallion carrying a double burden with the body of Dan Griswald draped behind the saddle. The wolf pup was riding comfortably inside Tom's shirt.

He reined in out front of the sheriff's office and stepped down stiffly. He pressed his hands against the small of his back and stretched, trying to work the stiffness out. The stallion hung its head wearily. Curious people began to crowd around.

"Someone go find Reverend Hancock," Tom said. "And the undertaker."

He climbed the steps and entered his office. Bob met him and glanced out the window.

"This isn't going to go well with Griswald," he said, shaking his head. "No, sir. Not going to go well at all. Going to be big trouble over this."

"I know," Tom said, slumping down in his chair. He

took the pup from his shirt and placed it on the floor. "Would you get some milk for this little fellow? I could use a cup of fresh coffee too."

"Yes, sir," Bob said, and scurried out the door.

Moments later, the door opened and Fred Wilson walked in, shotgun cradled in one arm. His face was grim.

"See you got back," he said.

"Looks that way," Tom said. He yawned and tried to rub the scratchiness from his eyes. He nodded at the window. "I didn't want it that way. Tried to talk him out of it."

"I know," Wilson said. "But Griswald won't see it that way. And some others too, I'm reckoning. There's going to be trouble over this. Dan may have been arrogant and a Griswald, but there were many who just saw him as a head-strong boy. I know he had a streak of meanness in him, but people ain't going to believe me because I work for you."

Bob came in, carrying a small can of milk and a pot of coffee.

"Ma Lagerfield sent this over to you. She also says that there's a steak and eggs waiting for you when you feel like eating."

"Thanks," Tom said. He took the can and poured a little milk into a saucer and placed it on the floor. The pup lapped at it greedily. Tom leaned back and smiled, then took a long drink of coffee, scalding his tongue. But it felt good as it settled in his stomach, and he cautiously sipped again.

"What are you going to do?" Wilson asked.

"I don't know," Tom said. "I really don't know. Send Reverend Hancock out to tell Griswald that his boy is here and what happened to him. After that, I haven't the foggiest idea."

Hancock came in and heard the last of Tom's remarks. He came over and stood beside Tom.

"Don't revile yourself for what happened," he said gently. "When you went out after Dan Griswald, you knew something like this would probably happen."

"Maybe I could have handled it differently," Tom said.

"None of us can be such judges," Hancock said. "We try, but once something like this is done, there's no going back and no use wearing a hairshirt over what you could have done differently."

Tom looked up into the kind eyes and shook his head.

"You told me not to go. Amy told me not to go," he said.

"Yesterday's gone and there is nothing we can do to turn back the time and make all things right. The loss of a life is always bad, but once it's lost, it's lost for good. Joe Griswald's going to grieve and grieve hard over this. It might be that he'll try to extract vengeance for this, but you cannot give back pain for pain. You know that. You come from Tennessee where feuds are commonplace, and you know that there is no such thing as getting even in the death business. It has to stop somewhere. Despite how good you are with a pistol or rifle, there's always someone better or bigger or stronger. Or a snake might startle your horse and throw you and break your neck. Or someone will shoot you in the back. Maybe you'll just get old and die. That's the way life works. Trying to get even for the loss of one life does not make an even measure."

"Why do men always feel that they have to justify death?" Tom asked. "Is it arrogance? Or a sense of pride?"

"It's a need," Hancock said. "We must always try to justify what we do not understand."

"Perhaps. Right now, however, I'd like you to go out and tell Joe Griswald that his son's waiting for him at the undertaker's. Tell him that I didn't have any choice in the matter. Dan had already made up his mind about what he was going to do."

"I'll tell him," Hancock said.

"I was you, I'd take someone with me," Wilson said. "Griswald's less likely to do something if you have someone along with you."

"God will go with me," Hancock said peacefully.

"Yeah," Wilson grunted, "but God won't be carrying a Winchester. Griswald might take it so bad that he kills the messenger without thinking."

Hancock smiled and shook his head.

"I shall be all right," he said. He looked at Tom. "I shall try and get him to understand that there's been enough death in Walker lately and there's no need to add to the tally."

"I wish you luck," Tom said. "I tried to talk to him a week or so ago and he wouldn't listen then. Neither would his boy."

"I will remind him of the Lord's words to Malachi: 'I hated Esau, and laid his mountains and his heritage waste for the dragons of the wilderness.' Perhaps if Joe Griswald had been a better man, this would never have happened."

He smiled again and left. Wilson waited until the door closed behind him, then said, "Yeah, and if wishes were bricks, we'd have a strong shithouse."

He shifted the shotgun in his arm.

"You go and get you that steak and eggs. Probably wouldn't hurt you none to get Devlin's porter to pull a hot bath for you too. Then get some rest. You need it and you're going to need it more later. Bob and me can hold the fort a bit longer. If Griswald comes into town loaded for bear, we'll let you know."

Tom yawned. His stomach rumbled. He rose, stretching.

"Well, I reckon that's about the best advice I've heard

so far today," he said. He looked down at the pup, who had finished lapping the milk and was lying on the floor, looking up at him patiently. Wilson noted his attention.

"Where'd you get that wolf pup?" he asked.

"Griswald killed its mother," he said, bending and picking the pup up. "Left the little guy out there to die."

"Why'd he kill the mother?" Bob asked. "That ain't right to kill a mother. Makes no difference whose mother. Ain't right to kill a mother."

"It was in his nature," Tom said.

He walked out the door, stepping around the black stallion. Dan Griswald's body had been taken away, but no one had thought about the horse. He called, and Bob poked his head out the door.

"Take Griswald's stallion down to the livery stable and tell Ben to brush him and give him a bait of oats," he said. "At least we can return the horse in good condition. Although why a man'd value a horse over his son is beyond me."

Obediently, Bob untied the black and led the tired horse down to the livery stable as Tom crossed the street to Ma's Place. The people he passed refused to meet his eyes. A tiny bell tinkled when he entered the restaurant. Two men looked up to see who had come in, then dropped their gaze back down to the large wedges of apple pie in front of them. Ma came in from the kitchen, wiping her hands on her apron.

"Well, I was wondering when you'd get around to getting over here," she said, scolding him. "Mercy, but men can be the most stubborn creatures."

Tom removed his hat and ran his hand over his dusty black hair. "Yes, ma'am, I reckon that's true enough. I too late for a bite to eat?"

Ma pulled a chair out and pointed sternly at it. "You just sit yourself right down here, Tom Cade, and I'll have a steak and eggs out to you before you get settled. And I got a fresh wild plum cobbler just out of the oven to put a topping on your meal. Ain't nothing better than a wild plum cobbler for what might ail you." She noticed the wolf pup, and pointed at it. "Where'd you get that?"

"Dan Griswald killed its mother," he said.

"That gives you an idea about what that boy would turn into. A copy of his father, if I'm any judge, and I've seen enough to judge most men. The fruit don't fall far from the tree, you know, and Joe Griswald's a man that God should have had second thoughts about."

She patted his shoulder and bustled out into the kitchen, only to return within seconds with a fresh pot of coffee and a mug. She plopped both down in front of him, put a saucer of milk for the pup on the floor, and disappeared again into the kitchen.

Tom placed the pup on the floor. The pup sniffed the milk, lapped a little, then lay down next to it. Tom sighed and poured himself a cup and leaned forward, elbows on the red-and-white checkerboard tablecloth, to sip the hot brew. His muscles began to relax and he sighed deeply.

The bell tinkled, and he looked up to see Amy enter. She came over to the table. He stood and pulled back a chair for her.

"Are you all right?" she asked anxiously. "I heard about what had happened with Dan Griswald. That's a terrible thing!"

"Yes," he said. "I'm all right. He didn't leave me much choice."

She grabbed his arm with both hands and said, "You had to do what was necessary. I know that."

He shook his head. "I can't keep thinking I could have handled things better."

"Hindsight is always better than foresight," she said. Then, she changed the subject. "You got some mail. I think from your brother. Matthew Cade?"

Tom nodded.

"I had my uncle put it up in your room. That's not exactly the way it should be, but there was a package as well and I thought it would be better that way."

"Thank you," Tom said as Ma came bustling out of the kitchen, carrying a thick steak piled high with eggs and a loaf of fresh-baked bread.

"This is from my own sourdough starter," Ma said, plunking the food down in front of Tom. "That starter came down to me from my great-grandmother."

She looked at Amy. "Would you like a cup of coffee and something? Pie? Mr. Cade's gonna finish off his meal with some wild plum cobbler."

"I'll wait for that, please," Amy said. "Thank you."

Ma beamed and nudged Tom with an ample hip. "You take my word, Tom Cade, and marry up with this young thing as soon as you can and give up sheriffing. You've done what was wanted. That's enough. Now, get on with your own life."

"I'm not certain what that could be," Tom said.

"Well, think about it anyway." She patted his shoulder. "Now you just give a shout when you're ready for that cobbler."

She hastened into the kitchen. Amy smiled at Tom.

"She has a good heart," she said.

Tom nodded, his mouth full of steak and eggs. He swallowed, washing it down with a swallow of coffee.

"Yes, she is," he said. "But I wonder what the rest of the town is thinking."

"I don't care," she said.

A tiny smile crossed his lips, but there was no humor in the smile.

"You should," he said. "It'll reflect back on you if you stay with me."

"I'll stay with you," she said firmly.

"That's good to know," he said. "But I don't know what I'll be doing."

"You could farm," she said.

"I could," he said. "But right now, I don't know. This affair isn't over yet. It won't be until Griswald lets it be alone. The choice is his."

"You could give up carrying a gun," she said, her eyes looking down at her hands folded demurely in front of her.

"Could I?" he mused. "I wonder. I told a man once that I thought the world would be a better place if there were no guns in it. But if I hadn't been wearing this gun, then I wonder what would have happened to Walker."

"Another man would have come along," she said. "It doesn't have to be you."

"Why should I be different from another?" he asked.

"Because I love you," she said simply.

"That might be enough," he said.

At that moment, Ma came out with the wild plum cobbler and a fresh cup for Amy. And a good thing it was that she did, for Tom had been starting to lean across the table to plant a kiss on Amy's lips and hanged be any who might have seen the sparking. And stranger still, Amy had been leaning toward him too, bent on helping him make the short journey over the checkered tablecloth.

19

WHEN Tom got to his room, he discovered the package and letter waiting for him. He sighed, unbuckled his gunbelt, and carried the package to the table by the window. He opened the letter.

Dear Thomas,

Pa is dead. He was kilt by accident or sos those around say when he went and tried to stop Wylie Johnson from shooting Cousin Ruban. I weren't there no were any other cept the Johnsons so we have to take their word for it. The sheriff says there ain't nothing we kin do by it but I don't think this is going to end all. You know the Johnsons. Eula had her baby and it don't look nothing like you but like Ed Watkins up over in Sleepy Holler but that don't mean nothing to the Johnsons as theys set on you being the father. I don't think you shuld come

*home and sides we buried Pa yesterday over by Ma. I
know he wanted you to have this stuff so I send it on to
you. Things are bad here and I'm going to head out
soon as I can for New Arluns. Mark and Luke are comin
too. I heard you were sheriffin in Walker so I'm sending
this to you there. Take care. Watch your back.*

Yr lovin brother

Matt

Tom laid the letter aside and opened the package. He
found his father's black coat and Wesley collar and the
Bible he had used in the pulpit. He stared at it for a long
time, then picked it up and opened it at random, reading.

"Thou shalt not be afraid of the arrow that flieth by day
nor the terror that cometh at night."

He closed the book and placed it on his father's coat. He
picked up his father's watch and wound it. Then, tears
came to his eyes and he rose and went to his bed and
stretched out. Within minutes, he was asleep. The wolf pup
sat on its haunches for a minute, then whined and stretched
out on the floor beside the bed.

• • •

Joe Griswald didn't make an appearance that day, but the
next day, he came into town with ten of his cowboys and the
cook driving a buckboard to take Dan Griswald and his cof-
fin back to the Box G. The townspeople had been cool toward Tom despite Hawthorne's assurances that killing Dan
Griswald had been unavoidable. Many of the people under-
stood that, but were afraid of what Griswald might do.

As he watched the solemn Box G procession, Tom's
thoughts merged into a cold, thoughtful earnestness and he

felt a darkness begin to flow in his veins. He felt troubled by this feeling, making him aware of some part of himself that was trying to rise to the surface despite his desire to keep it buried deep inside.

Griswald saw him standing beside the door to the sheriff's office and rode over to him. His face was set with fury.

"You are dead," he said quietly.

Tom nodded. "We all have to die sometime."

"Soon," Griswald promised. "Very soon."

Viciously he reined his horse around and went back to the head of the procession, leading them out of town.

"I think you'd better have eyes in the back of your head," Wilson said quietly from beside him. "That man will kill you if he can. And he won't give a damn how he does it. He's had a free hand on the range for quite a few years. A man like that gets used to doing what he wants and when he wants."

"Handy to know," Tom murmured.

Wilson spat into the street and shifted his shotgun so he could roll a cigarette. "Well, the way I see it, you got two choices: leave town or kill him."

"That's about the way I see it too," Tom said. "But either choice galls me."

"Well." Wilson scratched his head under his hat and leaned against the hitching post holding the overhang off the duckboards. Tom glanced at him; he looked embarrassed.

"Spit it out," Tom said. "You got something unpleasant to do, best get at it and put it behind you."

Wilson took out his tobacco and makings and deliberately began to roll a cigarette from the rice paper.

"There's talk going around town. Down in Tent City. Up here." He gestured around the town.

"Talk? What about?"

"You gettin' too handy with that piece of yours. How many's it been? Countin' him?" He nodded at the procession.

Tom sighed. "Too many."

"Uh-huh. There's some who're saying you're gettin' to likin' it too much."

Tom stared hard at Wilson. "What do you think?"

Wilson shrugged and put the cigarette between his lips, lighting it with a kitchen match. He shifted the shotgun.

"You had a job to do. There's consequences to havin' to do that kinda job."

"Had?" Tom asked softly.

Wilson blew a cloud of dirty gray smoke.

"We haven't had much trouble in a few weeks, outside of the occasional drunk and the section worker who gets a little frisky when he comes back to Walker instead of going to the new railhead down the line. But trouble just seems to follow you around."

"I know," Tom said quietly. "That's got me wondering too. Sam told me that once you start using a pistol, that word travels fast and there's always someone somewhere thinking they can buck you."

"It's gonna get worse. Devlin and McCoy are starting to build holding pens outside of Tent City. They're counting on the trail herds coming up from Texas. But they're afraid that the ramrods won't come to Walker if there's a chance that their cowboys will get in trouble. Bad trouble, I mean."

"They won't. As long as they shuck their guns," Tom said. "A man doesn't need a gun in order to have fun. He can shoot off steam other ways without shooting up the town and maybe some innocent bystander. Guns aren't the answer. Not anymore. Not in town anyway."

"They're afraid that the trail herds will swing over to Abilene or Hays or even Omaha to avoid Walker. Some are saying you're getting too hard. Harder than Hickok and Mather. They're feeling that maybe you ought to be relaxing some of your rules some."

"That's money talking," Tom said. "A man can't serve the right and Mammon. It just isn't possible."

"That's what the reverend keeps reminding them. But you know how stubborn people can get when they think they're right. 'Course, that right is usually governed by what they want now despite what they wanted in the beginning. Now, they know that if the herds come in here, why, those cowboys will be figuring that they ought to have a real run for their money."

"What do you suggest?" Tom asked.

Wilson sighed and flipped the cigarette out into the dust of the street.

"I don't rightly know. I think you've been doing a good job the only way you coulda done it in the first place. But people are thinking that maybe it would be a good idea to open Tent City up again. Keep the cowboys down there."

Tom remained silent for a minute, then sighed and said, "The problem is that once the cowboys start hitting that Who-flung-John, they'll be trying to spill over into the town and then we'll be right back where we started. It's going to be hard enough when the herds begin to arrive to keep the fools from the respectable and the respectable from the fools. We don't need a harness slapped on us while trying to do our jobs."

He stared gloomily out into the street.

"I guess I'm going to have to have a talk with Devlin

and McCoy," he murmured. "I seem to be spending more and more time with the politics of this job than doing it. Maybe I ought to ask for a raise."

"Yeah," Wilson said dryly. "And you got as much chance of getting that as horses have growing wings."

"Pegasus did," Tom said. "Where it happened once, it could happen again."

"Yeah, well, I don't know nothin' about no Pegasus, but I do know that gettin' McCoy to open his purse strings a little wider ain't gonna happen. And he's gonna have somethin' to say about what's been happening here in Walker too. That Devlin will back him, sure as the sun rises in the east. Don't know why Devlin should be comin' up short against you, but he has been lately."

"He's afraid," Tom said.

"Afraid? Afraid of what?"

"Afraid that the people in town will get to know more about him than he wants knowing," Tom said, stepping around Wilson and heading toward the bank.

"Now, what the hell could that be?" Wilson asked.

But Tom didn't answer. He knew that some things were better left unsaid, and knew that the truth about Lismore's father and mother was best kept private until Devlin wanted to make it known. Which, he reflected as he opened the door to the bank, was something that obviously was not going to happen. The next best thing would be to get rid of Tom as the sheriff and bury the problem as deeply as it once was.

He glanced over at McCoy's office and noted the door was shut. He felt a smile coming, but closed it down as he glanced at Roy Jenks, the teller, waiting on Ma Lagerfield. He nodded at Ma, who gave him a smile.

"McCoy in?"

Jenks looked up. He wore sleeve garters and his hair looked like it had been slicked down by the contents of a lard can. His thin lips pressed together. Tom didn't like him. Jenks usually walked around as if he was trying to sniff the air of the moon.

"He's busy," he said loftily.

"Well, he's going to get busier," Tom said.

He pushed the gate open and walked through as Jenks started to protest, then thought better of it and went back to taking care of Ma's transactions. Tom crossed to the door, knocked once, then opened it and stepped in.

McCoy sat behind his desk, his muttonchop whiskers bristling. Devlin sat in one chair, looking hard at Tom. Hawthorne sat in the other, his face red and mad from what appeared to have been an argument going on in the room before Tom's entrance. Next to him sat Hancock, his eyes troubled, but his face calm.

"Morning all," Tom said. "Looks like I interrupted something."

"You always do," McCoy said, annoyed. "You're getting a bit rough around the edges with your manners."

"That's what I hear," Tom said, pulling another chair over between Devlin and Hawthorne and sitting. "And I think it's something that we need to talk about."

Devlin and McCoy exchanged glances, and Tom knew that they had been talking about him.

McCoy cleared his throat and said, "Now that you mention it, maybe it is time we had a talk. We"— he swept his hand around the room—"have been thinking that maybe you're becoming a bit too zealous with your job."

"I think you're going a bit far, Mr. McCoy," Hancock said softly. "You're not speaking for all of us here."

"And you're not speaking for me either," Hawthorne

said hotly. "Not in this. We asked Tom Cade to do an impossible job, one that could have gotten him killed and almost did. But he did it. And he did it the only way he
could. You know as well as everybody in town that he tries
to avoid gunplay whenever he can, but there just isn't reasoning with some people."

"Figured that you would take his side." Devlin smirked.
"He's sparking your niece."

"That is not called for," Hancock said.

A coldness settled in Tom's stomach as he turned toward Devlin.

"You're overstepping yourself, Devlin," he said quietly.

"I'll remind you that we are the town council here,"
McCoy said huffily.

"Self-appointed, if I understand right," Tom said.
"When was the last election? But that doesn't matter. What
does matter is Devlin has no right saying what he just did."

"And why not?" Devlin said. He gestured at Hawthorne.
"He's sticking up for you because you are courting his
niece. That colors his judgment in my book. And a man
does foolish things when a woman is involved."

Tom settled back in his chair, but his face was hard and
cold as he held Devlin's angry glare.

"That experience talking, Devlin?" he asked softly.

Devlin's face went white; then red slowly started crawling up from his starched collar. McCoy noticed that and
leaped into the silence that had come into the room.

"It's this way," he said. "Tom, you've done a good job.
There's none here that won't say that, despite where their
interests lie. But it's time for Walker to move on now, to
build something that we wanted when we came here.
Something good for Walker."

"And that good is allowing the trail herds to come up?"

Tom asked. "I don't disagree with that. But my job isn't finished yet. The trail herds will be bringing new problems to Walker that are going to have to be dealt with and I intend on keeping the peace. The trail herds will only be part of the answer to building Walker into a respectable town. And they won't be permanent. They'll only be temporary as more and more railroads are built. Soon, you'll have railroads going down into Texas, so there won't be any reason for ranchers to drive their herds up north."

"But," McCoy emphasized, leaning forward in his chair, "they will bring prosperity to this town."

"Call a spade a spade, not a shovel," Tom said. "What you mean is they'll bring money into this town and some people here are going to get rich off that. Now, I don't have anything against someone becoming rich. It's the way they go about it that begins to bother me some."

"I think he's right," Hancock said. "Mr. Cade has done an impossible job. One that was asked of him to do. I do not wish to offend, but this whole affair is becoming something that is beginning to appear self-serving. Mr. Cade has shown that he is a God-fearing man. He comes to church regularly and has shown kindness to many in this town."

"I'd appreciate it if you left God out of this," Devlin said sarcastically.

McCoy shook his head. "The truth of the matter is that we needed you at the time. But now"—he spread his hands—"things have changed."

"They're changing," Tom said. "They haven't changed. You're still going to have problems with Griswald and you're going to have problems with the cowboys when they hit Walker and decide to let off a little steam. Then, you're going to be right back where you were when the railhead was here and the section men came into town to have a good time. You didn't like that when it happened. And the same situation is going to exist once the herds arrive in town."

"You're making a mountain out of a molehill," Devlin said contemptuously.

"Cowboys carry guns," Tom said quietly. "Most railroad workers don't. It'll get worse before it gets better. You need to nip trouble in the bud before it becomes a flower."

"Yes, it's true that railroad workers don't normally carry guns. But how many did you have to kill anyway?" Devlin challenged. "Seems to me that you've gone a bit further than you should have with that. What are you going to do when you have more gun-packing cowboys around? It seems to us that a sheriff who has your ideas will just encourage that, not stop it. You went off after young Griswald and brought him back dead. You didn't have to do that."

"How would you know? Were you there?" Hawthorne asked angrily.

Devlin shook his head. "I don't have to have been there. It just seems natural to me that Cade has taken to his gun as the answer to all problems."

"I tried to tell you a gun wasn't the answer when I took this job," Tom said. "But I also told you that a gun would have to be used on occasion."

"I agree," Hancock said. "I know that Mr. Cade does not fall back upon his pistol to solve problems. Many occasions have arisen when he did not resort to his pistol to resolve them."

"I disagree. It seems to me that the occasion is coming up more than necessary now," Devlin snapped. "We need a sheriff now who is used to using a bit more reasoning than pulling his pistol each time a situation comes up. You are beginning to scare people. Shooting Dan Griswald has bothered a lot of people."

"Why?" Tom asked. "You ever read Thomas Paine?"

Devlin exchanged looks with McCoy. "What the hell's that got to do with anything?"

"Sometimes a man has to make sacrifices for the greater gain," Tom said. "And sometimes, those sacrifices affect people differently. Of course, that all depends on what a person has in mind as the end result of what those sacrifices are going to lead to. In your case, and yours," he added, nodding at McCoy, "it seems to me not to be better for Walker, but for your own interests. You've got a relatively clean town. Buildings are starting to go up in Tent City now, which is going to make Walker even bigger. Apparently, some of those people have decided to give up following the railhead and settle here. There has to be a reason for that. Maybe they feel that this is a place where they can build good lives. Maybe they're simply believing the same thing that you do: that this is a place where money's going to be made in the near future. But the funny thing about money is that trouble usually comes where the money begins to gather. Look at what's going on over in Missouri since the end of the war. When a man gets a load of money, there's always going to be someone who's going to want to take it away from him."

"We need this man now more than we did before," Hawthorne said stubbornly.

McCoy shook his head. "I don't think so. And as mayor, I'm going to have to do what I think is proper for Walker. I'm going to have to ask you for your badge."

The room grew quiet as Tom stared first at McCoy, then at Devlin. A tiny smile played across his lips.

"No," he said quietly.

"What?" Devlin shouted. He almost leaped from his chair, then thought better of it. "Who the hell do you think you are?"

"The sheriff," Tom answered. "As much as you are the mayor, McCoy, and you a member of the council, Devlin. You folks appointed yourselves as the town's watchdogs and hired me to take care of the town. Well, that's just what I'm going to do. Until a proper election is held. Then, we'll let the rest of the people decide. Pick a date and have Parsons print up what's needed. But," he said, leaning forward and tapping a finger on McCoy's desk, "it'll be a full election. Mayor, council members, sheriff, everything. And until then, I'm going to keep the peace around here."

The others looked thunderstruck at his words. Hawthorne shifted uneasily in his chair and coughed.

"Tom, I don't know if this is quite right," he said uncomfortably.

"It's the only way that things will be right," Tom said. "A fair election. I'll step down then. But only after a fair election when the right men are chosen for the job according to the wishes of *all* the people and not just a few self-chosen protectors of the town. That's little more than vigilante rule. So, I'm appointing myself sheriff as of this moment. I'm not going to see Walker go back to the way it was just because a couple of men want to use the town to make themselves better off than they already are. Sorry, Mr. Hawthorne, but Pa told me that there would come a time when I'd have to stand up for those who can't stand up for themselves. I reckon this is one of those times."

He rose and settled his hat upon his head. "You want my badge, then you hold an election. Get the right people in office and I'll step aside. You have my word on that."

"Your word?" Devlin gave an ugly laugh. "What's the word of a gunfighter?"

"I'm a gunfighter because you made me one," Tom said softly. "And don't you forget that, Devlin. Or you, McCoy. I was little more than a kid when you came into my room a little over a year ago and said you needed someone like me. I didn't want the job. But I remembered what Pa told me when I left home. He told me that there would be some men who would be working against the commandments given them. And he told me to trust God above what others tell me and I wouldn't go wrong. He said I wouldn't be the most popular among men, but I'd be right and that's enough for any man." He paused. "My pa was a good man, and I know now that he knew what he was talking about."

Hancock stood and shook his head. "I think you two should listen to what Mr. Cade is saying. Walker has grown. Now, we need to have elections to see who will be leading the town from this point on in its new direction."

"I'll remind you, Reverend, that we are the town here," Devlin said. "Not you. And not this gunfighter."

"They are as much of the town as I am," Hawthorne said, rising. "And I cast my vote with Tom Cade. That makes it two against two, and since Tom is a citizen here as well as the sheriff, that makes it three against two."

"What?!" Devlin shouted.

"You heard me," Hawthorne said. "And I'm leaving now to see Parsons." He glanced at Tom and Hancock. "One month. We'll have those elections in one month."

"I'll make the announcement at church as well," Hancock said. "There'll be some who may want to run for office." He looked at Tom apologetically. "Maybe even as sheriff."

Tom shrugged. "They can have it. As long as it's a fair election."

The three of them walked out of the office, leaving the door open and Devlin and McCoy staring after them, open-mouthed in dismay at what had happened so swiftly that neither of them could muster a defense.

• • •

Wilson looked up as Tom stormed into the office, his face like a storm cloud.

"I take it things didn't go like you thought," he said.

"We're going to have elections," Tom said.

Wilson reached automatically for his tobacco.

"And," he asked carefully, "how did they take that? I'm surprised they didn't take your badge."

"They asked for it."

"And?"

"I told them no. Not until after the elections." Tom paused, then added, "You might want to think about staying on as deputy now."

"You told them they couldn't have it?"

Tom nodded.

"Wisht I could've been there to see that," Wilson said wistfully. "This means that you're by yourself then. You know that, don't you? You won't be gettin' any help from Devlin or McCoy. Just the opposite. They'll try to raise the town up against you. That might not be healthy."

"You want out?" Tom asked. "I won't take it personal if you do. Fact is, probably would be a smart thing to do."

Wilson grinned. "Nope. I think I'll stick around and see how things shape up."

"Thanks," Tom said. "Now, I reckon I'd better make the rounds. Hawthorne's already down at Parsons's, setting up things and getting things printed. The election's in a month."

"Things are going to be poppin' over the next couple of weeks," Wilson said, rising. He lit the cigarette and picked up his shotgun from the desk. "So, I think I'll just mosey around town and see what's happening."

"I'm going to make rounds," Tom said, reminding him. "Maybe you need to get some sleep."

Wilson said, "I'm sorta used to getting along on little lately. The older I get, the less it seems I need. And when you were down, I got to feeling I was a hundred and ten. No amount of sleep in the world is gonna make me feel like a spring rooster again." He paused. "How about I take the town and you take Tent City. Them roosters you left will be starting their crowing around this part of Walker first to rile the people up some. They'll talk a bit freer around me than you, I'm thinking."

"Doubt that," Tom grunted. "They'll see that badge on you and know that you are working with me. They'll think we're one and the same."

"That may not be all bad," Wilson said. "Might make my job easier come night."

Tom laughed and together they walked out, splitting on the duckboards, with Tom heading down to Tent City while Wilson began to make his way around the town proper.

• • •

Wilson was right. Tom could tell that when he crossed the line into Tent City. People greeted him, some cheerful, others a bit curt, but he knew that word had already spread within the hour, and made a point of keeping himself as taciturn as possible. He walked into Daid's Place and found Willie polishing glasses behind the bar while a couple of gunless cowboys sat at a table with a bottle between them, playing with a pack of greasy cards that had seen better days two towns down the line before Walker.

Tom nodded at them and crossed to the bar, slipping his hat back from his forehead as he rested an elbow on the bar and smiled at Willie.

"So," he said, "what's happening?"

"About what you'd expect," Willie said, adding, "Devlin was in here about fifteen minutes ago. I think he's making his way on down the street. Didn't have much good to say about you 'cept that you was gettin' a bit uppity for the job and thinkin' that you were the king or president or something like that here."

"What do you think?"

Willie raised his eyebrows and continued wiping glasses.

"Someone's gotta make decisions. Seen you work. You do a fair job even when I don't agree with it." He rolled his head on his massive shoulders. "Might as well be you as someone who thinks he don't leave the same droppings as a cow or horse."

Despite his black feeling, Tom had to laugh. "I'd take it favorably if you'd just remind folks that things aren't changing until after the election. We still have the same law."

"One day at a time," Willie said soberly.

Tom nodded at the two cowboys. "Know them?"

"They work for the Box G. Some of the Box G wanted to come into town after they planted young Griswald, but the new foreman stopped them. He said the problem was the boss's and he could damned well take care of it."

"Who's the new foreman?" Tom asked with interest.

"Ryan Sloan," Willie said.

Tom's eyebrows raised in surprise. Willie smiled faintly.

"You may not know it, but there's some who'll back your play. Sloan made it known that if Griswald wants something done about his boy, he needs to take care of it himself. Those cowboys were hired to work his ranch, not take care of his feuds for him. You took care of Bodeen, so now they got a real foreman up there who's more worried about cows than he is in what happens in town."

"That won't make him popular with Griswald," Tom observed.

Willie shrugged. "A good foreman's hard to find. And Sloan's a good cowhand who knows his stuff. May be a bit wild, but he'll keep those cowboys under control and Griswald knows that."

"That's gratifying," Tom said.

"Figured it would be," Willie said. "That doesn't mean they'll step in and help you. But they won't get involved. Most of them are good people. A couple of hardcases, but they know about Bodeen and the others and they'll behave themselves in town. None of them want walking papers with winter coming on. Hard to find a bunk when the snow flies."

"I appreciate it," Tom said.

He tugged his hat brim down and left, making his way on down to the cribs at the end of the street, looking for Devlin. But he found himself walking in Devlin's trail at the saloons he stopped in. When he got to the cribs, he found the girls sitting around at the tables, playing cards and waiting for customers. They looked up when he entered; then their faces dropped down to the cards, knowing he wasn't there for sporting.

Tom walked over to the bartender and stood facing him until the bartender gave up and raised his face to meet Tom's eyes.

"You want to stay in business?" Tom asked.

Alarm spread across the bartender's face.

"You can't shut us down," he protested. "We done nothing wrong."

"Didn't say you did," Tom said. "But if you're gonna stay in Walker, then I want this tent and those cribs gone. Put up a proper house so men can have a little privacy. And get your girls checked by the doctor once a month. A girl shows up unclean, she's not working until that problem is taken care of itself."

"That'll cut into our take!" the bartender said.

"Too damn bad," Tom answered. "I may not be around much longer, but damned if I'm going to leave Walker until it's proper. As long as a man's got an itch, he's gonna want it scratched. But that doesn't mean that he has to become an animal to do it."

He raised his head and sniffed.

"And another thing. Put a bath in. This place stinks like a buffalo camp. I mean it," he said, lowering his eyes. The bartender flinched. "I want to see a building going up by tomorrow."

He turned and faced the room and raised his voice.

"Just because you're whores don't mean you can't start being ladylike. Might not hurt if you went to church as well. Of course, I won't make you do that. But you want to work here, you'll start conducting yourselves with a little bit of digniiy."

"That would depend upon those who come in, won't it?" a buxom red-head with tired eyes asked.

"You get what you let others have," Tom said. "You behave the way you want to be treated. You want to be camp followers, then hire or buy a Texas wagon and hit the trail and take your business to those types you want in your bed."

"What about you?" a blonde asked boldly.

Tom shook his head. "I just want a decent town. That's all."

He turned and walked out, leaving a stunned crowd in his wake. He bumped into Ryan Sloan and stood back. His eyes dropped automatically to Sloan's hip, and he nodded when he noticed the absence of a pistol. Sloan stood back warily, watching.

"I heard about what you said," Tom said. "I appreciate it."

"No sense in more getting killed than already have been," Sloan said. "I can't run a ranch with dead cowboys."

"There's truth in those words," Tom answered.

Sloan nodded and glanced over Tom's shoulder at the cribs.

"I take it you're spreading a bit more law," he said.

Tom shook his head. "Decency. That's what I'm spreading now. The law's already here."

He looked around Tent City. Some had already started converting their tents into buildings. He looked back at Sloan.

"This is going to be a good town," he said quietly.

He turned and walked away, pacing his way down the middle of the street. The tents had to go; it was time for it. He made his way to Parsons with a new order for the printer to fill.

20

TWO weeks passed, and Tom could feel the tension building in the town as election day started drawing near. McCoy and Devlin were working with some of their friends, trying to convince the voters that they needed to vote them back in and choose someone else for sheriff as Tom had gotten out of hand. Hawthorne, however, had enlisted the other merchants in town and had started rallying them behind him.

Tom continued his work grimly, enforcing the law and personally delivering notices to the residents of Tent City that the ramshackle tents and skeleton buildings were to disappear and respectable buildings appear if they planned on staying in Walker. He met with resistance from some, but many agreed with him. Some had already made plans to pull out and follow the railroad on down the line, but others were willing to follow his demands if it would mean that they would become a part of Walker and not be designated as Tent City. Tom promised them that when the new council was elected, Tent City would be brought into the town as well and the deadline would disappear. He warned them, however, that if things got out of hand in any of their establishments, he would close them down permanently. They took this news thoughtfully.

Hancock made good his promise, announcing to his congregation the new changes that were being planned and following up with visitations to the homes of those who attended his church. He spent long hours riding out to the homesteads, carrying the message of what was happening in Walker to those who farmed around the edges of the Box G, and to some of the single-loop outfits that the Box G no longer would be holding the town in an iron fist. Tom saw new people come into town each day to buy supplies and see for themselves what changes were being made.

One late afternoon, Tom, bathed and freshly shaved and wearing his father's black coat, walked over to Hawthorne's store and asked if he could see Amy. Hawthorne grinned and went upstairs to get her. When she came down, Tom stood awkwardly, hat in hand, twisting the brim around in his hand.

"Well, Thomas," she said. "What can I do for you?"

"It's been a while since you and I managed to have a little talk," Tom said.

"Yes," she said. "I was expecting you before this."

He pulled at his ear, feeling his face redden before her steady gaze.

"There's been a lot to do lately and, well, uh, would you like to take a ride? That is, it looks like it's going to be a nice evening and I thought we might take a little drive out along the creek. That is, if you would like," he added hastily.

"Why, Thomas Cade! Are you asking me to go out with an unmarried man without someone along?" she asked. Her lips quivered, but she kept a poker face as she faced him.

He heard Hawthorne snigger and Molly hush him from the back room. His face felt as if he was running a fever. He shifted his feet, then nodded and said, "Yes, ma'am. That's what I'm asking."

"A proper lady wouldn't think of such a thing," Amy said. His face fell and she smiled. "But you are the sheriff and all, so I think that I would be safe. Yes, Thomas, I'd like to take a little ride with you. As long as you're not practicing with that."

She pointed at the Schofield.

"No, ma'am. Nothing of that sort. I mean, I work in the mornings, not the evenings, and Wilson said he'd go make the rounds for me and—"

"You told Fred about your plans? Why, what must he think about me?" she asked, placing her hand at her throat.

"Oh. Er. Nothing, nothing," Tom said hastily. "I mean, well, he said he'd be happy to as long as I got out for a spell. I mean, well, how about in an hour? It should be cooler then. I'll go see Reverend Hancock and see if I can borrow his buggy."

"All right," she laughed. "An hour then."

"An hour," Tom said.

He turned to go, stumbling a bit. He heard giggling behind him and fled the store, making his way down to the small house beside the church. Thankfully, a light shone from the window, and he made his way up to the door and knocked.

The door opened and Hancock stood in front of him, a

finger marking his place in the Bible he'd been reading. He
raised an eyebrow.

"Yes, Mr. Cade? What can I do for you?"

"Well, Reverend, if it isn't too much trouble, I was wondering if I could borrow your buggy for a couple of hours
this evening," Tom said.

"I see. Amy Hawthorne?" he asked.

Tom felt himself blushing again.

"Yes, sir. I thought she might enjoy a little ride out
along the creek this evening. Things have been pretty quiet
in town for a while and I thought that it might be . . . a fine
thing," he added lamely.

"I was wondering when you would get around to this,"
Hancock said, smiling.

Tom was astonished. "You were?"

"Mr. Cade. I think you must be the only one in town
who doesn't know that you care for Miss Hawthorne. Including herself."

"What?"

"You may borrow the buggy," Hancock said, smiling.
"And about time too, I'd say. But remember, don't keep her
out too late. The proprieties must be observed."

"I won't," Tom promised. "And thanks."

He walked around the corner of the house to the small
stable that Hancock kept. The back door of the house
opened and Hancock stepped out, closing the door behind
him.

"I'll give you a hand," he said.

"I can manage," Tom answered, but Hancock brushed
his protest away.

"Besides, I want to show you something," he said.

He led the way into the stable. There stood the buggy
and Jupiter, the gelding Hancock used to pull his buggy,

and a gray mare with a streak of white down her forehead. She had a deep chest and a fine head that turned to consider the two men who had just entered her domain.

"What do you think?" Hancock said, gesturing at the mare.

Tom studied her critically, noticing how her lines blended gracefully. She tossed her head and snorted and went back to nibbling on a little hay that Hancock had thrown into her manger.

"A nice-looking mare," Tom admitted. "Where'd you get her?"

"I was out visiting some folks down along the Teapot," he said, mentioning a creek that ran twenty miles south of town. "An Indian had come by leading her and offered her in trade for some supplies. Stebbin, that's who I was visiting, took her in, but she's proved too much for him to handle. So he gave her to me. I suppose he was thinking that she could take the place of old Jupiter, but I can't handle her. Stebbin said that he and a couple of other cowboys have tried to settle her, but they only got a licking for their troubles."

"She'll make someone a fine horse," Tom said wistfully.

"Then, she's yours," Hancock said.

Tom looked at him, frowning. "I can't take your horse, Reverend."

"Last I knew, you didn't have one," Hancock said. "Didn't young Griswald kill that bay you were riding?"

"I've been meaning to get another," Tom said. "But I just haven't had the time. When I need a horse, I just get one from the livery and send the bill to Devlin or McCoy."

"Which I'm certain pleases them to no end," Hancock said dryly. "But the fact is, I can't do anything with her and you need a horse. So, she's yours."

"I'll pay you," Tom said. "A fair price."

Hancock laughed. "There'll come a time when you can do something for me and we'll call it even. But right now, we'd better get old Jupiter in the traces if you're going to make that buggy ride."

"What's her name?" Tom asked.

Hancock shook his head. "As far as I know, she doesn't have one. So, I guess that's up to you."

Tom gingerly approached the mare. She stopped eating and turned to look at him suspiciously. He put his hand out and touched her neck. She jerked away, sounding a warning. Tom began to croon to her and tried again to place his hand upon her neck. She cocked her head and watched him curiously. The skin under her mane trembled, but she let him run his hand down her neck before she flipped it off and went back to eating.

"Sheba," Tom said.

Hancock frowned. "Sheba?"

"Yep. She has to be Sheba. Look at her. She has a lot of riddles to her and that's what Sheba brought to Solomon. I figure she and I are going to have to spend some time together to figure each other out."

"You continue to amaze me, Mr. Cade," Hancock said.

He led Jupiter from his stall and backed him into the traces as Tom began snapping the leads together.

"I'm afraid that I haven't had time to wash the trail dust from the buggy," Hancock apologized. "But I don't think we have time for that now."

"No, sir," Tom said, climbing into the buggy. He picked up the reins, slipping them through his fingers. "Not at the moment. Fact is, I'm a little pushed right now."

Hancock laughed and slapped Jupiter gently on the

rump. "Then, you'd better be getting over to Hawthorne's. You don't want to keep the lady waiting."

"I appreciate this, Reverend," Tom said gratefully.

"I'll expect to see both of you in church on Sunday," he said.

"You will," Tom promised.

He gently slapped the reins on Jupiter's back and drove around in front of the cottage and down to the store. Amy stepped out of the store as Tom climbed down from the buggy. She wore a small bonnet that matched her pale blue dress and carried a white shawl folded over one arm. Tom caught the hint of lavender as he handed her into the carriage.

"You're on time," she said. "That's nice."

"We want to enjoy the evening at its fullest, don't we?" Tom asked as he slapped the reins against Jupiter's broad back.

"By all means," Amy murmured. She resettled herself so they sat close together as Tom drove out of town and turned along the path that followed the creek.

"There's going to be a full moon," she said, bending forward to look out from under the fringed top of the buggy.

"A new month," Tom said.

"A hunter's moon, I think," Amy said. "Isn't that what they call it when the moon looks orange?"

"Yes," Tom said. "That's what we called it back in Tennessee. But the Cherokees used to call it a harvesting moon."

"What should we call it?" Amy asked mischievously.

"I don't know," Tom said, carefully guiding Jupiter around a pothole. "What do you think?"

"Oh, look!" she said suddenly, pointing at a gray shape that glided across their path. "A coyote."

"They come down close to town at night to try and find something to eat," Tom said. "It's easier than hunting for their food. Sometimes Ma Lagerfield puts out a couple of bones for them."

"It doesn't seem right," Amy said. "I mean, they were meant to live out here on the prairie and not hang around town looking for handouts."

Tom clucked to Jupiter and said, "That's what happens when a town comes in and establishes itself. The wild things have to go."

"Yes," she said. She slipped her arm in under his. "The wild things have to go. Sometimes, that isn't a good thing. But they still have to go."

"I know," he said roughly.

"Do you?" she asked softly. "Do you really understand?"

He looked down at her face in the moonlight. Her lips looked full and inviting, and some invisible force made him suddenly bend down to kiss them. For a moment, she kissed him back, then broke away and hugged his arm tightly to her.

"I've wanted to do that for a long time," he said huskily. "I'm sorry if I offended you."

"I wasn't offended," she said.

And that was all it took for Tom to loop the reins around the whip socket and turn to take her in his arms and kiss her while Jupiter plodded his own way along the faint trail that led along the creek.

• • •

Sunday came, a warm and cloudless day with a sky so blue it hurt the eyes. Tom dressed in his best clothes before walking to Hawthorne's place to pick up Amy for church. She was radiant, dressed in a pale yellow dress with matching bonnet. She smiled and kissed his cheek when he appeared, hat in hand, to escort her. Hawthorne and Molly were dressed in their best, beaming at Tom and Amy together.

"Oh, but this is going to be a happy occasion!" Molly exclaimed, straightening Tom's tie. "Reverend Hancock is making the announcement, and we'll have a picnic later in the week when the newspaper comes out with the banns published. Why, I bet it will be the best picnic of the year. You'll be surprised how many people will be coming."

"Well," Tom said dryly, "I wouldn't count the chickens before they're hatched. I'm not exactly the most popular man around."

"You might be surprised," Molly scolded. "There's a lot of people who are grateful for what you have done over the past year, Tom."

"And what you are going to do," Hawthorne said, clapping him on the shoulder. "There's been a lot of talk about you and the coming election."

Tom glanced at Amy and smiled. "I'm not certain— *we're* not certain that this is the job for the two of us."

"What will you do?" Hawthorne asked, frowning.

"Maybe take up farming. Or ranching. Or maybe a general store," he added with a mischievous gleam in his eye.

Hawthorne clapped a hand to his heart and looked pained.

"Oh, the ungrateful young!" he exclaimed.

Amy and Tom laughed at the look of misery upon his face.

"We'll see you at church," Amy said, tucking her hand under Tom's arm. She felt Tom's pistol and frowned.

"You're wearing your pistol?" she asked.

Tom smiled. "I'm still the sheriff. I'll leave it in the vestibule before we go into the church."

"I don't see why you should have to wear a pistol on Sundays," Amy replied. "Isn't Fred Wilson on duty?"

"He is. But this is the time to take a little precaution," Tom answered.

He opened the door and led her out onto the boardwalk. A great contentedness came over him as they walked slowly toward the church, enjoying the Indian summer morning. People greeted them and smiled as if they knew the announcement that was going to be made by Reverend Hancock that morning.

Amy hugged Tom's arm a little closer. "This is a beautiful day, isn't it?"

He smiled down at her. "It is. A very beautiful day."

"I—"

She jerked, and a puzzled look came into her eyes as she clutched his coat.

Tom heard the gun report a fraction later. Then another as a bullet whizzed like a bee past his head.

He whipped his head around and saw Joe Griswald levering another round into his Winchester from the side of the hotel. Tom palmed his pistol and fired two rapid shots. Griswald threw up his arms and fell to the ground as one bullet struck his shoulder and the other his knee. He writhed in pain on the ground.

"Thomas!" Amy said faintly.

Tom holstered his pistol and lowered her to the ground. Blood began spreading rapidly over the front of her dress as a crowd gathered around them. Hawthorne pushed his way through and knelt beside Tom.

Amy lifted her hand and touched Tom's face.

"I'm so sorry," she murmured.

Then her eyelids fluttered and closed and her hand fell away.

"Amy!" he shouted sharply. He shook her, but there was no response.

"She's gone, Tom," Hawthorne said in a choking voice. "She's gone."

Gently, Tom lifted her and held her out to Hawthorne.

"Take her home, please," he said softly.

Hawthorne took her from Tom's arms and turned away, tears streaming down his face. The crowd parted as Tom walked down toward the hotel where Griswald had pulled himself to the side, propping himself up against a rain barrel. He was trying to pull the Winchester to him.

"Griswald!" Tom shouted.

The rancher looked at him, then reached inside his coat and pulled a pistol from a shoulder harness. Tom drew and shot him in the other shoulder, and the pistol flipped away from him. Then, Tom deliberately drew the hammer back and shot him in the leg. Griswald yelled in agony as Tom continued to empty his pistol slowly into Griswald, listening to the man scream as each shot hammered into him.

Tom paused when he came up to Griswald. Blood was spreading slowly around him. Tom slipped the spent cartridges from the Schofield and methodically reloaded it.

"I—said—I'd—get you," panted Griswald.

"You didn't, though. You killed a woman," Tom said stonily.

"I'm—not—finished yet!" Griswald said through gritted teeth.

"Yes, you are," Tom said. He raised the pistol and put a bullet through Griswald's forehead.

He turned, holding the pistol at his side, and started down the street. He heard another gunshot and turned, dropping to one knee as Devlin stepped out of his hotel, a pistol held in his hand. He raised it and pointed it at Tom. Tom fired rapidly three times, watching Devlin jerk back as each bullet struck him. He fell, slumped against the front of his hotel.

Slowly, Tom rose and looked around. The crowd of people had spread to each side of the street, looking at him strangely as he turned and made his way down to Hawthorne's place, reloading the pistol again as he walked.

21.

THEN came the days of blackness when the sun seemed to hide behind dark clouds. Amy was buried and Tom patrolled the streets of Walker with a vengeance, a menacing figure with his hand only inches away from his pistol. People looked at him with pity, then fear, and began to avoid him.

Hawthorne and his wife tried to ease the pain within Tom, but he continued to blame himself for Amy's death, and seemed to court death on his walks through Walker and Tent City. He stopped more and more at Daid's Place, where he had a couple of drinks, but the whiskey seemed to have no effect upon him

"There was something to the way you killed Joe Griswald," Wilson told him one day. "You didn't so much kill him as assassinate him. You could have arrested him, Tom. And Devlin. People were a bit unsettled when you killed Dan Griswald, but killing his father as well by shooting him to pieces and reloading before you killed him, that was going a bit too far. People are beginning to wonder if you aren't becoming what you were hired to get rid of."

"That's none of their concern as long as I do my job," Tom said angrily.

Wilson shook his head. "No. No, that's where you're wrong. It *is* their concern. This is their town, not yours. And they're afraid of you. Afraid that what you did to Griswald and Devlin you could do to them just as easily. You need to back off."

But Tom ignored him and continued to stalk the streets like a wraith.

Ryan Sloan came into town and talked with him about the Box G. With the deaths of both Griswald and his son, the future of the Box G had been open. But then a distant cousin was found in Chicago, and the cousin decided that the Box G would be run with Sloan in charge while the cousin, a lawyer, stayed in Chicago.

"It sounds like you got yourself a good opportunity," Tom said.

"Maybe," Sloan answered. "But I'd like to be certain that when my boys come into town that there won't be any trouble."

"As long as they follow the law," Tom said.

Sloan smiled and stuck out his hand. Tom took it.

"I know we didn't get off to a good start," Sloan said, "but I'd like to have another chance at that."

"Sounds good to me," Tom answered.

Election Day came, and by sundown, Hawthorne had been elected mayor, and that evening he told Tom that he wanted him to stay on as sheriff. Tom listened quietly to the storekeeper, then shook his head.

"Sorry," he said. "But I think it's time for me to step down."

"Amy wouldn't want that," Hawthorne said quietly. "Not like this."

"If I hadn't been sheriff, then she would still be alive," Tom answered.

"You don't know that. As long as you're Tom Cade, then there'll be a need for you," Hawthorne insisted.

Tom walked to the window of the store and pointed out at the people moving quietly up and down the street.

"There's your answer," Tom said. "They're afraid of me now. That might be a good way for the peace to be kept, but it's not the right way."

He took the Schofield from its holster and held it up, examining it.

"I wonder what would have been if it hadn't been for this," he said.

"We would still have the town that we had before you became the sheriff," Hawthorne said.

"If I stay sheriff, you won't be a very popular mayor," Tom said. "At the next election, McCoy or one of his underlings will get elected. You know that. When I killed Griswald and Devlin, people began to step aside from me. I go to church and people shift around until no one has to sit with me. I think it would be best if I gave up the badge."

"Then, who'll take it?" Hawthorne said.

"Fred Wilson," Tom said promptly. "He's a good man and will do a good job for you."

"Think about it," Hawthorne said pleadingly. "Give it a week."

Tom hesitated.

"One week. That's all I'm asking," Hawthorne said.

"One week then," Tom answered.

Tom took to working with the mare Hancock had given him, letting Wilson take over the duties of the sheriff. Wilson complained good-naturedly, but made the rounds that Tom had normally taken, letting Bob Lismore handle the day rounds when little trouble could be expected.

The wolf pup began following Tom around the town. Folks looked at it curiously but said nothing.

Then, trouble came again to Walker when another Hardesty rode into town.

Tom was down at Hancock's, trying once again to break the mare to a saddle while the wolf pup sat panting, safely away from the mare's flying heels. So far, the mare had managed to kick Tom into the stable and throw him three times over the top rail of the corral. But Tom kept coming doggedly back, refitting the saddle time and time again.

"Mr. Cade!"

He turned and watched as Bob hurried up to the corral, panting from his run.

"What is it?" he asked.

"There's gonna be trouble. I'm certain of it. There's a man down at Daid's and he's carrying two guns he refuses to give up."

Tom sighed. "Well, you'd better tell Fred. He'll take care of it."

"He's askin' about you," Bob insisted. "Says that you owe him a death."

Slowly, Tom turned away from Sheba and stared at Bob.

"He give his name?"

"Jason Hardesty," Bob said promptly. "And he looks like he can handle them pistols. Wears them tied down low like."

Resignation came over Tom, and he slipped through the corral fence and took his pistol belt, which he'd hung on the top rail, and buckled it around his waist, settling the Schofield into place just over his left hip.

"All right," he said softly. "Reckon I'd better go down there and see if we can't resolve this thing once and for all."

He walked down the street, watching the people slip away from him and the pup as they crossed down into Tent City and made their way to Daid's Place.

When he entered, the saloon was quiet. A man in a dirty red shirt and trail-worn pants leaned against the bar, nursing a glass of whiskey. He wore two pistols hung low. Tom walked up to the bar and nodded at Willie.

"Looks like you got a little more trouble," Willie said in a low voice. "For what it's worth, I think he's right-handed."

"Thanks," Tom said. He moved down the bar until he was close to the stranger.

"You'd be Hardesty," he said.

The man turned his head and looked hard at Tom. His eyes dropped down to the star on Tom's chest, then back up to his face. His eyes were cold and hard, like anthracite. He nodded.

"And you're Tom Cade. I've heard about you."

"What have you heard, Mr Hardesty?" Tom asked. He indicated the pistols. "I hope you heard that it's against the law to carry pistols in Walker."

"That I heard," Hardesty answered. "Also heard that you were a friend of Sam Kilian."

"True."

"And you killed a couple of Hardestys."

"Three," Tom said. "But there's no reason to make it a fourth. Just shuck your guns."

"I don't think so," Hardesty said. "It's family."

He moved away from the bar and grinned wolfishly at Tom. "But look at it this way; when you're gone, then there's no other problem."

"Might be," Tom said. "I have three brothers."

Although he knew that the chances of Matthew, Mark, or Luke coming out to continue the feud were slim, he held a slight hope that mention of a possible coming feud might ease matters some. But the hope was useless.

Hardesty shook his head. "Then, there'll just have to be three more graves. The Hardestys don't take much to people steppin' on their kinfolk. And there's a passel of us. Most down on the Brazos, but we go back a ways as well."

"Not Tennessee, I hope," Tom said.

"Kentucky. But that's close enough, I reckon."

Without warning, his hand dropped down to the walnut handles of his pistol. He drew, bringing his left hand back to fan the hammer. But before his pistol came level, Tom flipped the Schofield from its holster and put a bullet in his throat.

Hardesty spilled forward onto the floor, coughing and grabbing at his throat. Tom watched him as he died, then silently replaced the Schofield and walked from the saloon. He paused outside the door, then resolutely made his way up to Hancock's cottage. The minister was waiting on the porch for him.

"I heard a gunshot," Hancock said soberly.

Tom nodded. "Another Hardesty. I don't think we're ever going to run out of Hardestys. Or Johnsons," he added.

He sat on the top step and pushed his hat back from his forehead. He stared at a bare wisteria bush planted at the side of the steps.

"I am getting very tired of this," he said, rubbing his hands across his eyes.

Hancock sat down beside him and nodded.

"It's hard to take a man's life," Hancock said. "You've borne the brunt of that responsibility for quite some time now. Maybe it's time for you to give the job to another."

"I told Hawthorne that, but he asked for me to wait a week and think about it some more," Tom said. "But"—he motioned toward Tent City—"I think waiting any longer is just an effort in futility. I think it's time for me to move on."

"If you stay here, there'll only be more killing," Hancock acknowledged. "What will you do?"

Tom shrugged. "I'm not good at much except this pistol. Oh, I suppose I could drive cows or work in a store someplace else."

Hancock turned so he faced Tom squarely. "Maybe you should take up your father's occupation."

Tom laughed. "Me? A minister? The roof of any church I preached in would cave."

Hancock placed his hand on Tom's arm and said seriously, "Thomas, you're a good man with a good heart. I think you've got a lot to offer to people out here. People and towns need ministers now, more than ever. I think you could find a church somewhere, and given what you have done in the past, I think that you would have an extraordinary insight into the souls of men. Put what you have done to good work now. The Lord's work."

Tom stared out at the town, watching Fred Wilson hurry up the street.

"I'll think about it," he said.

22.

A WEEK later, Tom Cade resigned as sheriff of
Walker, leaving the town in the hands of Fred Wilson.
Wearing his father's black coat and Wesley collar, he
mounted Sheba, the riddle-made mare, and with Sam, a
half-grown wolf pup trotting at their heels, rode away in
the early morning before the streets were peopled. In his
saddlebags, he had the Schofield rolled up in its gunbelt
along with his father's Bible. The Spencer was tucked in its
scabbard under his leg. He paused at the cemetery, staring
at the crosses of those he had placed there. He said a silent
prayer, asking for wisdom, then rode away, leaving Tom
Cade behind and taking the name of Amos Hood with him
into the West.